1 2 3 4 5 6 7 8 9 10

OAKBRIDGE
K040424
ISBN 9781739549619 (paperback)
ISBN 9781739549626 (eBook)
A CIP catalogue record for this book is available from the British Library

Black, Peter Jay
Murder at Vanmoor Village / Peter Jay Black

London

RUTH MORGAN INVESTIGATES...

MURDER
at Vanmoor Village

PETER JAY BLACK

1

A giant motorhome barrelled down a snow-laden hill, faster and faster, racing past trees, fences, and a dilapidated red phone box. At the corner of the road the motorhome didn't slow, nor did it bother to turn. Instead, it trundled straight on with zero concern for public safety, ploughed through a stone wall, and plummeted twenty feet into an icy river.

Standing at the top of the hill, Ruth Morgan's grandson, Greg Shaw, remained rooted to the spot, eyes wide, open-mouthed, as if he struggled to believe what he'd witnessed.

Excited squirrels jumped from branch to branch in a nearby tree as though they too had a hard time grappling with the reality of the situation.

Greg licked his dry lips and said in a hoarse whisper, "You forgot the handbrake, didn't you?"

Ruth—dressed all in black, save for a pink beanie, scarf, and gloves—clutched her cat, Merlin, and her cheeks drained of colour. "Um."

They'd only stopped off for a breath of fresh air because Greg felt travel sick. To be honest, he always felt travel sick.

However, Ruth had grown sympathetic of his retching and pulled over to let the poor lad offload without fear of staining upholstery.

While Greg threw up with reckless abandon, Ruth had admired a spectacular view of a picturesque snow-dusted village nestled in the valley below.

Although she'd appreciated the short stop-off, she itched to get moving again. They were on their way to Scotland, driving up the west coast of England, and still had another hundred miles to go.

Ruth's food consultancy business had gone well until her last assignment on board the *Ocean Odyssey*, so she was keen to get things back on track, *after* she solved a decades-long mystery on Ivywick Island.

A few moments later, their entire world, *literally*, rolled past them.

Merlin let out a raspy meow.

Ruth sighed, "Come on," and made her way down the hill.

Greg traipsed after her. "It might not be too bad, Grandma."

At the bottom, they stepped over the rubble of the wall and peered at the river below.

"On the other hand." Greg cringed. "That looks pretty bad. I don't think it's going to buff out."

Ruth stared as a mixture of shock and disbelief washed through her veins like ice water.

Jagged rocks had staved in the front of the motorhome, shattered the windscreen, removed the front bumper, along with driver's-side wing mirror, and as a final insult had also shredded Ruth's jaunty "*Home is where you park it,*" sticker. It now read, "*Home is you,*" which on any other day she would have thought was rather profound.

Ruth stood rooted to the spot and tried to grasp the magnitude of the situation. Apart from her house in Surrey, which Ruth's daughter and granddaughter currently occupied, everything she owned was in that tin container.

The stupid handbrake had never been quite right, and Ruth cursed herself for not putting the motorhome in gear when she'd parked.

She looked about. No one else was around, no witnesses to her stupidity, thank goodness, but also no one to help them. They had to act fast—the rear of the motorhome was submerged to above the wheel arch, likely now with copious amounts of water pouring in.

Great.

She let out a long breath, and the cold air traced it for her in a cloud. "Okay, Greg. Go get it."

He gawked at the carnage, and then at Ruth. "Get what?"

"Merlin's box. We can't leave it in there. You know how cross he gets without it."

As if in agreement, Merlin let out another raspy meow and glared at the teenager.

Greg's eyebrows lifted. "You expect me to swim?" he said in a shrill voice, and thrust a finger at the river. "In that?"

"Well, I certainly can't." Ruth gave him an incredulous look. "Anyway, it's shallow. No swimming required." She shrugged. "A little bit of wading, sure."

Judging by the chunks of ice floating past, the river flowed slowly, so he'd be perfectly fine.

"I'm not going in there," Greg said. "You're crazy."

"Why not? You are far more agile and spritely." Ruth raised her eyebrows. "It's a no-brainer. I'm in my early fifties, and you're twelve."

Greg blinked at her. "First of all, you're sixty-five, and I'm nineteen." He glanced at the river. "And secondly, I'll drown, or freeze to death, or both."

Ruth rolled her eyes. "So dramatic. I have no idea where you get it from." Another chunk of ice floated past. "Your grandfather would have jumped in without a second thought."

"Yeah, well," Greg muttered. "Grandad was a lunatic."

Although John had died over a decade before Greg had even been a twinkle in the ether, Ruth had to agree; her late husband had thrown himself at every task with little regard for his own personal safety. Now she came to think about it, it was a wonder he'd lived for as long as he had.

"Hold on." Ruth looked about for a length of rope to tie around her grandson's waist—not that he needed a safety line, but to put the lad's mind at ease. However, none were handy. She then pointed at a strip of rocks crossing from one riverbank to the other. The spritely teenager could leap across them with the surefootedness of a mountain goat. "Go. You'll be fine."

Worst-case scenario: if Greg slipped into the water, there were plenty of other rocks for him to grab on to. After all, those currently prevented her beloved wheeled palace from floating down the river and winding up in the ocean, where it would become the world's worst submarine.

Ruth wore a silver cat pendant on a fine chain around her neck. With her free hand, she rubbed it between thumb and forefinger.

Greg may come out a little sodden, a bit cold, perhaps with a few minor bruises, a couple of scuffs, but certainly alive and whole for the most part. Which his mother, Sara, would be glad of.

He mumbled a few swear words as he removed his

trainers and socks, then rolled up the legs of his jeans. "If I die, I'm coming back to haunt you."

"Duly noted." Ruth massaged Merlin's ears.

"And that stupid cat too." Greg edged down the snow-laden riverbank and screwed up his face. "It. Is. *Freezing*." He spat the last word through clenched teeth.

Ruth wrapped her coat around herself and Merlin. "It's not that bad." She contained a shiver.

"My feet are already blue."

"You're doing great."

"Mum will kill you if I get hurt."

"Your mother is a fine one to talk," Ruth said. "She once got her head stuck in a railing while showing off to a boy. We had to call the fire brigade, and they cut her free. Drew a crowd. It was all over the news." She shook her head. "I wouldn't have minded, but Sara was twenty-three at the time."

Greg gave her a hard look.

She grinned.

He then put a toe in the water, and yanked it out again. Greg scowled at Ruth.

Pretending not to notice, she waved to the line of ice-covered rocks. "See if you can make your way over using those. They look sturdy." Ruth removed a lip balm from her pocket and applied it as he traversed them.

More by luck than any real skill or judgement, the rake-thin teenager clambered over the boulders on all fours, like a drunken monkey learning to walk, periodically slipping a foot into the water, almost falling in, and shooting her a nasty glance each time.

Ruth pocketed the lip balm and gave him an encouraging thumbs-up.

She only hoped Merlin's bespoke oak box had suffered

no lasting damage, because his midnight-furred lordship would never forgive her.

Greg sat on the biggest boulder, slipped into the water, screamed himself hoarse, and then waded the last couple of feet to the motorhome. He opened the side door and stepped on board.

Ruth waited, her heart in her mouth, but sighed in relief as Greg reemerged with the bespoke oak box—sixteen inches wide and tall, twenty-two long, with a brass handle. He held it high above his head, slipped back into the water and waded across the river.

"Careful," Ruth called. "Don't drop it."

Greg picked his way over, taking his time, minding not to slip. Finally, he made it ashore and traipsed up the embankment. Greg handed her the box and bent double, hands on his knees, panting. "There's no water inside the motorhome."

"Thank goodness for small mercies." Ruth checked the exterior of Merlin's box, then she flipped open the clasps and peered inside. It had several grated vents but everything looked dry—his tailored cushion, the personalised bowls, and the rose-scented litter tray underneath . . . Ruth set the box on the ground. Merlin hopped in, circled a few times, then dropped to the cushion and closed his eyes.

"Great." Ruth let out a long breath. "Brilliant work, Greg. You make Grandma proud." She secured the clasps, and then pointed to the motorhome. "Now get my handbag and our suitcases."

Greg's face fell.

～

After two more trips across the icy river of doom, and at least a hundred muttered swear words of increasing originality and complexity, Greg made it back to Ruth with her handbag and their suitcases: all dry for the most part, but a little damp around the edges, and bulging at the seams. Luckily, they'd already packed for their visit to Ivywick Island.

Ruth opened her mouth to comment about the fact Greg could have carried one suitcase at a time, rather than both, but closed it again. After all, the lad didn't seem in any fit state to take a soupçon of constructive criticism.

After he dried himself with a towel, and changed his trousers, Greg's mood brightened, along with the colour in his cheeks.

Ruth slipped her phone from her back pocket and, with some reluctance, called her sister, Margaret.

She picked up on the fifth ring. "I told you that bloody thing is a death trap. What on earth were you thinking? I mean, seriously, Ruth. You both could have died."

Ruth shot her grandson a look. Clearly, Greg the traitor had sent a text to his great-aunt when he was inside the motorhome. "It's nothing," she said through clenched teeth. "A scratch. And we weren't in it when it crashed. Stupid thing did that all by itself."

"Oh, well, that's a relief," Margaret said in a sarcastic tone, which was pretty much her default. "How long will you be sorting out your mess?"

Ruth gazed at the battered vehicle. "I'm not sure."

"You promised you would help me," Margaret said.

"And I will."

"When?"

"As soon as I can."

"I can't do this without you, Ruth. I've made that very clear."

"Can't do what?"

"We've tried and failed."

Ruth ground her teeth. "Tried what?"

"Plus we have an uninvited guest showing up in less than a week," Margaret said. "I need you here before then."

"Who?" Ruth said. "You still haven't told me what's so urgent or what you're trying to do." The only thing she knew was Margaret's father-in-law had passed away, leaving Ivywick Island to Margaret and her husband, Charles. Ruth sighed. "We'll be there before next week."

"Get a taxi," Margaret said. "Lord knows you can afford it. Or is this a principle thing? You want us to pay?"

"I'm not abandoning my motorhome." Ruth had waited almost forty years to return to Ivywick Island, so a few more days wouldn't hurt.

However, Margaret wasn't interested in the past unless it affected her in the here and now. And the here and now presented its own set of problems.

"I'll call with an update as soon as I know," Ruth said. "Say *hi* to Charles." She hung up before her sister could moan any more or suggest something absurd, like hiring a helicopter.

Ruth glowered at her traitorous grandson, but he now checked a map on his phone, and mumbled, "I told you to sign up for roadside assistance."

"*Roadside*," Ruth said. "Not *in-river*." Despite the dire situation, she smirked. "Maybe I should have gotten boat insurance."

Greg squinted at the map. "We're not far from a place called '*Smuggler's Cove.*'"

"Smugglers?" Ruth's eyebrows arched. "Pirates too?"

"Doesn't say."

"Bandits?"

"No idea."

Ruth looked about. "We're by the coast, then?" Navigation had never been her strong suit.

"It's about a mile away." Greg pointed down the road. "And there's a mechanic's place in that direction."

"See?" Ruth slung her handbag over her shoulder. "The motorhome gods are smiling on us after all." A loud grinding came from the river, and the motorhome slid a few feet along the jagged rocks. She tensed. "Perhaps we should hurry."

The pair of them, Ruth carrying the oak box, Greg with a suitcase in each hand, marched along the road, following its twists as it descended into the snow-covered valley.

Ruth took deep breaths of crisp country air. "We have to do this more often, Greg."

He gave her a sidelong glance. "Crash?"

"We didn't crash," Ruth retorted with a hint of annoyance. "The motorhome did that all by itself. No, I mean, a lovely relaxing walk in the countryside. Your grandfather and I used to go hiking all the time. Rain or shine."

"What about snow?"

"That too."

Greg adjusted his grip on the suitcases. "You had to walk. They didn't have cars back in the eighteenth century."

Ruth's eyes narrowed. "I tell you what, let's enjoy this walk in silence from now on, shall we?" Besides, their unfortunate accident could have absolutely happened to anyone. "Don't tell your mother," Ruth added as she pictured Sara's face twisting with that usual look of disapproval. "Or your sister." She cleared her throat. "Or your dad, either. In fact, I think it's best you hand over your phone. No more sneaky texts." She motioned for it.

Greg pulled away from her.

"And while we're on the subject," Ruth said. "I've noticed you locking your phone. I don't lock mine. What are you hiding?"

"Nothing." Greg huffed. "And you really should."

"Should what?"

"Lock your phone."

"Why would I do that?"

"It's not safe."

"I'd never remember the combination thingy."

"If you get a new phone, you can unlock it with your face."

Ruth's step faltered. She slipped her mobile from her pocket and smooshed her face against the display. "Like this?"

Greg let out a low growl. "I know you do it on purpose."

"Do what?" Ruth asked in an innocent tone. "Whatever will they think of next?" She returned the phone to her pocket. "Dialling with your nose? Sending texts using your tongue? Ooh, taking pictures with your teeth?"

Greg squeezed his eyes closed for a second and mumbled something incoherent.

Ruth chuckled. She loved winding him up from time to time.

They continued to follow the winding road down into the valley, and then came to a sign that read:

WELCOME TO THE VILLAGE OF
VANMOOR
PLEASE DRIVE WITH CARE

As he waddled past with the suitcases, Greg snorted.

Ruth snarled. "I. Wasn't. Driving."

The two of them reached a fork in the road. Greg set the cases down, consulted the map on his phone again, pointed to the right, and on they continued.

A third of a mile down a lane flanked by oak trees and tall bushes, the road opened to a thatched cottage with a manicured front garden, surrounded by a white picket fence.

To the left of the house sat a wooden garage with peeling paintwork and a faded sign that read:

Jones & Sons

Motor Mechanics

Greg and Ruth made their way over.

Inside the garage, various rusty metal signs and car badges lined the walls and rafters, along with oil tins, chests of tools, mechanics' testing equipment, and a colourful landscape painting of the nearby village. Up on a hydraulic car ramp, in stark contrast to the surrounding clutter, sat a sleek deep blue sports car.

Greg's eyes popped from their sockets. "That's a Ferrari." He abandoned the suitcases and staggered toward it.

Ruth couldn't tell the difference between a Lamborghini and a Lada, a top-of-the-range Jaguar, and a battered Jeep, but the sports car certainly was pretty. It could probably get up enough speed to leap the river in a single bound.

Mouth slack, Greg waved a finger at it. "Ferrari J50."

"Only ten in the world, by all accounts." A man in his late sixties, with tufty white hair and a bulbous nose, wearing tatty overalls, wiped his hands on an oily rag as he approached. "Afternoon." Although clearly softened over time, he still had a Cornish accent, which had to be unusual so far north.

Greg remained transfixed by the car. "This is amazing."

"I'm no expert on sports cars," the mechanic said. "I just fix things when they go wrong." He shrugged. "Dun matter if it's a go-kart—as long as it's got an engine and four wheels, I'm yer guy. Not too sure about all these new-fangled onboard computers, mind."

"Amen to that," Ruth said.

He looked between them. "What can I do yer for?"

"I'm Ruth Morgan." Knowing what they were about to discuss, she offered him her best smile. "And this is my grandson, Gregory."

"Greg."

The mechanic nodded. "Trevor. Nice to meet yer both."

"Are you the *Jones* or one of the sons?" Ruth gestured at another hand-painted sign in the rafters.

"Neither," Trevor said, and he didn't elaborate.

"Right." Ruth took a breath. "So, we were passing by, on our way farther north, but had a minor accident."

Trevor the mechanic's bushy eyebrows lifted, and he stared at Greg. "Oh, yeah? What 'appened?"

"I wasn't driving," Greg said in a defensive tone.

"Came off the road." Ruth opted to leave out that she hadn't been behind the wheel either. There was nothing wrong with remaining a little ambiguous in the explanation. She gave Trevor a coy look. "Went a little way into the river."

"All the way." Greg brought up the map on his phone and held it out to the mechanic. "Right here."

"Ah, yeah. Krangan's corner," Trevor said in a sage tone. "Notorious spot. Many a 'orse and cart come a cropper there."

"You get horses and carts round these parts?" Ruth asked.

"Nope," Trevor said, and again he didn't elaborate. He tossed the oily rag onto a workbench. "Well, then, what were yer drivin'? A family car? SUV? Not one of those new-fangled electric ones, is it?"

"A motorhome," Greg said. "A giant, massive, colossal motorhome. Think double-decker bus, only bigger and uglier."

"Hey." Ruth glared at him.

However, this didn't faze Trevor the mechanic one bit. "In that case, gonna need a crane." He eyed a Pirelli clock on the wall above the double doors. "Can get Bill 'ere in about an 'our for yer. He's the village 'andyman. Knows 'is stuff, does Bill."

"A handyman has a crane?" Greg asked with an incredulous look.

"What can I say? Bill is *very* 'andy."

"Thank you," Ruth said with more than an ounce of relief. "Do you have an idea of the cost involved?"

"Yer leave Bill to me," Trevor said. "I can 'aggle him down to a few pints of ale and a packet of pork scratchings." He winked.

Ruth's cheeks flushed. "That's very kind."

Greg rolled his eyes.

Trevor's attention moved to him. "Did yer do much damage, young fella?"

"I don't even have a licence."

Trevor studied him. "That explains the accident."

Greg opened his mouth, but Ruth cut across him. "It was my fault. I wasn't paying attention." She cleared her throat. "Rocks caved in the whole front of my beloved motorhome, I'm afraid. Bumper came off too. Smashed windscreen." She gave Trevor another apologetic look, hoping it may help. "A few other parts probably lost too. Not sure. Ooh"—she clicked her fingers—"wing mirror's gone. Likely on its way to France by now."

"Well, I don't know about the bumper." Trevor scratched his rough chin. "But I can order in a windscreen, right enough. Will be 'ere in a day or two. As long as the engine ain't damaged or taken on water, I'll get yer back on the road in no time. Won't be pretty, but it will run at least."

"That sounds perfect." Ruth was thankful they'd found someone nearby to help. "I'll also need to speak to the owner of the wall and come to a financial agreement regarding its repair."

Trevor shook his head. "Not privately owned. Part of the village. Yer'll need to speak to Ms Jacobs."

Ruth's eyebrows arched. "One of the cracker people? Jacobs Crackers?" She smacked her lips.

"Head of the parish council. Elsie Jacobs." Trevor frowned at the floor. "Although, come to think of it, she is a bit crackers, yeah."

"I'll seek her out," Ruth said. "And is there somewhere we can stay for a couple of days?"

Trevor's gaze moved to their suitcases.

"We were on our way to Ivywick Island," Ruth elaborated. "My sister and her husband recently inherited it. It's a couple of hours north of here."

"Never 'eard of the place," Trevor said. "Yer on 'oliday, then?"

"Between work assignments," Ruth said. "Well, sort of. Away for pleasure." Although she'd hardly call staying with her sister for any amount of time a pleasure. "I'm a food consultant."

Trevor considered her. "Is that like Doctor Dolittle,

except yer consult with carrots?" His mouth pulled into a crooked grin. "Liaise with leeks? Chat with cheese?"

Ruth giggled. "All of the above."

Greg pinched the bridge of his nose.

"Well, yer'll want Molly's Bed & Breakfast. No finer establishment. Come to think of it, there's no other place to stay in Vanmoor." Trevor gestured past their shoulders. "Back the way yer came, up the 'ill, and 'ead into the village. Molly's is at the far end of the 'igh street, on the corner. Pink sign. Can't miss it."

Ruth thanked Trevor again and left her mobile number.

As they headed up the lane, he called, "I'll see yer at the pub tonight, shall I? I'll buy yer a brandy. Yer might need it."

Ruth waved, then whispered to her grandson, "He's lovely. A rugged type. I like rugged types."

Greg let out a low moan.

2

When she was a child, no older than six or seven, Ruth's mother and father had taken her and Margaret to York: a city in the north of England. In some parts, its Tudor buildings, with their second and third floors staggered, jetties overhanging the narrow lanes, gave the streets an enclosed and cozy feel that Ruth never forgot.

Vanmoor Village reminded her of that place: its cobblestone high street flanked by rows of Victorian fronted shops, packed in close, white and silver bunting strung between them—even though Christmas was a month prior—giving everything a heightened quirkiness.

Every lamppost advertised a winter fete due to start the next day, and Greg was deliberately ignoring the flyers, averting his gaze every time they strode past one.

There were various shops, including an antiques market, a bank, a greengrocer with crates filled with fruits and vegetables out front, a post office, a hardware shop, and a chemist. Some people peered into windows, others came and went with bags of shopping, running errands. There was even a police station with an old-fashioned blue lit sign out front.

To Ruth's eyes, Vanmoor was frozen in time.

She stopped outside a shop called *Malcolm's Groceries*. It had two large window boxes, and several gnomes lounged about between the plants, their brightly coloured hats and faces poking out of the snow.

Ruth chuckled and pointed to one of them.

The gnome lay sprawled facedown, clutching a bottle of whiskey, his bare bottom showing above his bright red trousers.

"He reminds me of my dearly departed Uncle Norman." Ruth waved at the gnome. "Hello, Uncle Norman. I've missed you."

Greg shook his head in apparent exasperation.

Halfway along the high street, opposite a village hall, sat the pub Trevor must have been referring to, called, "*The One-Legged Purple Horse.*" As if to drive the point home, the painted board that hung out front did indeed depict said horse, with a violently purple mane, and the animal balanced on a solitary leg. An impressive, if not slightly unbelievable feat.

Greg frowned up at the sign as they walked underneath. "This place is weird."

"I think it's delightful." Ruth peered through the front window of an art gallery.

Beyond sat an assortment of portraits and landscapes on easels, painted in oil and acrylic, all finely detailed.

One canvas depicted a court jester dressed head to toe in red, seated in a high-backed wooden chair, slouched, his fingers interlaced, with a downcast expression. Behind him a party was in full swing.

Another painting drew Ruth's attention; nothing more

than blocks of colour overlaid with intersecting black lines.

She recalled her own brief failed dalliance with the arts. When Ruth had turned ten years old, she'd joined the Girl Guides, by which time her sister, Margaret, had already made it to patrol leader at the ripe old age of twelve.

The guides stated you didn't have to be *"loud or super confident"* to be a patrol leader, but Margaret was both, in spades. Plus, she'd earned so many badges and sewn them on, she could hardly bend her arms. In fact, when Margaret wasn't wearing that shirt, it was so stiff that she stood it up in the corner of her bedroom like a display piece.

Margaret had also done everything in her power to convince the adults not to place Ruth in her patrol. Any other patrol would have been perfectly fine. She'd even resorted to bribery, but the leaders seemed to get a kick out of watching Margaret's obvious irritation.

"Don't embarrass me," she had warned Ruth on her first day.

But Ruth had failed in that department: she'd tried to create a picture of a tree with tissue paper but had wound up gluing her skirt to her leg.

From then on, Margaret's second-in-command, Patsy, a girl with braces and a lazy eye, was under strict orders not to let Ruth out of her sight or near anything remotely flammable.

It had taken Ruth almost a year to earn her first badge —*crafting*—and even then, her handmade stuffed bear had resembled a deformed and rather sickly elephant with three legs, one ear, and two trunks. Although, in her defence, that second trunk was meant to be a leg.

"What's with all the security cameras?" Greg pointed above their heads.

Sure enough, someone had mounted two CCTV

cameras back-to-back, high on the wall above a hardware shop. Ruth looked about. Now he mentioned it, several more cameras stood out on buildings and lampposts, covering every conceivable angle of the high street.

She battled the urge to start asking questions of the local residents. The events back on the *Ocean Odyssey* had awakened something in Ruth: an innate curiosity she'd buried since her husband's murder and subsequent firing from the police force.

The only problem was Ruth's nosiness often got her into trouble. "Maybe they had a spate of burglaries." She eyed a compact jewellery shop and imagined a gang of octogenarians in beige cardigans raiding the place, and then escaping with bags marked "*swag*" slung over their walking frames and rollators.

"Grandma," Greg said in an impatient tone. "You're daydreaming again."

Ruth shook herself, weaved in and out of people, and hurried after him. "I hope Trevor can fix the motorhome."

"Me too." He adjusted his grip on the suitcases. "I was looking forward to exploring Uncle Charles's and Aunty Margaret's island."

"Maybe you could find some local ruins while we're here?" Ruth said.

"There aren't any. I already checked the map. Just an old mansion house only open to the public for a couple of weeks a year."

At the far end of the high street, next to a village green, sat an imposing church, complete with spire stretching skyward.

However, true to Trevor the mechanic's word, the last building on the corner opposite had a pastel pink sign that declared it *Molly's Bed & Breakfast*.

Greg set the suitcases down and opened a gate. Its hinges groaned in protest. He stepped aside as a woman in her thirties stormed down the path. She wore a black puffer jacket, jeans, and white trainers.

A man, also in his thirties, wearing a long military jacket and a woolly hat, caught up with her. "Caroline."

The woman spun to face him and snapped, "She stole the locket from our room." Her gaze moved to the front door. "I know she did. Why won't you believe me?"

"Okay. Fine. I do," the man said in a placating tone. "Let's go back and ask her again. I'm sure it's one big misunderstanding. Probably moved it while cleaning."

Caroline stared at him for a second. "I'm getting something to eat, and if my locket's not back in our room by the time we return, I'm calling the police." She stomped down the road.

"Caroline, slow down." He trotted after her. "Let's talk this through. No need to make a scene."

Ruth watched them go. "That explains the security cameras: this place is obviously a crime hot spot." She laboured up the front path with Merlin's oak box, while Greg brought the suitcases.

Ruth rang the doorbell, and a faint tinkling came from deep inside the building.

A minute later, an elderly woman in her nineties answered. She wore a dark floral dress, a thick hand-knitted jumper, and hiking boots. Deep lines etched her face, and she stooped so low that she had to turn her head to look up at them. "What do you want?"

"Are you Molly?" Ruth asked in a bright tone.

"No." The old lady went to close the door, but Ruth put her hand out.

"Is Molly in?" She forced a smile.

"Molly died in 1887," the woman croaked, and pointed to her left breast. "Can't you read?"

Ruth frowned at the woman's jumper.

The old woman glanced down. "Where the hell has it gone now?" She looked at the floor about her feet, then headed back inside, muttering as she went.

Ruth nudged the door open with her foot and followed her.

The gloomy lobby had an old threadbare rug and several armchairs with their horsehair stuffing exposed. A sitting room stood to the right, with more forlorn chairs, a chaise lounge, and a cold fireplace.

Paintings filled every inch of wall space and—like the art gallery in the high street—covered a bewildering array of styles: everything from renaissance, baroque and neoclassicism, to abstract modern art, surrealism, and cubism.

Ruth wrinkled her nose at a musty smell as she peered at a painting of a chimpanzee playing a guitar, and by the screwed-up look on Greg's face, he'd noticed it too.

She peered at the signature: *A Pennington*. "Never heard of them."

The old woman hobbled behind an oak reception desk and through a door at the back. "Where is it? Bloody thing. Always vanishing."

Past the door was a compact office with more rooms beyond, and the corner of an iron bedstead could be made out. Paintings crammed every inch of the walls in there too.

Ruth studied another nearby painting, this one of a rowing boat on a storm-tossed sea. The artist's signature read, *A Pennington*. "Hold on a minute." Ruth looked round at the other paintings. They were all signed by the same person.

The old woman returned. She fished through the

contents of an old-fashioned biscuit tin, pulling out reels of thread. "Maybe I dropped it in here again."

"The same person did all these?" Ruth gestured at the paintings. "Who are they? They're very talented. A local artist?"

The old woman slipped on a pair of pince-nez. "Ah, here we go." She held up a brass name badge that read "*Dorothy.*" Instead of pinning it to her jumper, Dorothy banged it on the counter. "I own this place. Lived here for decades." She muttered, "So help me," and squinted at Ruth and Greg. "What is it you want?"

Ruth took a breath. "A couple of rooms, if that's no bother?"

"Did you book in advance?"

"No. Sorry."

Dorothy blinked at her. "Then I'll have to see. Can't promise anything. We're very busy." She hobbled back through the office door and closed it behind her.

Greg looked about. "Busy?"

"Ghosts," Ruth whispered. "Lots and lots of ghosts, ghouls, and poltergeists."

Greg glanced up at a chandelier burdened with cobwebs. "Spiders too." He shuddered.

Ruth's grandson had a deep aversion to the eight-legged creatures, and there had been many times he'd run screaming from a room.

Dorothy returned with a dusty leather-bound ledger. She set it on the reception desk, licked the tip of a gnarled finger, and flipped over the pages. "Double room?"

"Two," Greg said. "Separate."

"Two rooms?" Dorothy glared at him as though he'd asked her to try out for a decathlon.

Floorboards creaked behind Ruth and Greg. Dorothy

peered over their shoulders. A man wearing a long coat and a baseball cap pulled low over his face carried a nightstand out the front door.

"Most people steal towels," Ruth murmured to Greg. "That's a little extreme."

Dorothy stared after the man with a look of unease.

"Everything all right?" Ruth asked.

Dorothy returned to her ledger. "Two rooms? I think we can manage that." She rotated the ledger and offered a fountain pen with a leaky nib. "Fill in your details and sign. No pseudonyms. Real names only."

Ruth did as she asked.

"How long are you staying?" Dorothy asked, as if it was a real inconvenience.

"As short a time as possible," Ruth said. "Do you have any of that whiffy stuff? My grandson is rather partial to it."

Dorothy's brow furrowed. "What did you say?"

"Grandma thinks she's funny," Greg said. "She means Wi-Fi. Do you have a password I can log on with?"

Dorothy's frown deepened and threatened to split her face in two.

"Internet?" Greg's shoulders slumped, and he murmured, "Never mind."

"Breakfast is at eight sharp," Dorothy said. "Elsie brings over fresh glazed buns every morning, or you can have cereal, toast, or a full English."

Ruth smiled at Greg. "I bet I know which one you'll go for."

"All of the above."

Dorothy handed over two keys with oversized wooden fobs. "Next floor up." She pointed to a rickety elevator with a rusty metal grate pulled across.

Ruth baulked at the idea of squeezing into that thing

and getting stuck between floors. "We'll take the stairs."

Dorothy eyed Ruth's silver cat pendant, and then the oak box by her feet. "I've not used anything else for fifty years. It's perfectly safe. What's the matter with you?"

By the look of the old woman, Ruth could understand why stairs might be a challenge. She picked up Merlin's box before Dorothy could enquire as to its contents. "We'll be fine. Thank you." Ruth wasn't claustrophobic, but her clei-throphobia—a fear of being trapped—would not allow her to go any other way.

"Constance will see you up, then." Dorothy turned her head and screamed, "Connie? Where are you? Get in here."

There came a clattering as if someone had dropped a saucepan onto a tiled floor, and then a girl in her early twen-ties, with curly red hair and a pale complexion, wearing a dark blue cardigan, bustled through a door at the back of the sitting room and over to them. She wiped her hands on an apron.

Dorothy eyed her with disgust. "Help these people up to their rooms." She vanished into the office, slamming the door behind her.

Constance reached for one of the suitcases.

Greg held up a hand. "We're fine. I can manage."

Constance looked taken aback, as if he'd slapped her across the face and insulted her ancestors.

Ruth strode across the lobby before they arm wrestled for the suitcases, and she stopped at the base of the stairs. "Oh." She turned back. "Why are there so many security cameras in Vanmoor?"

A flicker of puzzlement crossed the girl's face. "I— I'm not sure."

"Don't worry," Greg said. "Grandma used to be a detec-tive. She's naturally suspicious of everything."

Constance's face brightened. "Detective? Really?"

Ruth shifted her grip on Merlin's box. "You pointed out the cameras in the first place, Gregory. And I was never a detective, only a curious constable." She looked round the gloomy interior and shuddered again. "Come on."

As they headed up the flight of stairs, which also happened to be lined with old paintings, Ruth glanced back at Constance. She remained at the bottom, hands clasped, staring up at them with lamp-like eyes.

Greg muttered, "We're going to die here."

"Don't be so dramatic," Ruth whispered back. "This place is charming."

Although he could well be right.

They reached a darkened landing. One door stood open, and the room beyond had piles of clothes stacked on the bed, plus mounds of bric-a-brac spilling from boxes. A banner strung across the window read, *"Vanmoor Church Annual Jumble Sale."*

"Guess that's not our room." Ruth checked the numbers on the key fobs. "This way."

They found their doors at the other end of the landing— two adjoining rooms with sitting areas, en suite bathrooms, spacious wardrobes, coffee and tea-making facilities, televisions, comfy furnishings, and although paintings lined the walls here too, at least they were spaced apart. Also, unlike the rest of Molly's B&B, the rooms were well lit, warm, and inviting.

"Wow, this is a nice surprise," Ruth said. "No spiders. You're safe."

Greg peered into the hallway, as if he struggled to believe the contrast too. "Why's the rest of the hotel so run-down?"

"Maybe a lack of funding." Ruth thought about her

damaged motorhome and counted her lucky stars she had a regular income.

Sara had taken over John's business after he died. Ruth liked cats, but would never have made a good breeder, so was glad to hand over the reins. Her daughter had then turned an already thriving and profitable business into an empire. They even had their own brand of cat food, along with a booming cattery franchise up and down the country.

Ruth set Merlin's box on the floor and opened the front. The sleek, black cat stepped from it, stretched, and looked around the place like a king appraising his new digs, checking corners and under furniture.

Greg went to stroke him, but Merlin lashed out, claws missing the back of his hand by a fraction of an inch.

Ruth chuckled. "You never learn."

Greg pulled back. "Why does he hate me so much?"

"Don't take it personally," Ruth said. "Merlin hates everyone, apart from me, but I feed him. And water him. Clean up after him . . ." She inclined her head. "In fact, I'm not entirely sure what I get out of the relationship."

Merlin glared at Greg, as if daring him to try again, then returned to the familiarity of his luxury box and cushion.

"His Majesty's inspection is over." Ruth sighed. "Looks like we're all going to love it here." She rubbed her hands together. "Now, be a good lad and pop the kettle on, Gregory."

A couple of hours later, after settling in—which included a long soak in the bath and making sure Merlin was fed and had fresh water to hand—Ruth got dressed, knocked on the connecting door, and opened it.

Greg sat on his bed, feet up, laptop open.

"You found the internet?" Ruth asked.

"There isn't any," Greg murmured. "Surprise, surprise." He nodded at his phone. "Tethered."

Ruth cocked an eyebrow. "Am I supposed to know what that means?"

Greg didn't answer.

She let out a breath. "Okay. Come on, then."

He looked up. "What?"

"The pub."

Greg returned to his laptop. "I'm not going."

Ruth couldn't hide her shock. "You mean to say you're prepared to let your frail, vulnerable, and elderly grandmother go out—"

"You're not frail or vulnerable," Greg said.

"—on her own in a strange place, with strange men lurking down dark alleyways?"

"What strange men? What are you on about?"

"There may be some people your age at the pub," Ruth said. "Your mother would be pleased if you found a partner to accompany you through your days."

"I've not seen anyone under ninety."

"Don't exaggerate."

"Eighty, then."

Ruth huffed. "You can't mope all evening cooped up in here. It's not healthy. Get out. Have some fun. See the world." She considered her grandson for a few seconds, then knew exactly how to get the moody teenager into motion. "They'll have burgers and steaks at the pub. French fries too. Hot dogs?"

This got Greg's full and undivided attention. "For sure? You saw a menu?"

Ruth smiled.

~

Twenty minutes later, Ruth and Greg stepped inside *The One-Legged Purple Horse Public House*. The interior had a stone fireplace, a matching cobbled floor, and a low ceiling with oak beams. Various pictures filled the walls: everything from pencil sketches of farm animals to newspaper cuttings from World War II declaring V-Day.

Ruth made a beeline for an inviting set of high-backed oxblood leather chairs in the corner of the room.

Greg traipsed after her, and they sat at a table.

She handed him the menu. "Order whatever you like."

"Hello, darlin'." Trevor the mechanic approached with an equally dishevelled companion. "Bill 'ere got yer van out of the river."

"Thank you, Bill."

"No worries, my lovely." He winked.

Despite not looking up from the menu, Greg squeezed his eyes shut.

"Quite a job yer did on 'er," Trevor said to Ruth. "Goin' to take some doin', but I should have yer up and runnin' as I promised in the next couple of days."

A wave of relief washed over Ruth. "That's wonderful." That would get Margaret off her back. "How much?" She braced herself.

Trevor slipped a folded piece of paper from the top pocket of his overalls and handed it to her.

Ruth read the amount and almost fell off her chair.

"Want that brandy I promised yer?" Trevor asked with a crooked smile.

Ruth swallowed. "Better make that five brandies."

"I found a replacement bumper and side mirror," Trevor said. "Took some doin' too but they'll be 'ere tomorrow with the windscreen. As yer can see, that amount of glass don't come cheap."

"Yes. I do see that." Ruth's head swam. "I'll transfer the money directly to your bank account tonight. Greg has a tethered phone."

"You like fish?" Bill asked her.

"Excuse me?"

"Fish," he said. "Going fishing in a few days. Wondered if you'd like to come along? I already pulled your motorhome from the river, so fancied trying my hand at plucking a few of the natives from it too. If you haven't scared them off, that is. They're probably not used to having motorhomes dropped on their heads."

"That's a very kind offer," Ruth said. "But I'm not sure we'll have time."

Trevor's gaze moved to Greg. "What about it, young fella? Fancy a tipple?"

Greg looked up from the menu. "I'll have a cola, please."

"Yer blinkin' well won't," Trevor said. "Yer'll 'ave some of our local ale. Put some 'airs on that chest."

Bill gave a fervent nod in agreement.

"Careful," Ruth said to them. "The ladies won't be able to contain themselves once they spot a hairy-chested Greg on the prowl."

The three older folks chuckled, whereas Greg's cheeks flushed, and he sank in his chair, so only his forehead remained visible above the menu.

"Don't yer worry, fella, we'll drink away some of that shyness t'boot." Trevor slapped Bill on the back, and the two of them headed to the bar.

"They're absolutely delightful, aren't they?" Ruth beamed. "What charming, charming men."

3

Ruth peered around the pub and people-watched.

Greg moaned and grizzled something about there being no cheeseburgers on the menu, and wanting to try somewhere else, but Ruth's attention moved to a striking young woman as she entered.

The girl had long blonde hair tied back in a ponytail, and Ruth gauged her to be around Greg's age—late teens, early twenties. She wore black jeans, a white shirt, boots, and a leather jacket.

Greg glanced up from his menu, then did a double take, and his jaw dropped.

"See?" Ruth said through the corner of her mouth. "I told you so. She's nowhere near eighty. Grandma knows best."

The girl approached Trevor and Bill at the bar and showed them something in her hand. They both shook their heads, so she moved on to another middle-aged guy. He shook his head too, and the girl continued around the bar, getting similar results from other patrons.

Ruth leaned in to Greg. "And where's there one, there'll be more. Young ladies as pretty as that move in packs."

Greg didn't take his eyes off the girl. He tried to look casual about it, but failed miserably, and as she approached their table, he sat up and straightened the creases in his T-shirt.

The girl held out a photograph of a good-looking guy Ruth judged to be in his mid-twenties, with mousy blond hair. "Have you seen this person?"

Ruth shook her head. "Sorry."

Greg opened his mouth to say something, then closed it again and shook his head too.

The girl moved to the next table.

"Is he your boyfriend?" Greg blurted out.

Ruth winced and muttered, "Smooth."

The girl turned back with a look of confusion.

Greg swallowed and nodded at the photograph. "Wh- Who is he?"

"My brother."

"You're in luck." Ruth patted Greg's arm. "Not only is my grandson someone's brother, but he's also an expert in finding lost things. Mostly dead and buried things, but gifted nonetheless."

The girl's brow furrowed deeper. "Okay." She held the photograph out to three women at the next table.

Greg's eyes followed her round the pub.

"Seen something you fancy?" Ruth asked in a nonchalant manner.

Greg blinked and looked at her.

Ruth nodded at the menu.

Greg cleared his throat. "Can I have a homemade steak pie, please?"

"Oh, we're staying now? Despite the lack of cheeseburgers?" Ruth smiled and put on her best grandma voice. "Of course you can, my darling." She pinched his cheek. "Gonna need all your strength to help the damsel in distress."

Greg was on a gap year, or what his parents had lovingly referred to as a "*do naff all*" year. Greg had done well in his A-level exams: *A*s and *B*s, and Oxford University had accepted him to study history and archaeology.

Given the fact Ruth travelled the country and had a spare bedroom in her motorhome, Greg had asked to tag along.

The plan had been to explore the local history, visit a few dig sites, and maybe hunt for his own discoveries while she worked at being a culinary goddess.

The reality so far had been quite different. The last trip had seen Ruth spending her time on board a cruise ship in the middle of the ocean, and now came this unscheduled detour, with an apparent lack of archaeologically interesting places nearby.

"How about we recover your metal detector from the motorhome tomorrow and go exploring anyway?" Ruth said to Greg. "There must be a farmer nearby who'll let us check out their fields. Dig a few holes. Find a hoard of gold coins. What do you say?"

Greg's face brightened, and he opened his mouth to respond, when someone shouted, "Get off me."

A man with red hair and a goatee, wearing a dark blue sweater and black jeans, had the blonde girl's arm in a vice-like grip.

"Hey." Greg leapt to his feet. "You heard—let go of her. *Now*."

"Back off, boy." With his free hand, the bearded man pulled police ID from his pocket. It read, *Sergeant Fry*.

"That doesn't give you the right to manhandle her," Greg

said.

"I have to agree." Ruth got to her feet and stood next to her grandson, arms crossed, wearing her best scowl.

Sergeant Fry looked between them, then at the rest of the gathered patrons. "She's been causing trouble for two days. Had numerous complaints."

"I'm trying to find my brother." The girl pulled her arm free.

"We know," Sergeant Fry growled. "We *all* know. And we've told you a thousand times we haven't seen him. No one has. You're harassing the locals and need to leave."

"She's going nowhere." Ruth gestured to a vacant chair at their table. "This young lady is our guest."

The girl hesitated, then spun on her heel and left the pub.

Greg dropped back to his chair, deflated.

Trevor and Bill returned with the drinks as Ruth sat too, and for a moment Greg looked as though he was going to leap back up and punch Sergeant Fry squarely on the nose.

Ruth nudged his arm. "We don't want to cause trouble."

"Trouble?" Trevor said. "In Vanmoor?"

"Chance would be a fine thing." Bill raised a glass. "To the promise of mischief and mayhem."

There came several muffled thuds, five or six in quick succession, followed by silence . . .

Ruth pushed back the duvet, sat up in bed, and blinked herself awake. "What? What was that?" She looked about. "Merlin?"

He seemed to have heard the strange noises too, because

the cat had left the comfort of his box and now stared at the door.

Ruth yawned and rubbed her eyes. "Greg probably fell out of bed. Wouldn't be the first time."

Like his mother, Ruth's grandson was prone to the odd night terror. They both had active imaginations that went into overdrive as they slept. In fact, a few weeks prior, while parked at a Devonshire campsite full of retirees, Greg had escaped via his bedroom window, wearing nothing but *Ghostbusters* boxer shorts.

The sleepwalking teenager had then somehow navigated through *Jezzie's Crazy Golf Course* and made it halfway to the bingo hall before triggering security lights and a claxon so loud that people in the next county must have heard it.

Ruth frowned.

However, now she came to think about it, the thudding hadn't come from Greg's room, but somewhere else farther along the landing.

What Ruth should do in any situation like this was get back to sleep. It had been a long day, and whatever had happened was none of her business. She glanced at the bedside clock: 6:28 a.m. Ruth yawned again. Besides, sneaking about a creepy, unfamiliar house while it was still dark was a terrible idea.

She swung her legs out of bed, stood, and pulled on her dressing gown. "What am I doing?" Ruth grumbled as she tied a knot at her waist. She then slid her bare feet into a pair of fluffy pink slippers. "I'm insane. Officially lost it." Ruth eyed Merlin and whispered, "Back me up. If someone attacks me, scratch their eyes out." She padded through the sitting room area to the door. Ruth turned an ear to it.

Nothing. She held her breath, opened the door an inch, and peered out.

All was quiet.

Ruth looked back as Merlin slinked into his box. "Thanks for your help." He was the worst bodyguard in the world. "Knew I should have gotten a dog."

Mind you, Ruth's sister, Margaret, had a Chihuahua, and every time the miniature mutt saw Ruth, it would get overexcited and pee on her shoes. Now whenever Margaret came to visit, Ruth made a point of wearing sandwich bags on her feet.

She snatched her mobile phone from a side table, stepped onto the landing, and tiptoed to the top of the stairs.

The B&B was in darkness, save for a sliver of light from a streetlamp, creeping through the skylight above the front door.

At a glance, not a thing seemed out of place—the door closed, nothing disturbed—so Ruth was about to head back to her room when something caught her eye—a shadowy mass at the bottom of the stairs, twisted and hard to make out.

Then Ruth's breath caught in her throat as her gaze landed on an outstretched hand protruding from the form.

With her heart thumping against her rib cage, she raced down the stairs and knelt by a body. Ruth activated the torch function on her phone, leaned down and stared into a pair of cold, lifeless eyes.

"Dorothy?" Ruth clapped a hand over her mouth.

The landlady wore her nightclothes, a shocked expression etched into her face.

Instinct took over, and Ruth checked for a pulse. There was none. She dialled 999, and as she relayed information to the operator, she tried to revive the old woman with CPR, but it was to no avail.

"Stay where you are," the operator said. "We'll have someone with you as soon as possible."

Ruth ended the call and, with reluctance, gave up her fruitless attempt to revive the departed landlady. She sat back. "I'm sorry." Holding the phone in her shaking hand, Ruth used the torch to scan the body and the area around it.

One of the old woman's shoes had slipped from her left foot and wound up near the front door, and apart from what appeared to be dried paint on several of Dorothy's fingers, nothing seemed out of the ordinary.

Ruth stood, found the light switch, and flicked it on. Then she checked each of the stairs as she headed back up.

When Ruth reached the landing, she bent and examined the carpet, but it looked in place—no ruck that could have tripped Dorothy and sent the poor woman tumbling to her death.

Ruth hurried back to her bedroom to get changed.

A few minutes later, after Ruth woke Greg and explained what had happened, the two of them stood on the landing.

"Let me check something." Ruth strode over to the elevator, opened the door, and pulled the grille aside. "Come here."

Greg stepped in.

Ruth closed the door and headed downstairs.

When she reached the reception desk, Greg appeared from the elevator.

"It's working." He glanced over at Dorothy's body, and quickly looked away. Greg's attention moved to a plate of glazed buns on the countertop, and he clapped a hand over his mouth.

"If you're going to be sick, find a bathroom." Ruth pursed

her lips, faced the reception desk, and recalled the bedroom beyond the office. "Stay here." She was about to check out the rooms when the front door opened.

The red-bearded police officer from the pub strode through, along with a younger female officer with dark hair.

Greg let out a low groan.

Sergeant Fry stared down at the body for a long moment, and tears formed. "Dorothy." His eyes rose to meet Ruth's, and he cleared his throat. "You're the lady who called?"

Ruth edged over to them with a heavy heart. "I am." She extended a hand. "Ruth Morgan."

The female police officer stepped forward and shook it. "PC Karen Bishop."

Ruth stepped aside. "My grandson—Greg Shaw."

He kept his gaze averted from the twisted body and shook Constable Bishop's hand too.

However, Sergeant Fry stared down at Dorothy.

"I take it you knew her?" Ruth asked.

"Wait for us outside." He gave Greg a hard look. "Both of you." He then faced PC Bishop. "Go wake Constance."

Ruth and her grandson left the house and stood on the path out front as the police officers set to work.

"What do you think happened?" Greg asked in a low voice. "She sleepwalked?"

"Perhaps she had an early morning urge to play a round of crazy golf." Ruth couldn't help herself, despite the dire situation.

Greg's cheeks flushed. "It wasn't an urge. It just . . . happened. I had no control." He lowered his voice. "And you promised never to mention that again."

"You're right." Ruth raised her hands. "I'm sorry. My lips are sealed." At least until the next time she met a stranger and needed to fill some awkward silence with an amusing anecdote.

Ruth stared through the open front door as the officers checked the scene. Images of her past career in the force flashed back to her—finding a body, the reaction of relatives and neighbours, searching for clues, and hunting a suspect.

"Why did she use the stairs?" Ruth murmured to Greg. "Dorothy told us when we arrived that she always takes the elevator. Made a big song and dance about it. Remember?"

"Maybe she tripped and fell."

Ruth shrugged. "Maybe." Her brow furrowed. "She wasn't carrying anything. What was she doing?"

If Dorothy had lived in the house for decades, and by her own account only used the elevator, then truth was, Ruth suspected foul play.

Greg's gaze flicked to her face, and he tensed. "Please, no."

"No, what?" Ruth said in an innocent tone.

"Investigating." He waved a hand in the direction of the police officers. "It's their job. It's always their job."

"Fine. Understood."

Greg didn't look convinced.

He was right not to believe her.

Police officers are human, and mistakes happen. During her time on the force, Ruth had made plenty, but a couple still haunted her.

One such event was a call out to an apartment building in Central London. When they'd arrived on the scene, they'd found the body of an elderly gentleman near the front entrance.

Ruth's subsequent investigation and interview with his wife had revealed he'd been putting the washing out to dry on the balcony when he'd slipped and fallen.

Two years went by, the lady had remarried, and then her new husband had suffered a similar fate, only this time falling into the Thames and drowning.

CCTV evidence showed the lady had pushed him, and she later confessed to the balcony gentleman too.

Of course, Ruth blamed herself, and vowed never to assume an unexpected death was an accident.

Sergeant Fry and Constable Bishop left the B&B with solemn expressions, and closed the door behind them.

"You say you're the one who called this in?" Sergeant Fry asked Ruth.

Constable Bishop jotted notes in a leather-bound pad.

"I am," Ruth said. "How's Constance?"

"Taking it hard." Sergeant Fry eyed Greg with suspicion and then refocused on Ruth. "How did you come to find Dorothy?"

"I heard a noise," Ruth said. "Went to investigate. I found her at the bottom of the stairs, checked to see if she was breathing, then called you right away. Tried CPR too."

Constable Bishop scribbled this down with enthusiasm.

"And the last time you saw Dorothy alive?" Sergeant Fry asked.

"When we got back last night," Ruth said. "We had dinner at the pub. She gave us our room keys, and we went to bed."

Sergeant Fry looked between them. "What time was that?"

Ruth faced her grandson. "Would you say around ten?"

He nodded.

Ruth turned back to Sergeant Fry. "Ten."

"Can anyone else corroborate that?" he asked.

Greg glared at him. "You saw us in the pub."

"I mean here. Did anyone else witness your arrival?" He seemed doubtful they were telling the truth.

Greg's scowl deepened. "You're not suggesting we shoved her down the—"

"As I said," Ruth interrupted. "Dorothy gave us our keys, and we went to our rooms." She sighed at the horrible memory of what had happened next. "Then a little before six thirty, I heard a noise and came down to investigate."

"Did you hear it too?" Sergeant Fry asked Greg.

"I was asleep."

Sergeant Fry smoothed his goatee. "You heard nothing at all? Not a peep?"

Ruth couldn't understand why he suspected Greg of having a hand in this, but put it down to their run-in the night before.

"I was asleep," Greg repeated through tight lips. "Grandma woke me up and told me what had happened."

"After I called you," Ruth said to the sergeant. "We got dressed and came straight down."

Does he not like strangers in his village? Is that the issue?

Constable Bishop flipped over the page of her notebook.

"Any other guests?" Sergeant Fry asked.

"I have no idea," Ruth said. "We signed the book when we arrived, but I took no notice of the entries. Oh, wait." She clicked her fingers. "There were a couple when we arrived yesterday, a man and woman in their thirties, but I haven't seen them since."

"And some guy stole a nightstand from his room when we arrived yesterday," Greg said.

"We'll look into it," Sergeant Fry muttered. "The pathologist is on her way. She's an hour out." He eyed Ruth and Greg in turn. "Although, it's clearly an accident."

Ruth inclined her head. "Are you sure?"

His gaze moved to the front door for a second, and then he pointed down the path. "I'll need to ask you to stay local for the time being, in case I have more questions."

"We have no choice but to stay in Vanmoor," Ruth said. "My motorhome is with Trevor the mechanic."

Sergeant Fry's eyes narrowed. "I heard about that."

"Should we get our stuff from the rooms?" Ruth asked before he could arrest her for property damage. After all, if he'd heard about her motorhome accident, he knew about the wall.

"No need," Sergeant Fry said. "Once we're done with the scene, you can return."

Greg screwed up his face. "We can?"

He obviously didn't relish the thought of occupying the same building as a recently deceased landlady.

In a way, Ruth couldn't blame him.

"Constance will take over for the time being," Sergeant Fry added. "She's Dorothy's grandniece." A crinkle furrowed his brow. "She'll inherit this place." He shook himself. "Now, if you'll excuse us . . . Bishop?" Sergeant Fry stepped inside the house.

Constable Bishop smiled at Ruth and Greg, mouthed, "*Thanks,*" then followed him in and closed the door.

Greg looked at his phone. "It's a little before eight. Will anywhere be open yet? I'm hungry."

"Nice to see you're over your sickness," Ruth said as she followed him through the gate. They rounded the corner and strode up the high street. "That poor woman." Dorothy's lifeless gaze would haunt Ruth forever. Sure, she'd seen more than her fair share of corpses over the years, but she remembered them all.

"Dorothy was very old," Greg said, as if that might ease Ruth's pain. "Ancient."

She shot him a look. "She wasn't that old."

"At least a hundred."

"No way."

"She had to be," Greg said. "Maybe older."

Ruth huffed out a breath. "How do you figure that?"

"Dorothy had a sewing kit in a biscuit tin. Only people at least a century old have stuff like that."

Ruth pressed her lips together. Back at her house in Surrey, she was pretty sure she not only had a biscuit tin with a selection of coloured threads and needles, but another one with an impressive assortment of random buttons. By Greg's logic, that would make her at least two hundred years old.

They walked past a bistro, but paper covered its windows, along with a sign that said it was "*Opening Soon.*"

A flyer taped to the door advertised the Vanmoor Village Winter Fete. Ruth tapped it. "That's today." She beamed.

Greg muttered, "Good to know," and nodded to The One-Legged Purple Horse. "They look open."

4

Having stuffed themselves full to bursting with an English breakfast and several mugs of milky tea, Ruth started out asking Greg nicely whether he would do her the honour of accompanying his dear old grandmother to the fete, and then she'd resorted to all-out bribing him with the promise of junk food.

The latter had sealed the deal.

Yay.

Ruth shrieked with delight as they passed through a gate at the end of the high street and strode into a snow-covered playing field packed full of stalls, open-sided tents, and various fun activities for the whole family to enjoy.

Ruth waggled her eyebrows at her grandson. "Extreme, awesome, radical fun, huh?"

Despite his obvious best efforts to remain grumpy and aloof, the corners of the teenager's mouth twitched into a smile. His gaze then scanned the attractions, landing squarely on a van selling chocolate-coated mini donuts. "Dessert."

"All in good time," Ruth said. "Let our breakfast settle

first." Besides, one good prod in the general direction of her tummy and she'd explode.

"—absolutely terrible what happened to Dorothy," one elderly woman said to another as they passed.

Ruth leaned in to Greg. "News travels fast."

A man in a flatcap scowled at them.

"Looks like they all blame us," Greg whispered back.

However, several other people smiled as they made their way deeper into the fete.

Ruth spread her arms wide. "Who needs one of those fancy PlayBox consoles when you have all this?" She skipped to the first stall, which comprised of several pasting tables pushed together.

A sign behind them read:

Vanmoor Village Homemade Jam Competition
Finest in the world
First prize is a trip to Tahiti!

"Tahiti?" Ruth's eyebrows shot up. "Wow. If I'd known, I would have entered."

Unfortunately, the contest was already in full swing. She sniffed the air, catching a bewildering cacophony of fruity bouquets.

Thirty jars lined the tables. There was all-natural wild grape, crab apple, peach, plum, raspberry and strawberry, and even one called "*Arabian Nights Among the Stars,*" which, given its dark red, almost black hue, Ruth guessed was mulberry.

Bleh. No way that one will win.

Behind the tables stood a line of hopeful Tahiti-venturing wannabes, all wearing wool hats and thick coats, hugging themselves as they waited.

Each possible future jam champion watched on in anxious silence, some wringing their gloved hands, others stamping the ground, trying to get feeling back into their toes, while two official-looking judges in brown overalls sampled their offerings.

The first judge was a vicar dressed in the customary black attire, complete with dog collar, beneath his overalls; the second was a slender, pale lady in her eighties, who looked in desperate need of a sandwich before she evaporated.

The judges swirled jam around their mouths as though tasting wine, smacked their lips in quiet contemplation, made a few appreciative "*Mmhmms*" and nods to one another, then stared up at the sky for a moment before making notes on their clipboards.

Culinary scientists hard at work.

A contestant at the end of the row—a woman in a bright red hat with oversized bobbles—leaned toward a man next to her and murmured from the corner of her mouth, "I don't know why I bother to enter. She wins every year."

He nodded and peered at another contestant farther along the row—a plump woman with an impressive purple perm styled into a beehive. She wore a psychedelic flowery apron over the top of a faux fur coat.

As Ruth scanned the jam jars, she fought off the urge to hunt down a loaf of bread and work her way through the whole darned lot.

Well, apart from the mulberry.

Seriously, what were they thinking?

However, Morris dancers dressed head to toe in white, matching the compacted snow beneath their feet, drew her attention from the nail-biting competition.

The men also wore straw hats covered in flowers. Wide

ribbons and colourful trimmings crossed their chests, while they held large white handkerchiefs in each hand and waved them about with reckless abandon.

Bells strung around their arms and shins tinkled and jingled as they danced to a band made up of several accordion players, a drummer, a flutist, a violinist, and an overeager old guy in a wheelchair. He had a blanket over his legs, and shook a tambourine as though it were a bottle of sauce.

The gathered crowd roared their appreciation every time he matched the beat, but then he'd drift off again into random spasms, as though possessed by a percussion demon.

Greg laughed at three ladies seated in garden chairs. They had fabric screens between them, blocking their views of one another. On their laps were bowls filled with apples, pears, oranges, and bunches of cherries. Twenty pence bought you a pull on a wooden handle, which caused the ladies to select a random item of fruit and hold it up. If you got all three cherries, you won the jackpot: a shiny pound coin.

"There sure is a lot of gambling here," Ruth muttered. "Love it."

Greg now stared in the opposite direction, his expression serious again.

Ruth followed his gaze.

The young blonde girl from the pub the night before worked her way through the crowds, holding up the photograph of her brother, and receiving vehement shakes of heads before moving on.

"Got to hand it to her," Ruth said. "She doesn't give up easily." She glanced at her grandson. "If I ever vanish, will you spend that much energy looking for me?"

"I've spent that much energy trying to get you to vanish," Greg said. "But you keep coming back."

Ruth clutched her chest. "Your words can be so wounding. From a member of my own family too. I don't know where you inherited such an acid tongue. Wait until I tell your mother."

Although, knowing Sara, she'd only find it funny.

The blonde girl moved to a family standing in front of four exercise bikes. Each was connected to a complicated network of pulleys, controlling a series of cardboard racehorses on a makeshift track.

VANMOOR DERBY

Greg hurried over, glancing at the girl as she moved to another group of people. He fished in his pocket and handed over a fifty-pence coin to the amusement operator before climbing onto a vacant exercise bike with a blue flag.

Once other jockeys had joined, the lady stepped to a lever. "On your marks, get set, go." She pulled it toward her, and they were off.

Greg and the others peddled for all their worth.

Sergeant Fry walked past, looked over at Greg, frowned, and then turned that glare on Ruth.

She gave the officer a little wave.

Sergeant Fry sneered and continued to the other side of the fete ground.

The gathered people laughed as the horses raced round the track. Even the blonde girl now watched, which had obviously been Greg's plan.

Ruth smirked.

For most of the way, it looked as though Greg would

lose, but one last excited burst of energy saw him edge in front and then cross the finish line in first place.

One round of applause later, he stepped from the bike, head held high, but the blonde girl had already moved on.

With a crestfallen expression, Greg returned to Ruth, red-faced and clutching a teddy bear key ring. He thrust it toward her. "Yours."

"Thank you. Very generous." Ruth pocketed it.

While Greg caught his breath, they moved along bric-a-brac and book stalls, plus a *"hook a duck"* game.

Ruth held up a pound coin to him. "Go on, then. You know you want to."

He frowned. "What's that for?"

With a straight face, Ruth nodded in the direction of a bouncy castle—a multicoloured inflatable where several small children, judging by their high-pitched squeals of delight, were currently having a grand old time. "Remember to take your shoes off first."

To Ruth's surprise, Greg snatched the coin from her and marched in the opposite direction.

"Hey," she called after him. "I was joking. I need that for the tombola."

However, Greg joined a group of people gathered around another attraction.

Ruth panted as she caught up with him. "What's gotten into you?"

He pointed through the crowd. "Sergeant Dick."

Ruth gasped. "Language."

"What?" Greg said in what he clearly thought was an innocent tone. "That's his name. I heard someone in the pub call him Richard. Sergeant Richard Fry. Dick Fry."

Ruth stood on tiptoes.

Sure enough, Sergeant Fry sat on a chair suspended over

a deep pool of water. An arm attached to the chair connected to a mechanism and a target with a bullseye.

Children took it in turns to throw beanbags at the target, but they all missed because someone had set the oche so far back the poor kids didn't stand a chance.

Bearded Bobby Sergeant Fry wore a smug grin.

Greg pushed through the crowd and thrust out a pound coin to the stallholder.

"Oh no," Ruth murmured.

Greg received three beanbags in exchange and joined the line of kids, now with a deep scowl carved into his features.

Ruth edged through the crowd and over to him. "Excuse me. Sorry. Coming through." She stepped beside Greg, leaned in, and lowered her voice. "Are you sure you want to do this?"

"Positive."

"It could start a war."

Greg squeezed the beanbags. "He started it last night by grabbing that girl's arm without her consent."

"True," Ruth said. "I only want you to think about what you're doing."

"Noted."

"So, you're sure?"

"Yes."

"Okay." Ruth held up her hands. "Glad we cleared that up." Tensed, she stepped back.

When Sergeant Fry spotted Greg, his face fell.

Ruth muttered, "This should be good."

Greg threw the first beanbag.

It missed the dunk tank target by a foot.

Sergeant Fry's shoulders relaxed, and his smirk returned.

Greg threw a second beanbag.

That one missed too.

Sergeant Fry now grinned from ear to ear.

Ruth cupped her hands around her mouth and called to him, "You know he's toying with you, right?"

Sergeant Fry's smile faltered again, and he smoothed his beard, clearly to cover his unease.

Greg spun on his heel and marched away.

"My grandson played cricket for his county," Ruth said in response to the confused expressions on the gathered crowd. "I watched him most weekends. He's excellent. Quite gifted, really."

Greg turned back, paused for a second, then ran toward the oche in big, loping strides. He launched the beanbag overarm, and it hit the target with a heavy thwack.

Sergeant Fry dropped into the dunk tank, and his head disappeared under the water. The crowd roared with laughter and clapped as he surfaced, spluttering, and flailing his arms about.

Clearly, the water had been deeper than he'd expected. Probably colder too.

A lady with a giant hook dragged him to the edge, where he caught his breath and shot daggers at Greg.

Several people smacked Greg on the back and congratulated him. Which told Ruth they weren't fans of Sergeant Fry either.

"Thank you," came a soft voice.

Of course, it was the blonde girl.

Greg's ears turned pink.

Ruth extended a hand to the girl before he passed out from giddy excitement. "Ruth Morgan. And this is my grandson, Sir Donald Bradman."

The girl shook Ruth's hand. "Mia."

M.I.A., Ruth thought. *Missing in action, like her brother.* Although she chose to keep that distasteful joke to herself.

"I— I'm Greg."

"Pleased to meet you," Mia said. "Wait. Who's Donald Bradman, then?"

"A cricketer," Greg said. "My grandmother is under the delusion she's funny."

"I am funny," Ruth said. "Any luck finding your brother?"

Mia glanced about. "Not yet."

"Why do you think he's here?" Greg led the way from the crowd as several people dragged the soaked police officer from the pool and covered him in towels. "I mean, we could help you find him, if you like?"

"That's okay. Thank you anyway." Mia went to leave.

"Hold on," Greg said. "I'm serious. We'd be happy to. Right, Grandma?"

Ruth wasn't sure they had the time to take on a missing persons case, not when they planned to leave in a day or two. She considered paying Trevor a visit to see how he was getting on, but Dorothy's suspicious death still weighed on her.

Perhaps they should return to the B&B and do a little more poking about. After all, Ruth had at least that one past mistake to atone for.

"Grandma used to be a detective," Greg said.

"I was en route to becoming a detective," Ruth corrected. "But they sacked me before I had the chance to complete my training. That should tell you everything you need to know."

Mia cracked a smirk but then must have realised Ruth wasn't joking.

"Come on," Greg said. "We might find something you've overlooked. What's the harm?"

Ruth nudged her grandson's arm. "Greg is very good at finding things. If your brother is around here someplace, he'll track him down in no time."

That was true. When he was three years old, Ruth had taken Greg and his twin sister to a supermarket. When they'd arrived back home an hour later and packed away the shopping, something had seemed off. Ruth couldn't quite put her finger on it. It was only when her daughter enquired as to Greg's whereabouts that Ruth remembered last seeing him with his face pressed against the glass at the cold meat counter.

Sara had flipped out, of course, and was about to call the police when there came a soft knock at the front door.

Ruth opened it, and in walked Gregory.

So, as far as Ruth was concerned, if her grandson had managed to find his way home when he was three years old, he could sure as heck locate a missing person in a day or so.

Mia looked about and lowered her voice. "I can't talk about it here. Will you meet me this afternoon? One o'clock at the campsite just outside the village? It's at the top of the hill."

"Absolutely." Greg smiled. "Be happy to. I think we drove past it on our way here."

"You would know," Ruth murmured to him. "You had your head stuck out the window most of the time."

"Thank you," Mia said. "I'll see you later."

As Greg watched her go, Ruth said, "See how fate plays its part at the fete? A fateful fete, you might say." She pictured a spring wedding. "Ooh." Ruth pointed at the next stall along. "Crochet animals. Love me some crochet animals." She clapped her hands and made a beeline for them. "I wonder if they have a stuffed mouse for Merlin. Might give him something to do other than sleep all day."

Although, Ruth had a box overflowing with toys the picky feline had shown little interest in. She could've set up her own stall and made a killing.

"You're helping, right?" Greg asked.

"Helping with what?" Ruth examined one of the crocheted creations. "Is this a tiger or a chicken?"

"We're going to help Mia find her brother. Both of us."

Ruth set the *tiger* down and picked up a frog. "You're more than capable of dealing with that on your own. I want to go back to the B&B and speak to Constance." She had to tread carefully, but the girl had been close to Dorothy and might have some useful information. Or at least could put Ruth's mind at rest.

"Please," Greg said. "We'd find him in half the time."

Ruth set the frog down. "I think this one could be a dragon."

"Grandma?"

"What?"

"Will you help or not?"

Ruth faced him. "This is your chance to be alone with a girl. Why would you pass that up?"

His cheeks reddened. "I've been alone with a girl before."

"Sure you have." Ruth put an arm around his shoulders, and they strode to the next stall—one selling bags of potpourri. "Did your mother give you the talk?"

Greg shrugged free. "I'm being serious."

"I really want to satisfy myself that I've done what I can for Dorothy, and after that, we're back on the road." Ruth pictured Ivywick Island with its mansion, run-down lighthouse, beaches, heath land, and a cave she was eager to explore. But then Margaret's scowling face superimposed the whole lot and ruined the mood.

"Trevor said it will take him at least a couple of days to fix the motorhome," Greg said. "Can't we speak to Constance, *and* help Mia?" He gave Ruth his sweet puppy dog eyes. The look he and his twin sister had also perfected at an early age, and one Ruth struggled to rebuff.

She ground her teeth. "Fine."

Greg smiled so wide his face looked about ready to split in half.

Ruth returned to perusing the craft stalls.

Merlin could do without another toy.

5

The day had barely touched eleven o'clock in the morning when Greg, a junk-food-seeking bloodhound, found a burger van in the field's farthest corner and bought himself an early lunch, comprising two double cheeseburgers and fries, while Ruth was more than content with a small pre-lunch hot dog.

They sat in a couple of plastic patio chairs and watched the hustle and bustle of the fete, while families laughed and amused themselves at various attractions.

Apart from the odd suspicious glance in their direction, most people were friendly and welcoming.

Ruth's attention moved to a couple of villagers as they approached.

The first was the vicar from the judging panel. He walked with a rod-straight back and thrust out a hand. "Reverend Collins, at your service." He had a deep, yet soft voice —an Irish accent, mixed with some Northern English.

Ruth swallowed the last mouthful of hot dog and stood. "Pleased to meet you." Her gaze dropped to his polished shoes, and then back up, noting in his pressed trousers and shirt. Reverend Collins took pride in his appearance.

The other person was the lady from the jam competition; the one with the purple beehive perm and flowery apron. She now wore a giant "*First Place*" rosette and smiled at Ruth as she gave her hand a vigorous shake. "I'm Elsie. Elsie Jacobs."

"Head of the parish council?" Ruth asked.

"That's me."

"Nice to meet you," Ruth said. "And congratulations on your victory."

"Seventh year in a row, I'm told," Reverend Collins said. "Elsie won't share her secret. I'm new to the village, so I've yet to gain her trust."

Elsie beamed, and said in a hushed voice, "I use a special recipe passed down through my family for generations." She tapped the side of her nose. "A magical ingredient."

"Let me guess," Ruth whispered back, "it comes as a white powder, beloved by celebrities and stockbrokers alike?"

A flicker of a frown crossed Elsie's face, and she stepped back. "I don't understand."

Reverend Collins stared at Ruth.

She cleared her throat. "Doesn't matter." Ruth motioned to Greg. "This is my grandson."

He waved and mumbled something through a mouth full of burger.

Ruth refocused on Elsie. "I was going to seek you out today. I owe you for a new wall. Complete accident. I'm sorry."

"Trevor tells us you're a food consultant?" Reverend Collins asked.

Elsie clapped and jiggled up and down. "Oh, please say you are. That would be wonderful."

This caught Ruth off guard, but she composed herself. "I am, yes. I advise restaurants and hotels on their menus, recipes, and anything else they could need." She failed to see the connection.

Elsie squealed in delight.

Ruth's brow furrowed. She enjoyed her chosen profession, but this reaction was unheard of. In fact, now she came to think about it, most people looked instantly bored the second she described her job in any detail lasting more than five words.

"Elsie is about to open our very first village bistro," Reverend Collins said. "We're ever so proud."

Elsie hyperventilated. "Oh, you're going to love it," she said to Ruth with sparkles in her eyes. "I've worked so hard. Spared no expense. Antique tables and chairs, oak, a new coffee machine . . ." She leaned in. "It's top of the range. So shiny. I have a kitchen to die for."

"Elsie would like you to check it out," Reverend Collins said to Ruth. "Give her advice on what you think works and what doesn't."

"I really want to make sure it's top notch before opening to the public. Vanmoor Village's reputation is at stake. It simply has to succeed, at any cost." Elsie gave her an imploring look. "A couple of hours of your time, and we'll call it even regarding Krangan's wall. What do you say? I'll see to the repairs, and we will hear no more about it."

Ruth thrust out a hand before Elsie could change her mind. "Deal."

They shook.

"Splendid," Reverend Collins said.

Elsie squealed again and beamed at Ruth. "Can you come when you're finished here?"

Ruth looked at Greg, who paid little attention to their conversation, and then back again. She checked the time on her phone. They had to meet the blonde girl in little under an hour and a half. "Is this afternoon, okay? Say four o'clock?"

"Perfect," Elsie said. "Thank you so much." She squeaked. "This day is amazing. I'm all of a dither."

Reverend Collins bowed his head, and the pair of them disappeared back into the crowds.

Ruth dropped into her chair, scratching her head. She couldn't quite decide if Elsie was amusing or annoying.

Probably a bit of both.

Oh, well. If it meant she'd get out of paying for damages, putting up with some overexuberance for an hour or two would be more than worth it.

As far as Ruth was concerned, that deal with Elsie was the first time she'd broken something and not had to spend a colossal amount of money to get it fixed.

Driving a land yacht through Britain's narrow lanes resulted in these minor accidents from time to time, so Ruth was thankful to have gotten away without having to pay for a wall on top of the other repairs.

She finished her soft drink and stood. "Shall we?" They still had the left-hand side of the fete to peruse.

Ruth and Greg sauntered along more stalls of bric-a-brac, books, and assorted raffles. They stopped at a lucky dip—a series of buckets filled with sand.

"I haven't tried one of these since I was a kid," Ruth said. "Quid a go."

Greg held a pound coin out to her.

Ruth chuckled. "It's okay." She turned to leave.

"Half price." The vendor was a young woman with bright red hair: Constance, the grandniece of the newly departed B&B owner.

Ruth blinked, surprised to see her here, given the tragic circumstances.

"You get two goes for that," Constance said in barely a whisper.

"Pardon?"

Constance nodded at the pound coin in Greg's hand. "Half price. Two goes."

"Go on then." Greg handed it to her. "One each."

"Sorry about what happened," Ruth said. "It's terrible. You must be devastated."

Constance baulked, as if Ruth had slapped her. "You— You're the one who found Aunty Dorothy?"

"I am." She was about to ask whether Constance had seen or heard anything suspicious the day before, or that morning, but thought better of it. Now was not the time. The girl looked fragile, so Ruth would have to choose her moment.

Constance picked up another bucket of sand and swapped it for the one in front of her. She then waved Greg to a second bucket and stared at Ruth with such intensity it was hard to tell if she was angry, upset, or something else.

Ruth hesitated, then rolled up her sleeves, pushed her hand deep into the bucket, and felt about the sand until her fingers touched a buried parcel. She grabbed hold of it and pulled out a packet wrapped in a ball of brown paper, around the size of an egg.

Greg did the same.

Ruth forced a smile at Constance. "Thank you." She softened her expression. "Can I see you later? This evening, perhaps?"

Constance's eyes went wide. She looked around at the other people milling about, then hurried off.

"She's a charmer," Greg muttered.

Ruth shook her head. "Grieving." She, better than some, knew exactly how that felt.

As they sauntered through the fete, they opened their prizes. Greg's turned out to be a plastic dinosaur. He held it up with a look of disgust.

"Ooh, excellent." Ruth suppressed a smirk. "That'll keep you entertained." She opened her own parcel to find a gold locket engraved with a seahorse.

Greg's jaw hit the floor. "Not fair." He reached for it, but Ruth pulled away. "Grandma." Greg held out the plastic dinosaur. "Bagsy swap you."

"Why do you want it?" Ruth asked. "Present for Mia?"

Greg frowned. "Technically, it's mine. I gave you that quid. Meaning I bought it with my own money."

"And where did you get that pound coin in the first place?" Ruth asked.

"Mum." He reached for the locket.

Ruth pulled away from him. "Not true," she said. "That was mine. I gave it to you earlier."

"I spent yours on Sergeant Fry's bath," Greg said. "A fair price for that level of entertainment, I think. That pound you spent on the lucky dip was from the money Mum gave me last month."

Ruth put her hands on her hips. "And who brought your mother into this world?"

"Grandpa John."

"And me," Ruth said. "Mostly me. So, I'm entitled to at least half. That's fifty pence, which I used to buy this lovely surprise locket."

Greg stiffened.

Sergeant Fry stood before them with a towel draped over his shoulders. He glared at Greg, and then his attention moved to the locket in Ruth's hand. "Where did you get that?" He looked over at the lucky dip stall.

Ruth pocketed it. "Won it."

Sergeant Fry's brow furrowed. "You need to give—"

"There he is." A woman in a blue dress and rain mac hurried over to him. "Thought you could escape?" She hooked her arm through his and led him to a ferret-racing stall.

"What was that about?" Greg murmured.

"I'm not sure," Ruth said. "But I have a strong feeling the locket is stolen property." Although, if Constance had taken it, Ruth had no idea why the girl had gone to all the trouble of now giving it to her.

Greg looked shocked. "You think it's stolen?"

"When we first arrived, remember that couple arguing?" Ruth said. "The woman, Caroline, I think her name was, mentioned someone taking a locket from their room."

"Constance did it?" Greg glanced over his shoulder.

Ruth looked back too, but the girl was nowhere to be seen, and a man in a green bowler hat now tended to the lucky dip stall. "I'm not sure what's going on." Ruth had no idea why Constance wanted her to have the locket, but she vowed to track down the couple and ask them about it. *But first things first* . . . "Let's finish up here and go meet with your future bride."

Greg's ears tuned pink.

～

Ruth and her lovesick grandson strode from Vanmoor Village, through the valley, following the river, and then up a winding road on the other side.

Greg kept urging her to hurry, but Ruth kept a steady pace, enjoying the quiet walk, allowing herself a breather after such a horrific morning discovering Dorothy's body. She wanted to clear her head before they spoke to Mia about her brother's disappearance.

A twinge in the pit of Ruth's stomach told her something odd was going on, and Mia's Brother's disappearance might have a connection to what had happened to Dorothy.

Two odd events in such a short space of time?

Definitely strange.

"Mia will still be there," she said in response to Greg's scowl and the millionth time he'd muttered for her to quicken her pace.

"We're going to be late," he grumbled as they passed a forest on either side of the road.

"We'll be right on time," Ruth said. "I need a minute to think about Dorothy." If it was murder, rather than an accident . . . She tried to visualise someone shoving the frail woman down the stairs, and what evidence they may have inadvertently left behind.

"Don't tell Mia that Dorothy died," Greg said.

Ruth applied some lip balm and frowned. "Why ever not?"

"She's worried about her brother. She might think—"

"That someone's murdered him too?" Ruth's eyebrows lifted. "So, hold on. Are you saying you also think someone murdered Dorothy?"

"No one murdered Dorothy," Greg said. "It was an accident." He stared at her. "Wasn't it?"

"How are you so sure? She wasn't carrying anything. Did you notice that?"

Greg blinked. "Huh?"

"Dorothy," Ruth said. "She wasn't holding anything when she fell. No tray, not even so much as a mug of tea."

Greg now looked confused. "So?"

"What was she doing on the landing in the small hours of the morning?" Ruth said. "If she was that frail, carrying something or not, why wouldn't she use the built-in elevator? That's what it's there for. Why even attempt the stairs?" They crossed the road and strode past a farmhouse. "Plus the elevator was on the next floor. Which means she took it up there, but then decided on taking the stairs back down?" Ruth shook her head. "She was in her night things too, and yet Dorothy's bedroom is on the ground floor, beyond the office."

Greg's brow furrowed. "How do you know that?"

"I saw the corner of a bed when we arrived. The door behind reception stood open. I could see all the way through both rooms."

Greg shrugged. "Might not be her bedroom."

"I bet it is."

Greg's face dropped, and he whispered, "You really think she was murdered?"

"I can't say for certain without evidence," Ruth confessed, but something still didn't sit right with her. "The pathologist will get to the bottom of it, I'm sure, but I also want to look about the B&B as soon as we get the chance. See if we can get Constance to open up too."

Given Greg's expression, he wasn't convinced.

Ruth forced a smile. "Maybe Dorothy's death and the brother's disappearance are separate events, with no links whatsoever."

Greg gaped at her. "Are you suggesting Mia's brother killed Dorothy?"

Ruth stared back at him. To be honest, she hadn't thought of that. He was currently missing. Although Ruth wasn't so sure the events were indeed linked, she had to follow each avenue.

A single odd thing happening was a one-off; she could put two down to a coincidence; *but three?* That was if Ruth counted the stolen locket as another strange event, which she did.

They continued up the hill.

"I really hope he's not dead." Greg winced and looked away, as though frightened Mia may have overheard.

"I'm sure he's absolutely fine," Ruth said. "And that there's a perfectly logical reason behind his disappearance."

Even so, she didn't hold out much hope. After all, Ruth knew from her time on the force, a fair percentage of disappearances didn't result in happy outcomes.

"Anything could have happened to him." She sighed. "Maybe he got lost in the woods, broke his leg, and has survived by eating beetles and dead squirrels. Or he's chosen to live off-grid as a hermit somewhere."

Greg rolled his eyes. "Why do you always have to be weird?"

"He could have fallen down a well," Ruth continued. "Perhaps aliens abducted him, or he snuck out of the country on a secret spy mission. Got lost in a cave, deep in a remote Madagascar forest." She glanced about. "Or a ravenous bear might have eaten him whole."

"A bear ate him?" Greg's eyebrows arched. "In the English countryside?"

Ruth clicked her fingers. "He entered a witness protection program because he snitched on a big-time Mafia family. Now he's living on the Isle of Wight under an assumed identity."

Greg stopped and turned to her. "Can we be serious, please?"

"I am serious," Ruth said in a defensive tone. "One should not mess with the Mafia, aliens, and bears. Especially when they work together. A very dangerous combination."

Greg snarled and resumed walking.

Ruth plodded after him. "Look, I'm sure everything will turn out fine. We'll ask Mia to explain, find out what she knows, and you can then put your famous navigation skills to good use." She passed the entrance to the forest on their right and peered in at all the various trees. "You'll track the guy down in no time and be Mia's knight in shining armour." Ruth batted her eyelids. "Oh, Sir Gregory," she said in a high-pitched voice, "how can I ever repay you?"

"Grandma," Greg snapped.

"Fine," Ruth said. "I promise we'll do absolutely everything in our power to help Mia find her brother. We'll make that our priority."

As the road crested the hill, they reached an old farmhouse constructed from Portland stone, with ivy, a slate roof, oak door, and leaded windows.

A sign out front pointed the way to the campsite.

Ruth and Greg followed a gravel path around the house to the first of several fields.

A solitary dome tent sat in the corner, next to a blue Mini. Mia leaned against her car, mug of coffee in hand, and seemed agitated.

6

As they approached Mia at the campsite, Ruth raised a hand. "Sorry. Totally my fault." Even though she and Greg were on time, as Ruth had predicted. "Wow. I'm out of shape." She panted and looked about. "Just you?"

Mia set her mug down. "A family were here for the fete, but they left already."

"What did they look like?" Ruth asked.

"An Asian couple with a young son. Why?"

"Doesn't matter." Ruth took a breath. "Tell us everything about your brother, and let's see what we can do to help in your search."

Mia gestured to a side gate, and they followed her into a second field with hills and forests on all sides.

As they continued along a path next to the hedgerows, Mia said, "Scott came to Vanmoor last week. Sunday. I haven't heard from him since he left home."

"Why was he here?" Greg asked.

"Scott's an artist," Mia said. "The Vanmoor Gallery were interested in purchasing some of his pieces. He was only supposed to be here for one night."

"Was he staying at the bed and breakfast?" Ruth asked, already guessing the answer. When Mia nodded, she said, "Do you know the room number?"

Mia scowled. "The landlady denied Scott stayed there. Said she'd never heard of him, but I know that's not true. I was with Scott when he made the reservation. He planned to stay there for one night and then head back home." She took a breath. "When I confronted the landlady again, she continued to deny he'd visited, and she wouldn't let me check the rooms or the guest book."

"Well, I don't think that will be a problem now," Ruth said. "We can search as much as we like. She's dead."

Mia clapped a hand over her mouth.

"It was an accident," Greg said in a soft tone. "That's all. She fell down the stairs. A tragic accident."

"Or maybe it wasn't," Ruth murmured.

Greg shot her a look.

Mia's eyes widened. "What do you mean?"

Ruth waved the question away, and they continued their stroll along the field. "Did your brother drive here?"

"That's the thing," Mia said. "He did. But no one I've spoken to remembers seeing Scott's car, which I find very hard to believe."

"What car does he have?" Greg asked.

"A black Land Rover Freelander with a white stripe down the side."

"That sounds like a large vehicle." Ruth imagined a big 4x4 trundling along Vanmoor's narrow high street. It would be sure to draw attention. "How do you know Scott definitely came to Vanmoor? That's what he intended to do, sure, but how do you know for certain that's what happened?"

People often told their family one thing while they did

something else entirely. It had also been a common occurrence during Ruth's time as a police officer.

Mia pulled a phone from her inside jacket pocket and held it out.

Greg took it from her and examined the display. "A tracking app?"

"Tracking?" Ruth said.

"GPS," Greg said. "It shows other people your location."

"Why do you have that?" Ruth asked Mia.

"All my family do," she said. "We each have it installed. Stops my mother from worrying if we're late home. It was Scott's idea. Only we can see it."

Greg studied the display. "According to this history, he stayed at the B&B, then visited the art gallery the next day." Greg frowned. "After that, looks like he went back to the B&B. His car was probably parked outside. Then the app stopped tracking him." He handed the phone back to Mia.

"Someone else must have switched it off." She returned her phone to her jacket pocket. "Scott wouldn't do that. He knows better."

"Maybe it ran out of battery," Greg said.

Mia shook her head. "He wouldn't allow that to happen either. Scott's very conscientious. Mum is always telling me to be more like him."

"I get that from my parents too," Greg said. "I've got a twin sister. They think she's perfect."

"You're both special in your own ways." Ruth stopped at the corner of the field and stared at a water tower in the distance. "Why haven't you gone to the police?"

"I did," Mia said. "Straight after I visited the B&B. Spoke to Sergeant Fry. Several times. Showed him the evidence."

Greg's face darkened. "He still didn't believe you?"

"That's why I asked you to come here, away from the village," Mia said. "I don't know who to trust."

Ruth ran through a few scenarios to explain Scott's vanishing act, but none stood out more than the others. She turned to Mia. "We'll start at the B&B."

The pathologist would have cleared the scene, and she could kill two birds with one stone.

Mia looked relieved to have people on her side.

Greg offered her a reassuring smile. "We'll find him."

Ruth believed him.

As the three of them walked from the campsite back down the hill toward Vanmoor Village, she said to Mia, "About your brother's car: a black what was it?" Ruth of course remembered but wanted to check Mia's story for consistency.

Not that she had cause not to trust the girl, but double-checking a relative's statement, especially when they were under severe stress, often turned up extra details, and clarified old ones.

"A black Freelander with a white stripe," Mia said.

"Ah, that's right." Ruth bobbed her head. "Quite a large vehicle, isn't it? Hard to miss?"

"Is it the five door or three door version?" Greg asked.

Mia glanced up at the sky for a moment. "Five door."

"Second generation?"

"I don't know. Sorry. Cars aren't my thing."

"In good working order, though?" Ruth asked. "No recent breakdowns?"

"Scott had it regularly serviced and cleaned."

"Do you remember the registration number?"

Mia shook her head. "He must have the documents at his flat, but I don't have a key."

"How far away does he live?" Ruth considered going

there and breaking in, not for the registration documents, but to look for any clues as to where he might have gone next.

"Great Yarmouth."

Ruth let out a breath. That was at least two hundred and fifty miles away on the opposite coast of England. She didn't fancy a five-hour trip in Mia's compact Mini. Although Greg would have probably leapt at the chance.

As they crossed the road and turned into Vanmoor High Street, Ruth scratched her chin and pictured the off-road car again. A large, boxy hunk of metal, like the royal family so often drove across their vast estates. "And you searched all over for it?" Ruth glanced down an alleyway between shops.

"Everywhere," Mia said. "Spent days looking. It's not in this village, as far as I can tell."

"If your brother was at the B&B," Ruth said, "then there's a few parking spaces across the road from there, next to the church. It's where I'd park if I had a sensible-sized vehicle."

Even if those spaces happened to be full when he'd arrived in Vanmoor, there were more of them farther up the road. *How precise is the tracking app?*

Scott's car should have been easy to find, which meant he'd either left the village of his own accord, or something else had happened to his car. Perhaps he had parked illegally, and someone had towed it. Ruth made a mental note to ask mechanic Trevor the next time they spoke.

She halted outside Vanmoor Art Gallery. "I think we should have a word with the owner first. After all, Scott's intention was to come here. That was the purpose of his visit, so let's see if he did."

"I already spoke to him." Mia screwed up her face. "He denies meeting Scott. Said my brother never turned up. Missed the meeting. Another liar."

"Let me have a try." Ruth went to open the door, but when Greg and Mia followed, she held up a hand and gestured at a bench seat across the road. "I'd like to go in alone, if you wouldn't mind. Less intimidating."

They hesitated and then backed away.

Ruth took a breath and entered.

With a polished parquet floor and plain white walls, the gallery was like a million others. Several paintings stood on easels, while more hung under spotlights. It seemed modern and out of place in somewhere quaint like Vanmoor, and would have suited a posh part of London better, where people had money to burn.

Ruth strolled down one side of the gallery and stopped at a vibrant portrait of a girl's face done in striking and over-lapping colours.

She glanced to her right, where a door stood ajar, the edge of an office desk inside.

Acting casual, Ruth returned her attention to the artwork, and put on her best "appraising" face.

"Elias Bradford." A slender man wearing a tight salmon pink suit strutted from the office. He had a pointed nose, pursed lips, and his cheeks sucked in, giving him a sharp, angular appearance.

He reminded Ruth of a flamingo. "Excuse me?"

"The artist." Flamingo nodded at the painting. "Elias Bradford. Total genius, of course."

"Of course." Ruth looked back at the painting. "Is Mr Bradford a local artist?"

"Oh, no," Flamingo said. "Elias is a metropolitan exclu-sive, of course."

"Of course." Ruth moved to the opposite wall to a painting of a bright red cow wearing a Viking helmet and military boots. If it hadn't been two-and-a-half grand, she would've bought it for Greg as a joke birthday present. "Do you invite artists to show at your gallery?"

"Now and again," Flamingo said.

"Recently?"

Flamingo tugged at his cuffs. "I couldn't say."

Ruth let out a small breath. It was clear that after only a couple of questions Flamingo was not about to share any information on his business dealings, which left her with no alternative beside a risky, clandestine plan that could well backfire and result in her immediate arrest.

Happy days.

As Ruth moved to the next painting, her step faltered. "Oops." She pressed her hand to her forehead, and her eyes unfocussed.

Flamingo's brow furrowed. "Are you okay, madam?"

"I'm fine." Ruth stared at a painting consisting of concentric circles, then staggered back. "Oh dear." Her knees buckled.

"Madam." Flamingo caught her under the arms. "I say."

Ruth gripped his tailored lapels, and her eyes rolled into the back of her head. "I don't feel so good." She slumped. "Need to sit down."

Flamingo glanced about and hesitated, before leading her through the back door into his office. He guided Ruth to a chair.

She dropped into it, slouched forward, and murmured. "Don't know what's come over me."

"I'll call an ambulance." Flamingo picked up a phone and dialled.

Ruth grabbed his arm. "Can I bother you for a glass of water? I'm sure I'll be fine in a minute."

Flamingo put down the phone. "Still or sparkling?"

"Still." Ruth closed her eyes. "So, so sorry."

Flamingo left through a back door.

Ruth jumped to her feet, ran round his desk, and opened a drawer. "What the hell am I doing?" she breathed.

Inside lay a ledger. She set it on the desk and opened it. There were lists and numbers, filling every page, hundreds, if not thousands of dated transactions.

"Wow. He sells a lot."

Also listed were the artist names: initials and surnames.

Ruth ran her finger down the pages, but Mia hadn't told them Scott's last name. She swore under her breath and used her phone to take pictures of a few of the latest pages before she slipped the ledger back into the drawer.

Ruth was about to close it when Flamingo returned, glass of water in hand.

She froze.

He glared at her. "What do you think you're doing?"

Ruth stood rooted to the spot in the gallery office, thoughts numbed as she stared back at Flamingo. Then she cursed herself for not thinking her slightly less than clandestine operation through properly.

A spy, she was not.

Flamingo's eyes darted to the open drawer and back again. "Well?" he said. "What are you playing at?"

Ruth unstuck her tongue. "Tissues." She closed the drawer with her knee. "I was looking for tissues."

Genius excuse.

Flamingo set the glass of water down on a side table and motioned to the door. "Leave."

"What?"

"There's no cash here."

"I—"

"Leave," Flamingo snapped. "*Now.*"

Ruth considered continuing to feign ignorance or

outright confront the man about his unfounded accusation, but something told her to back off.

So, on balance, Ruth chose to get out of here. After all, Flamingo had not caught her with his ledger in her hands, only standing over the open drawer.

She bowed her head, mumbled an apology, and traipsed from the office.

Flamingo shadowed Ruth all the way out onto the street. "Don't come back." He gave her one last nasty look. "*Ever.*" He slammed the door.

As she walked away, Ruth glanced over at her teenage companions and signalled for them to follow.

Once Flamingo had gone back into the depths of the art gallery, they crossed the road behind Ruth, and when they were a safe distance away, she let out a breath and faced them.

"What happened?" Mia asked.

Ruth looked about, then brought up the photos on her phone and showed them. "Is your brother's name listed?"

"What is that?" Greg asked.

"A ledger with all the gallery's transactions."

Mia pinched the screen and zoomed in. "Here."

Ruth took the phone back. "S. Riley?"

"That's him." Mia glared down the street. "Scott was there." Clearly, she felt vindicated. "I thought I was losing my mind. Why did the gallery owner lie?"

"I'm not sure," Ruth said. "But now we've proven Scott was in Vanmoor. That's a first step in the right direction."

Greg and Mia smiled at each other.

"See?" Greg said. "I told you Grandma's the best at this sort of thing."

"Next, we'll see what evidence we can uncover of his

presence at Molly's B&B." Ruth pocketed the phone and marched up the high street with determination.

As they reached the corner, she held up a hand and indicated for Greg and Mia to hang back. "Wait here while I check what's going on."

"Why can't we come with you?" Greg asked.

"It's my fault," Mia said. "People will recognise me and not want to talk."

"I'll be right back." Ruth hurried along the pavement and up the front path.

Inside, a mop leaned against the wall, along with a bucket.

"Constance?" Ruth called.

No answer.

Seeing as the police were done with the scene, it most likely meant they'd ruled Dorothy's death as nothing more than an unfortunate accident.

Ruth approached the reception desk. "Hello? Anyone here? Constance?" When she was sure no one was about, Ruth raced back outside and waved Greg and Mia in. "I don't know how long we've got. We'll have to be quick." Ruth hurried back to the desk and grabbed the guest logbook. She didn't have to scroll down the list very far. "Here he is. Scott Riley."

Mia leaned in, and her eyes went wide. "This proves she lied too. That landlady told me Scott hadn't been here." Mia balled her fists. "Why would she lie? I don't get what's going on."

Greg shrugged. "Maybe she didn't remember him. Dorothy was ancient."

"Wait a minute," Ruth said. "There's only one couple on here: Mr and Mrs Wilkinson. Room five. They checked themselves out an hour ago."

"Who are Mr and Mrs Wilkinson?" Mia asked.

"I . . . *found* their locket." Ruth took a picture of the page, including the Wilkinsons' phone number, and returned the logbook to the desk. She then eyed the keys on their hooks. "Greg, go get us the one for room four. That's where Scott stayed." She watched the front door as he stepped around the desk, then the three of them headed upstairs.

On the landing, Ruth took the key from Greg, unlocked room four, and whispered, "Keep behind me."

"Why?" Greg said. "Expecting zombies?"

"I don't know what to expect." But Ruth had a horrible hunch they were about to walk into another crime scene. One that involved Mia's brother. She gave Greg a hard look.

A flicker of understanding crossed his features, so he stepped in front of Mia and nodded.

Ruth held her breath, opened the door, and edged into the bedroom. Her face dropped, and she was more confused than surprised.

7

The guest room Scott had stayed in was a similar layout to Greg's and Ruth's, but it stood empty apart from a rug rolled up along the back wall. Someone had removed all the furniture, which must have included the bed, side tables, desk, chairs, and . . . "Nightstand," she breathed.

Greg scratched his head. "What?"

"When we first arrived. That man in the baseball cap." Ruth peered into the en suite bathroom. "He carried a nightstand, remember?"

"So?"

"I bet it's from this room." Ruth pointed at the rug. "It appears we interrupted his removal efforts."

"What have they done to Scott?" Tears streamed down Mia's face. "Someone's killed him, haven't they?"

Ruth took her shoulders. "Now you listen to me. We'll have none of that talk. I'm sure he's fine."

Mia sniffed. "How sure?"

"Very."

Greg crossed his arms, obviously recalling their conversation as they'd walked up the hill to meet Mia.

"Then why take out the furniture?" Mia said in a shrill voice. "They're getting rid of evidence."

Ruth released her. "Or it could be a coincidence." She cleared her throat. "We don't know what's happened, but we're sure going to find out. Until then, we keep calm and levelheaded, right? We follow the evidence."

Mia wiped her tears and nodded.

Ruth motioned for Greg to help her unroll the rug. They took an end each and worked their way back across the room until they had it flat.

"Keep back and don't step on it." She squatted and examined the pile.

Identical to the one in her room, this rug had an intricate floral pattern in repeating squares, set against a deep red background. An imitation of a Persian rug, but of low, synthetic quality, threadbare in a few spots. No doubt the owner of the hotel had purchased all the rugs in a bulk buy some years ago.

Ruth leaned in close. The rug appeared clean, save for a single green leaf on Greg's side.

He reached for it.

"Wait." Ruth hurried round to join him.

The leaf was oval with toothed edges and a pointed tip. Veins formed straight ridges at a forty-five-degree angle to the midrib.

Ruth took a picture with her phone. "Hornbeam."

"Could have come from anywhere," Mia said.

"Not so." Ruth stood. "In the village there's mainly oak with a few silver birch. There's only one place I've seen hornbeam so far. Perhaps it's somewhere your brother visited." She gestured to the door. "Let's go."

"What about the leaf?" Greg said. "Should we take it?"

"No, it's evidence." Ruth stepped onto the landing and almost bumped into Constance. "Oh, there you are."

Constance staggered back, her mouth hanging open. She clutched a laundry bag and looked from one to another.

"The door was open." Ruth smiled. "We were being nosey. Sorry. It has a delightful view of the high street and all the snow. Beautiful."

Greg slipped the room key into his pocket when Constance wasn't looking.

Ruth softened her tone. "How are you feeling?"

Constance's gaze moved to a spot on the wall.

"So sorry about your great-aunt," Mia said.

"Right." Greg swallowed. "If there's anything we can do to help?"

Constance kept her gaze averted.

"Well." Ruth considered asking her about the locket, but clearly now wasn't the right time either. She held up her room key. "Better be going. Catch up later?"

Constance pressed her back to the wall, and the three of them squeezed past.

As Ruth opened her room door, Mia glanced over her shoulder. "She doesn't look well."

"Very pale," Greg agreed.

"She's lost a family member," Ruth said. "We'll check up on her again in a little while." She hoped if she approached Constance alone, the girl would be more amenable to answering questions. "I'll be right back."

After making sure Merlin had ample food and water, plus a freshly plumped pillow, Ruth left the B&B with Greg and Mia.

At the end of the path, she stopped. "I think you two should wait here."

"Why?" Mia's brow furrowed.

"It's safer." Ruth would never forgive herself if something happened to either of them. She was better off going it alone. "Wait for me at the pub."

"No way," Greg said. "We're coming with you."

"It could be dangerous," Ruth persisted. "I can't—"

"You made me go into an icy river yesterday," Greg said with a look of incredulity. "I could have died. Several times."

"No, you couldn't. It was only a couple of feet deep and slow moving." Ruth cleared her throat. "Anyway, that was different."

Greg crossed his arms. "How so?"

"I—" Ruth looked at Mia, and then the floor. "Merlin's box was in there. You had to go. If you weren't around, I would have gone myself."

Greg snorted. "Our luggage too? That was worth risking my life for?" He shook his head. "You can't have it both ways, Grandma."

"I said no."

"I'm not a kid."

"You're my grandson, and I love you," Ruth said. "But in my eyes, you'll always be that sweet child."

"We are coming with you." Greg motioned to Mia. "You can't stop us."

Ruth went to argue some more, spotted the determination in their eyes, and let out a slow breath. "Fine. But I don't want to have to explain to your parents if something bad happens. Stay close to me. No deviation. Got it?"

They headed back out of the village, up the hill for a second time, but instead of continuing to the campsite, Ruth followed a path into the forest. A lot of the snow had already thawed, leaving large swathes of bare earth.

A little way in, she pointed at a tree, fifty feet tall, with a twisted trunk and pale grey bark. "Hornbeam. They're not as usual this far north." Ruth swung round and gestured to the other trees. "Oak, elm, over there is a silver birch, then another oak, and that, I believe, is a black poplar."

"How do you know all this?" Greg asked.

"Are you impressed?" Ruth grinned. "You are, aren't you?"

He shrugged. "Sure. If you like."

"If you must know, I did a project on trees when I was at school."

Greg leaned in to Mia and murmured, "Back in the eighteen hundreds."

She stifled a laugh.

Ruth glared at him. "The late sixties, actually."

Greg inclined his head. "Eighteen sixties?"

"You asked a question." Ruth put her hands on her hips. "Do you want the answer or not?"

"Sorry." Although Greg didn't sound very sincere. "Carry on." He smirked.

Ruth composed herself. "As I was saying; I did a project at school where I gathered as many different leaves as I could find, pressed them into a book, then made notes about each tree type." She strode over to the hornbeam and rested a hand on its trunk. "I'm sure this can't be the only one." She took a picture with her phone, then spotted another hornbeam farther into the forest. "Ah, here we go."

Ruth, Greg, and Mia headed deeper into the woods, and soon two hornbeams became three, then eight, and then they were everywhere.

"Hmm." Ruth looked about. It had snowed the previous day and now mostly thawed, so little chance of spotting fresh tracks. She let out a breath. "I suggest we spread out. A few meters apart. We'll cover more ground that way. But stay within sight of each other," she warned. "Understood? No wandering off." The last thing she needed right now was for one of them to go missing.

Ruth, Greg, and Mia fanned out through the forest, careful where they trod and scanning the ground as they went. Other than a few animal tracks, nothing seemed out of the ordinary.

A couple of hundred feet farther in, Greg called, "Grandma?" He pointed to a narrow road that cut through the forest, wide enough for a car, constructed of hard-packed mud, which had also thawed in places.

Ruth tried to get her bearings. She pointed to their right. "What's that way?"

"Main road," Greg said.

"Which means . . ." Ruth followed the track to the left, careful not to slip on the mud, and periodically glancing over to make sure Greg and Mia still followed.

Soon the mud road turned to gravel and loose stone, and then disappeared behind a cluster of dense bushes. Ruth circled round, then stopped.

Ahead stood an old railway tunnel, long since abandoned, and parked inside was a black car with a white stripe down the side. Letters on the back spelled, "Freelander 2," and above them was the oval green logo of Land Rover.

Ruth's heart skipped a beat. She hurried to the car, peered through the side window, and stiffened.

Greg rounded the bushes, and when he laid eyes on the car, he smiled. "We found it." He went to call for Mia.

"Stop," Ruth hissed.

Greg's face drained of colour when he spotted what she was looking at.

Inside, slumped over the steering wheel, was the body of a man with mousy blond hair.

Mia appeared behind Greg. "You've found it." She took a step toward the car, but Greg leapt in front of her, hands raised. Mia frowned at him. "What?"

Greg's mouth worked, but no words came out.

Mia stared at him, and then realisation dawned on her face. She shook her head and went to step around him again, but Greg blocked her path.

"Get out of my way," Mia snarled.

"Can't do it," Greg said.

Ruth edged into Mia's line of sight. "He's right. You don't need to see this." Despite herself, an image flashed into Ruth's mind, a horrific memory from thirty years ago: her husband, John, lying on the floor, shirt drenched in blood, his breathing shallow.

Ruth refocussed on Mia, surprised that anger now twisted the girl's face.

"Let me see," she said through gritted teeth.

Greg didn't move. "Look, Mia, I don't think—"

She shoved him out of the way, pushed past Ruth and hurried to the car. Mia peered through the side window and clapped a hand over her mouth.

Ruth stepped beside her. "I'm sorry," she said in a soft tone. "I know this is terrible for you. We'll call the police and—"

Mia's wide eyes turned to Ruth's, and she lowered her hand. "Who is that?"

Ruth blinked. "Excuse me?"

"That's not Scott." Mia backed from the car, her expression a mixture of relief and confusion.

"Are you sure?" Greg said.

"Of course I'm sure," Mia said in a shaky voice. "I know what my brother looks like, and that's not him."

With bewilderment as the overriding emotion, Ruth

looked back at the body. "Then who is it?" Mia couldn't be mistaken, the girl knew exactly what her brother looked like, but Ruth still couldn't grasp the reality.

"I don't know," Mia said. "I've not seen that man before." She backed against the tunnel wall, her eyes wide. "What does this mean? It's Scott's car."

The three of them stood in stunned silence for a few seconds.

"Check to see if he has a wallet," Greg croaked.

"We can't," Ruth said. "We'll contaminate the crime scene." She turned back to the car.

"Even though you're wearing gloves?" Mia asked.

Ruth shook her head. "We'd still be breaking the law."

"If we learn who that person is," Greg said, "it might help us figure out what's happened to Scott."

Mia staggered to the back of the car and peered through the rear window. "It— It's all here."

Inside sat several bags, canvases, and boxes of art supplies.

Ruth then hesitated, weighing their options. Surely, with the body not being Scott's, the people of Vanmoor would have to take Mia seriously, especially as they'd found his car. They'd have to accept something odd was going on in their little village.

This new turn of events meant the search for Scott was far from over, and Ruth wanted to continue looking for clues, but that was the job of the police.

This being a crime scene, they'd seal off the tunnel and investigate. However, that could take days, especially given the current weather conditions, by which time Scott's trail could have gone cold.

Also, it wasn't likely, given his dismissive attitude to date, that Sergeant Fry would do a good job. He'd already ruled

Dorothy's death an accident, and he could do the same here.

Ruth was at a figurative crossroads.

What she should've done was demand they back out of that tunnel and call the police immediately. What she shouldn't have done was risk contaminating a crime scene. Her time on the force had taught Ruth exactly the right course of action, the lawful thing to do, so she was as surprised as anyone when she opened the passenger door.

Although Ruth had suffered the misfortune of smelling death before, the odour at this crime scene hadn't yet reached the overpowering stage, which meant the body was still fresh. Relatively speaking. She wasn't a medical examiner or a coroner, but given the time of year with the cold temperature, Ruth guessed the body must have been here a few days, and not much more.

The man had a tanned complexion and appeared in his mid-twenties. *An utter tragedy.* Ruth's stomach knotted. Someone dangerous was on the loose, but she remained as detached as possible.

Mia kept her distance and looked in shock—hugging herself, skin pale—while Greg stayed close, seeming unsure what to do or how to help. He kept glancing between Ruth and Mia, and shuffled from foot to foot.

With the passenger door open, Ruth murmured, "If I do this, no one else can know, right?" She gave the pair of them a stern look.

They both nodded.

"I'm serious," Ruth said. "I'm not trained for this type of thing. I could go to prison if the police think I've tampered with a crime scene." Although, for the most part, she intended not to touch, only look.

"You were a cop, though," Mia said.

"In another life." Ruth considered demanding they leave her to get on with it. After all, if caught, they'd be accessories to a crime. However, they were here now, and she didn't want to waste valuable seconds arguing with them. The quicker she checked out the body and left, the less chance of getting caught, but she'd keep them at bay after she'd dealt with this crime scene. After all, she worked better alone, and there was no point risking their lives too.

She motioned for the pair of them to stay back. "Don't touch anything. Put your hands in your pockets." Ruth then checked the ground and walls of the tunnel. Hard-packed stone covered the floor, so no chance of finding any obvious footprints.

Despite wearing gloves, Ruth was still careful not to touch the car. She knelt, peered underneath, and swept the light of her phone from side to side. A patch of stones looked darker than the rest.

She angled the light and squinted. "Blood."

The patch was around a foot in diameter. No jagged bits of metal protruded from under the car, so she assumed that was not where the wound had occurred.

Ruth got to her feet and returned to the passenger side.

Blood soaked the jeans of the man's right leg, his socks, trainer, and the carpet too. She leaned across the passenger seat for a better look.

"If I didn't know better, I'd say someone shot him."

In the UK, it was illegal to possess a firearm for self-defense purposes, meaning gun crimes usually occurred with illicit firearms. Ruth couldn't quite picture the sleepy village of Vanmoor with such underworld connections, not unless someone had used an antique weapon.

There was an entry wound at the back of the man's calf,

with a larger exit hole at the front. It certainly did look like a gunshot wound.

"Hit from behind." Ruth screwed up her face. "Poor guy." She patted the man's nearest pocket, but it was empty.

The car keys were in the ignition, and there was no sign of any bullet holes in the car itself.

Fearing she'd disturb the crime scene, Ruth pulled back and closed the passenger door. "My best guess is he was running from someone."

"Why do you say that?" Mia asked.

"The blood on the ground." As Ruth circled to the driver's side, she checked for any bullet holes or damage there too. "I think someone shot him as he ran through the forest, but he made it to this tunnel." She then motioned beneath the car. "He hid under there until his assailant left."

Ruth pictured the injured victim scrambling from under the car once the coast was clear, opening the driver's door and climbing in.

"He was about to drive away when he fell unconscious. Probably a combination of shock and the loss of blood." Ruth sighed. "That's my best guess."

She leaned in to the driver's-side window, checked the body didn't rest against it, then opened the door.

The man's other jeans pocket was also empty.

"No wallet."

Unless he had ID in his back pocket, but there was no way to get to it without disturbing the body.

Ruth took plenty of pictures with her phone, covering as many angles and details as possible, and was about to close the driver's-side door when something beneath the seat caught her eye. She reached for it, but the snapping of a twig made her freeze.

"Someone's coming," Greg said in an urgent whisper.

8

With the crunch of footfalls on snow and gravel, Ruth closed the car door as quietly as she could, then hurried to the rear of the Freelander with Greg and Mia, and squatted.

"We should get out of here," Mia whispered.

Ruth looked behind them into the darkened tunnel. "We'll wait for them to leave."

"Why are we hiding, though?" Greg said. "We didn't kill him."

"But we don't want to get caught here because they'll think we did," Mia said.

"And hiding makes us look innocent?" Greg said.

Ruth put a finger to her lips.

A metal jingling at the end of the tunnel made all three of them freeze again.

Ruth closed her eyes for a second, running through different scenarios and excuses in her mind, but each one sounded more absurd than the last. Mia was right: they compounded any explanation as a lie by the mere fact they were now hiding.

Greg pulled back and almost knocked Ruth over as the jingling headed straight for them.

A golden Labrador with a blue collar rounded the car, its eyes bright, mouth wide, tail swishing at a million miles an hour.

Greg cringed and gave the dog an awkward pat on the head. "Nice doggy."

Despite the dire situation, Ruth smirked. "Don't encourage him, Gregory. He'll want to be your friend."

"What am I supposed to do?" Greg said through the corner of his mouth.

The Labrador sat in front of him, as if expecting a treat, or for Greg to throw a ball.

Mia looked at Ruth and gestured down the tunnel. "Shall we make a run for it?"

"Oh, thanks a bunch." Greg patted the dog again. "Abandon me, why don't you?"

"It's too dark," Ruth said. "We could trip and hurt ourselves." She suspected if they went too far into the tunnel, they'd struggle to get a phone signal if something went wrong.

A man whistled, then shouted, "*Milo.*"

Milo glanced in that direction but returned his attention to Greg, tail still wagging.

Greg said in a resigned tone, "We're done for." He went to stand, but there came a second whistle, and Milo bolted. "He'd better not grass us up," Greg muttered as he watched him go.

"How can he?" Ruth said. "He's not Lassie."

Greg frowned. "Who?"

Ruth's mouth fell open. "Please tell me you're not serious."

"I know who Lassie is," Mia whispered.

"Thank you," Ruth said, vindicated. "My grandson has zero culture. I blame his parents."

Mia peered round the car. "I don't think they saw us."

Sure enough, the footfalls grew distant, and the three of them straightened.

"How did they not spot the Freelander?" Greg said with a look of incredulity.

"Most likely they walk past the tunnel every day and don't peer inside," Ruth said.

Plus, a hedge obscured part of the entrance. You would have to cross the gravel road and look, which, she assumed, was why the car was here in the first place: somewhere people rarely ventured.

Ruth thought about that for a moment. Someone had deliberately hidden Scott's car. *So, where is he? What does that mean?*

"I think we should take it as a sign to leave." Mia hurried back down the tunnel.

"Hold on." Ruth returned to the driver's door. She opened it, stared at the sheet of paper under the seat, and wrestled with her conscience. "I really shouldn't touch this." She went to close the door but hesitated. Curiosity got the better of her: she had to know.

Ruth took note of the exact position of the paper, then reached under the seat and carefully slid it out between thumb and forefinger.

Scattered across the page, with no discernible pattern, were a series of symbols. Although recognisable shapes—a sun, a spiral, a cross, etc.—none seemed to have any apparent meaning, especially out of context.

Ruth rested the paper on the bonnet of the car. "And what are these, do you suppose?"

Greg peered over her shoulder.

"Recognise any of them?" she asked.

"No."

"What about you?" Ruth looked over at Mia, but she shook her head. Ruth then used her phone again to snap several pictures of the page, before returning it to its original spot under the seat.

She took one last glance around the interior of the car, snapped a few more pictures for good measure, then closed the door. After she'd taken yet more pictures of the exterior of the car, the floor and tunnel, she pocketed the phone. "Let's go."

The three of them jogged from the tunnel, and followed the track as best they could, heading back toward the road.

When they were a safe distance from the car, Greg stopped. "Now what do we do?"

"Are you sure you don't recognise that dead man?" Ruth asked Mia.

"I've never seen him before in my life."

"Well, whatever the case," Ruth said with reluctance, "we need to report what we've found."

"To whom?" Greg asked.

"The police, of course."

"We can't do that," Mia said. "Not yet."

"We've already broken the law by looking in the car," Ruth said. "It's a murder scene. I'm sorry, we can't not report it."

"But if we bring this to the police's attention," Mia said, her expression imploring, "whoever shot that guy could get spooked and hurt my brother."

"I agree." Greg gave a firm bob of his head.

Ruth opened her mouth to argue that the murderer might not have any links to Scott, but she closed it again.

Who am I kidding? The events are linked.

Greg stepped next to Mia and folded his arms. "They have a gun, Grandma. They're clearly okay with killing people."

"And if they realise we're on their trail, what do you think they'll do to us?" Mia added. "It's too dangerous to tell anyone what we've found."

Ruth took a breath. "Has it occurred to either of you that Scott might be the one with the gun?" The words tumbled out of her mouth before she had time to vet them.

Mia looked scandalised. "Three things." She held up a finger. "Scott doesn't have a gun. Never even held one. Well, not unless you count the water pistol he had when he was nine." She held up another finger. "My brother is the most laid-back, passive person in the world. Wouldn't hurt a fly. Literally. If there was a war, he'd be a conscientious objector." Mia held up a third finger, and her expression intensified. "He doesn't have a gun."

Greg leaned in, hushed. "Err, you said that one twice."

"I thought it was such an important point that I should repeat it." Mia stared at Ruth. "You really think my brother shot that man? You think he came to Vanmoor, parked his car in that tunnel, shot someone, then escaped on foot and vanished?"

Ruth studied her. "No. No, of course I don't. I'm sorry I mentioned it." Although she had no way to be certain. There wasn't enough evidence to formulate a solid opinion either way.

Besides, Ruth had never met Scott, let alone had time to ascertain his character. Killers came in all shapes, sizes, and personalities. Whenever Ruth attended murder scenes during her time as a police officer, the one thing they had in common was how shocked the neighbours were that such a normal, friendly person could do something so heinous, and right next door.

Ruth's logic so far seemed sound: the body was in the driver's seat, and there was blood under the car, which pointed to the fact the victim had hidden from his assailant, and once they'd gone, he'd climbed into Scott's car. Being behind the wheel, with the keys in the ignition, the man had likely intended to drive away, but had sadly bled out before he'd had the chance.

If only the poor fellow had thought about tying something around his leg as a tourniquet, he might have made it.

Ruth let out a slow breath and looked at her youthful companions. "I'm sorry. We must report this." She held up a hand before they could argue further. "But it doesn't stop us investigating." Ruth tapped her pocket. "I have all those pictures on my phone. We'll sift through the evidence and see what we can uncover." For a brief moment, Ruth cringed at the thought of someone getting hold of her phone and finding those images, but didn't want the hassle of a pass-code, so she'd need to be careful not to leave it lying about.

Mia's shoulders slumped.

"We're not giving up," Ruth said. "It's the right thing to do." *The only thing.* "Besides, the police will have no choice but to listen to you now." Instead of heading back the way they'd come, she followed the gravel road until it turned to mud, and Ruth kept going.

Once they reached the road proper, they'd be able to get their bearings and relay an accurate location.

She only hoped it wasn't too late for Scott.

Ruth leaned against a broken wooden gate at the end of the track, where it met the road. She huffed and crossed her arms. "Where are they?" She'd expected the police to arrive in five or ten minutes after her call, but now it was forty minutes.

As she hugged herself and fought to stay warm, Ruth considered calling again, and making sure she'd described their location accurately. She eyed a sign and the driveway to *Gilding Dairy Farm* opposite.

Is there another entrance to the forest? Have the police gathered there instead?

"Maybe we should go back to Scott's car," Mia said.

"There's no point." Greg checked the map on his phone. "This road is the only way to that tunnel." He eyed the steep embankments on either side of them. "It must have once been the railway line." Greg scrolled across the map to the tunnel's entrance, and then over the hill to the other side, some three or four miles away, but there was no exit visible. "They filled in the track. Now it's only fields that way."

Ruth addressed Mia. "You work?"

"Sorry?"

"Do you have a job?" Ruth asked.

"I started university this year."

Ruth winked at Greg.

Mia looked between them. "What?"

"Greg's on a year out," Ruth said. "Currently travelling the country with his grandma in her motorhome. It's been lovely so far. A real joy. Right, Gregory?"

"I have my own bedroom," Greg said in a rush.

"They're hardly bedrooms," Ruth said. "More like oversized coffins, but they serve our needs."

"We only sleep in the motorhome if we have no choice," Greg said. "Most of the time we stay at hotels."

"Are you retired?" Mia asked Ruth.

"I'm a freelance food consultant," Ruth said. "What are you studying at university?"

"Computer science and artificial intelligence."

Greg nodded as though he understood what that meant. "Has your brother always been into art?"

Mia smiled. "Started off by drawing on walls when he was two. Mum and Dad bought him his first sketchbook because it was cheaper than having to redecorate the house every week."

Ruth was about to ask another question when a police car pulled from the road and onto the track. "At last."

Greg's face fell.

Sergeant Fry climbed from the car and let out a long breath when he laid eyes on the three of them.

"Let me do the talking," Ruth said through the corner of her mouth. "We don't want either of you two annoying him again."

"He's the annoying one," Greg muttered back. "Guy's an idiot."

"I agree," Mia said.

"We thought you'd never arrive," Ruth said with a painted smile.

"Got here as soon as I could." Sergeant Fry looked between them and smoothed his goatee. "A report of someone asleep in their car?"

"Not asleep," Ruth said. "Dead. *Extremely* dead. And not their car either. Someone else's." She didn't buy that the emergency operator hadn't passed on accurate details.

"My brother's car." Mia folded her arms. "You know, the guy you said hadn't visited Vanmoor? Well, his car is back there."

A flicker of a frown crossed Sergeant Fry's face. "Where exactly?"

Ruth thrust a thumb over her shoulder. "A third of a mile that way."

Sergeant Fry's gaze moved from the mud road to his patrol car, and then back to Ruth. "What are you doing out here?"

"We went for a walk," Ruth said.

"Bit remote for a stroll." Sergeant Fry's brow furrowed as he looked at the snow-laden ground and then Greg and Mia.

Greg shrugged.

"It's a lovely forest," Mia said with a hint of sarcasm.

Ruth wanted to signal her to keep her cool but feared Sergeant Fry would see it.

He refocused on her. "Second reported death in as many days. That's quite some record."

Ruth sighed. "My bad luck."

His eyes narrowed, and he waved a hand. "Lead the way."

The four of them followed the track in silence, with Ruth hoping she'd not left behind any evidence that she'd looked inside the vehicle, rather than calling the police right away.

If Sara found out Ruth had gotten her son involved with another murder case, she'd demand Greg return home immediately and then would never speak to her again. Plus, if they wound up arrested and detained, delaying their visit to Ivywick Island further, Margaret would have yet another thing to hang over Ruth's head.

A few minutes later, a hundred feet after the mud turned back to gravel, they reached the railway tunnel, and Mia gasped.

Ruth hurried over to her and stared too. "What the—?"

Scott's car had vanished.

The three of them stood at the end of the old railway tunnel with expressions of puzzlement mixed with shock.

Something as big as a car, or anything else for that matter, couldn't vanish without a logical explanation. Even so, Ruth's brain worked through possible scenarios, including alien abduction and the dead guy coming back to life and driving off.

Greg looked about. "You got me. Where is it?"

"A good question," Sergeant Fry said through gritted teeth.

Mia pointed to the ground. "Scott's car was right here." Her voice turned shrill. "Someone's moved it. Why would they do that?"

Ruth peered into the darkened tunnel. "Perhaps we should look deeper inside."

"There's nothing in there," Sergeant Fry said. "It's blocked off." He gave them a hard look and marched back outside.

"What about the pictures on your phone?" Greg said to Ruth.

She put a finger to her lips.

Fortunately, Sergeant Fry didn't seem to have heard.

Something in the pit of her stomach told her to hold off. Especially seeing as her mobile held images containing proof Ruth had checked out a crime scene, when she should have done an about-face and called the police immediately. Sergeant Fry didn't seem like the type of person to take kindly to that admission.

He turned back. "What did the victim look like?"

"In his twenties," Ruth said. "Mousy blond hair."

"Seriously. You need to show him the photos," Mia whispered to her as Fry walked away. "It proves we're telling the truth."

Ruth shook her head. "I will, but not yet." She knelt and used the torch on her phone to examine the floor of the tunnel. "Someone's cleaned up." Ruth indicated wet brush marks. "Stones are damp. They washed away the blood."

"How did they know the blood was under the car?" Mia asked.

"Never mind that," Greg said. "How did they get past us? The track is the only way in or out."

"Scott's car is a 4x4," Mia said. "They could have driven through the woods before we got back here."

Ruth straightened. "Then we should look for tyre marks."

Back outside, they met up with Sergeant Fry and spent the next few minutes searching for any impressions in the mud beyond the gravel section of the track, or the snow on either side, but there was nothing of any note. No signs the car had cut across the forest.

They then headed back toward the tunnel again, scanning for any clues they may have missed, but found nothing to indicate the car had come this way. It was as if someone had snapped their fingers and it had vanished into thin air.

"Your brother might have come back for it," Sergeant Fry said to Mia, although he looked as though he still didn't believe a word they were saying.

"He would've needed to move the body to do that," Ruth said. "It was in the driver's seat."

Sergeant Fry folded his arms.

"And why would he clean up the blood?" Mia asked. "My brother would've called the police."

Ruth hesitated as a thought struck her: *Could Scott be the killer?* After all, it was his car. *But if that's the case, why was the body in the driver's seat?* For a moment, she pictured a carjacking gone wrong, but couldn't imagine a scenario where Scott had shot the guy in the leg, especially at that angle. *Where did he get the gun?* With so little evidence making sense, Ruth chose not to voice her concerns yet. "Try calling Scott again."

Mia did, but it went straight to voicemail. She also checked the tracking app, but his phone appeared to still be switched off.

"I need to get back to the village." Sergeant Fry's expression turned cold. "Don't waste my time again." He scowled at Ruth and marched off.

Ruth, Mia, and Greg returned to where the track met the road. Ruth motioned down the hill. "Let's get back to Vanmoor and take stock." She needed time to process.

"Where are we going exactly?" Mia hugged herself and looked about as if she expected them to run into the killer at any moment.

"We'll go somewhere quiet where we can figure out what the symbols mean," Ruth said. The sooner they made it back to the village and were surrounded by people, the better. "Come on."

As they walked, Mia asked Ruth, "How long were you a police officer?"

She pursed her lips. "Including training, fourteen years."

"And you were going to be a detective?"

"That was the original plan."

"What happened?"

"She was sacked," Greg said. "For investigating Grandad's murder."

Mia's face dropped. "You're not joking, are you?"

"He's not." Ruth did everything she could to keep the last memories of John from her thoughts. She didn't want to remember him that way, and he'd be furious if she held on to anything but the happy times they spent together. "How about we sing a song while we walk?"

"No," Greg said.

"A happy melody," Ruth suggested. "Something cheery and uplifting."

"No."

"Try to stay in tune this time." Ruth winked, and belted out "Bohemian Rhapsody" at the top of her lungs.

9

Vanmoor Village Library, situated next to the church, was a modern building compared to its surroundings: a single-storied construction with a low, angular roof, large windows, and a clean white facade that stood in stark contrast to the nearby graveyard.

The well-lit interior with its high ceilings was as contemporary as the outside, with large skylights and clusters of spotlights, plus a spacious study area. Metal bookshelves filled the primary space, crammed full of various fiction and nonfiction titles. The shelves themselves had built-in striplights, and stood on tracks in the floor, so someone could move and rearrange them.

As impressive as it was, the library sat empty, save for a librarian and an old guy reading a newspaper in a chair by the entrance. Ruth assumed everyone was still at the winter fete.

She had also thought the library may have some local archives that would shed light on the symbols. She was wrong. Having scanned the relevant shelves several times,

Ruth sat with Greg and Mia, huddled at a table in the far corner, away from prying ears.

Greg had fetched his laptop from the B&B while Ruth checked on Merlin, then from her phone she'd emailed him a copy of the page they'd found in the car. Greg used the library printer to run off a hard copy, and now researched the random symbols on the internet, muttering under his breath, shaking his head, then moving on to another website, growing more frustrated by the minute.

"What about this one?" Mia pointed to a symbol at the top corner of the page, and then the corresponding image on a website.

"That makes little sense either." Greg sighed. "Let's try a reverse image match."

After twenty minutes of futile searching, Ruth got to her feet and stretched. She sauntered over to the nearest window and peered out, taking in the view of fields and forests beyond.

The last she recalled seeing symbols as strange as these was during the time she'd spent decades ago with her husband. They'd gone on an off-trail archaeological tour of Saqqara in Egypt, climbed all over its stepped pyramid and temple ruins.

However, on one particularly scorching day, John had deviated from the group, drawn to a recent dig nearby that had uncovered a necropolis of burial chambers.

"Look at this, Ru-Ru." He jumped into the nearest pit, crouched, and examined the wall. "Amazing."

"John." Ruth hissed. "Get out of there."

"This is incredible. You can see the tool marks." John waved her down. "Come and look."

Ruth glanced about to make sure no one was watching,

took John's hand, and dropped beside him. "You'll get us arrested."

"Only looking, Ru-Ru, not touching anything. We'll be careful." He winked. "Now, look at this."

Time stood still as they examined the pits. At one point Ruth found the faint outline of hieroglyphs carved into the rock.

John let out a shout of excitement over that discovery. "To think someone carved this out thousands of years ago." He shook his head, and tears formed in his eyes. "I'm so happy we came here."

Ruth had to admit John's enthusiasm had been contagious, and ever since that day, Egyptian history had fascinated her.

However, by the time they'd left those burial pits, the group had gone, vanished, along with the bus they'd travelled in.

The two of them had been alone.

Greg huffed for the millionth time. "This is ridiculous."

Ruth ambled back to the table and dropped to the seat next to him.

"Symbols can have a load of different meanings," Greg said in an exasperated tone. He pointed to the drawing of a bird on the photo she'd taken. "If this is a dove, it can represent peace, divinity, freedom . . ." He then indicated a circle with rays. "This could be energy, life, or a literal representation of the sun." Greg sat back. "Same with all these symbols. Unless we have some context, some idea where they're from, it means we have no way to understand them."

Mia studied the screen. "There doesn't appear to be a common theme."

"Exactly my point," Greg said. "It's hopeless."

Ruth examined the image on her phone, as if it might

give her a new perspective, and then noticed the time. She stood. "Keep working. I need to go to the bistro. I'll be back as quickly as I can."

Greg closed the laptop and pocketed the sheet of symbols. "We'll come with you."

Back on Vanmoor High Street, Ruth stopped outside a shop with signs filling the plate glass windows, declaring Elsie's Bistro would have a grand opening that night.

Once Greg and Mia had caught up, she knocked on the door.

When this didn't get a response, she tried the handle.

Finding the door unlocked, Ruth opened it and stuck her head inside. "Hello?"

The bistro had a wooden floor and ceiling, with low-hanging beams. Black-and-white photographs of Vanmoor hung on exposed red-brick walls, while old wooden chairs with cushions surrounded circular tables with thick legs.

Ruth motioned for Greg and Mia to follow her in.

Someone had placed candles on each table, along with menus and cutlery. Edison lightbulbs hung from the ceiling at various heights, creating a warm and inviting atmosphere. Soft jazz music played from hidden speakers.

Ahead sat an oak counter, with shelves behind filled with condiments, white mugs hanging from hooks, and chalkboards listing specials.

Ruth eyed the counter, and called, "Elsie? Are you here?" She then stepped to a door and grabbed the handle.

"Grandma." Greg rushed forward. "What are you doing?"

"Elsie might have fallen over back there. Besides, I'm invited." She opened the door and strode into a kitchen, which stood in stark contrast to the bistro.

It had stainless steel worktops, bright working lights

overhead, and polished pots and pans hanging from the ceiling. A giant range cooker sat in the middle of one wall, with several hobs, and cutting boards stacked to one side.

Ruth whistled. "Impressive."

"Is Elsie a millionaire?" Greg said, wide-eyed. "How did she afford all this?"

"We don't know what job she did before," Ruth said. "Could have inherited the money." She sauntered down one side of the room, soaking it all in. Everything looked brand new, spotless, and in its place. Ruth opened a fridge. It was jam-packed with fresh fruits and vegetables, all arranged in size and shape.

Opposite, another door stood ajar.

"Anyone here?" Ruth held her breath and waited for a response, but still none came. "Elsie?" She nudged the door open with her foot.

Beyond was a narrow cupboard with shelves, each labelled and full of cans and packets with their own labels aligned and facing outward. However, that was not what drew Ruth's attention: a trapdoor stood propped open, with a set of steps leading down.

She hesitated, knowing she should not go down there, but curiosity drove her on. Anyway, if Elsie lay hurt somewhere, they wasted precious minutes.

Ruth looked back at Greg and Mia.

They both shook their heads.

Ruth gave them an apologetic smile, then went to descend the stairs, but a voice called,

"Hello?" Elsie stepped into the kitchen, clutching a wooden crate. "Ah, there you are."

"Sorry," Ruth said. "We thought you might be back here."

Elsie set the box down and gestured around her. "What do you think?"

"Very impressive," Ruth said, and meant it.

Elsie beamed. "I've spared no expense." She opened a drawer, pulled out a binder, and handed it to Ruth. "All my recipes and menus. Would love your opinion. It simply has to be perfect. I want nothing less."

Ruth flicked through its imposing bulk. Elsie had labelled each section with colour-coded tabs. "I'm going to need a comfy chair and a sweet cup of tea."

"I can do better than that. How about samples?" Elsie looked over at Greg at Mia. "Hungry? I have enough for you too."

"Thanks," they said in unison.

Elsie clapped her hands and ushered the three of them into the bistro. "My first ever customers. I'm so excited."

Ruth passed the binder to Greg. "I'll need to wash my hands."

Elsie pointed to a door in the corner. "Through there. Can't miss it."

Ruth strode into a hallway with three other doors. The first stood open: a cleaning cupboard packed full of shelves and supplies, everything neat and in its place, labels out.

Elsie certainly likes things tidy.

The two remaining doors had quaint wooden signs: the one on the left a pirate, and the one on the right a mermaid.

Even though she would've loved to choose the pirate, Ruth guessed the mermaid showed the way to the ladies'.

Sure enough, inside was a compact, tiled room with a toilet and sink. Above the sink sat a shelf with fourteen bottles of scented hand soap, everything from lavender and jasmine to sea minerals and cookie dough.

Soft music played, and a breeze tickled Ruth's ankle. She

looked down at the gap under the door and shivered. A draught excluder would make this room perfect.

She smiled to herself as she washed her hands. If Elsie was this organised, the bistro would be a roaring success.

Now to sample the menu . . .

Ruth, Greg, and Mia sat at a table next to the window.

They helped themselves to sandwiches and cakes, while Ruth worked her way through the files. Elsie had included all the cost breakdowns and projected profits, written next to each recipe in a neat hand. Elsie's meticulous record-keeping impressed Ruth, and she assumed the bistro owner may have trained as a company accountant in a previous life.

Elsie would periodically refill their drinks—Ruth's tea, coffee for Greg, and hot chocolate for Mia—and then back away with an anxious expression.

However, Ruth could find no reason for her apprehension. Sure, the scones could have done with a little less vanilla extract, and she'd made a few other minor notes for Elsie to consider on a few of the other recipes, but overall, the menu seemed perfect.

It included a selection of ten different sandwiches, everything from cucumber to salmon, with various choices of garnish. The rest of the cake recipes looked amazing. It was clear Elsie had a grip on the situation and knew what she was doing.

Ruth frowned. In fact, she wasn't sure why Elsie had wanted her input at all. She certainly didn't need it.

Clearly a perfectionist.

The front door opened, and Mia stiffened in her seat.

Greg tapped Ruth's arm as in stepped Milo, the golden Labrador with the blue collar. He now had a matching lead, and on the other end of that lead was . . . Reverend Collins.

Milo made a beeline for Greg, tail swishing in recognition.

"Afternoon," Reverend Collins said.

Ruth nodded, stunned that he had been mere feet from them and a murder scene.

Greg patted Milo awkwardly on the head.

Reverend Collins looked between Elsie and Ruth. "How are things progressing?"

"Great." Ruth cleared her throat and closed the binder. "Better than great."

"Really?" Elsie sighed in relief. "I'm determined to succeed at all costs, no matter what it takes. This has to be perfect. I've dreamt about opening my own place since I was a child, and it was Frank's dream too. He made me promise I'd see it through, so I'll do whatever it takes." She beamed. "It will be a success."

"I believe you," Ruth said.

"Elsie's the best, isn't she?" Reverend Collins pulled a folded sheet of paper from his pocket and handed it to her. "The list, as promised." He scanned the bistro. "Everyone's coming."

Elsie tucked it into the front pocket of her apron and addressed Ruth. "It's the grand opening tonight. Say you'll come."

"Oh," Ruth said, caught off guard. "That's very kind, but—"

"You're all invited." Elsie motioned to Greg and Mia. "I won't take no for an answer. After all, you've been such a big help."

Greg brushed crumbs from his shirt. "You're welcome."

Ruth stifled a laugh. "We haven't done much at all."

"Nonsense," Reverend Collins said. "Vanmoor appreciates help, big or small, from near or far." He nodded at Elsie.

"Tonight." Then he gave the lead a light tug. "Come, Milo." Reverend Collins opened the door but stopped. "Oh, Elsie." His face turned solemn, and he spoke in a hushed, somber voice. "Are you able to supply the catering for Dorothy's wake next week?"

"Of course," Elsie said. "We can have it here."

"Excellent. I'm writing the eulogy tonight, so I'll also list some suggestions, and you can go through it with me tomorrow."

"Tonight?" Elsie frowned. "What about the party?"

"I'll do it after. I'm a night owl. Always have been. Need very little sleep these days. A few hours at most. I'm often up past two in the morning." Reverend Collins smiled. "I find it's the time of day I write my best sermons. Nice and quiet. Peaceful. Anyway . . ." He gave Milo's lead another light tug, and they left.

Ruth stood and handed the binder back to Elsie.

She clutched it to her chest. "Thank you so much."

"I really haven't done a lot," Ruth said. "You clearly have a full grasp of what you're doing. I'm sure it'll be a roaring success."

"Oh, it has to be," Elsie said.

Greg stuffed two fairy cakes into his mouth and got to his feet.

Mia stood too and stared at his puffed cheeks. "That's quite impressive. Or disgusting. Maybe a bit of both."

"You should see him at a fast-food restaurant," Ruth said. "Food barely touches the sides of his mouth on the way down."

"Can I offer you more drinks before you go?" Elsie asked as she followed them across the bistro. "Fruit juice? Something carbonated? A fizzy pop? Iced tea?"

"No thank you," Mia said.

Greg opened the door.

Elsie let out a breath and arched her eyebrows at Ruth. "See you tonight, then? Seven o'clock? You can sample some more of my offerings and let me know your thoughts. Oh, wait." She hurried to the cash register, opened the drawer, and grabbed a stack of twenty-pound notes. She offered them to Ruth.

Ruth held up a hand. "That won't be necessary."

"Are you sure?"

"Positive. Thank you. The wall, remember?" Ruth smiled. "Tonight." She stepped outside before Elsie had the chance to insist they sample something else. Ruth rubbed her belly. "I think I'm going to explode."

As the three of them waddled away from the bistro, Greg said, "She's a bit weird."

"How can you say that?" Mia frowned at him. "Elsie's lovely. Really sweet."

Greg shrugged. "I suppose. She did give us free lunch."

Now they came to mention it, Ruth's opinion of Elsie was somewhere between the two extremes: although there did seem something not quite right with her, a tad overexuberant perhaps, extreme, competitive, a bit obsessed. Ruth put it down to nervous energy and wanting to do well.

"What now?" Greg asked.

Ruth's thoughts returned to Mia's brother.

In this modern world, with mobile phones, cameras, and satellites watching your every move, it was unlikely someone went missing unless they made a deliberate effort to, or someone else had seen to it.

Either way, Ruth didn't hold out much hope, and with his car now gone, no doubt moved by the killer of the stranger, they had zero clues to follow.

"I need a bath," she muttered.

Greg frowned. "Is now really the right time?"

"Best time," Ruth said. "Let's go back to our rooms and relax. Think things through. To mull over the day's events, I need heaps and heaps of fragranced bubbles." She sighed. "Let's see if we can figure out a new line of enquiry." Ruth looked over at Mia. "You're welcome to come back too."

She shrugged. "I've got nothing else to do. And I'm not leaving until I find Scott."

Greg smiled.

"Then it's settled." As they continued down the high street, Ruth remembered the locket. After her bath, she vowed to call Mr and Mrs Wilkinson and let them know she had it.

In the B&B, the three of them approached the reception desk, but all was quiet.

"Hello? Anyone here? Constance?" When there came no reply, Ruth circled the desk and removed both sets of room keys.

She had trouble dragging her overfull belly up the stairs, and along the landing, but when Ruth opened her bedroom door, all thoughts of indigestion evaporated. "What the—"

10

Some delightful specimen of a human being had taken time out of their busy day to ransack Ruth's bedroom —clothes tossed onto the bed and floor, suitcase open, cushions pulled from the sofa and chairs in the sitting area, drawers yanked free and tossed aside—total carnage.

The connecting door to Greg's room stood ajar, and his belongings also lay strewn about the place.

"Someone's robbed you," Mia said.

Ruth gasped. "Merlin." She rushed over to his box, held her breath, and peered inside. "I don't believe it." She shook her head.

Merlin lay curled on his cushion. He opened one eye and let out a raspy meow as if to say, *"What's your problem? Did I miss something?"* then went back to sleep.

Ruth sat back. "Great work, Merlin. Another successful day as a security guard. Remind me to give you a pay increase."

Greg appeared from his bedroom with a confused expression. "What were they after? Nothing valuable is missing."

Ruth looked about, brow furrowed. "They didn't take money because that's in my handbag. They weren't interested in Merlin. Which only leaves . . ." She held up the locket. "This."

Greg's eyes widened. "From the lucky dip? How would anyone know you have that?"

"Perhaps they saw me open it at the fete." Ruth pointed to the corner of her bedroom, next to Merlin's box. "Both of you, please stand there." Once Greg and Mia moved into position, Ruth got to her feet. "Don't move. I mean it. Touch nothing." With a rush of determination mixed with anger, she picked her way across the room, and then raced along the landing.

"Where are you going?" Greg called after her.

Ruth hurried down the stairs to the reception desk and hit the bell. Several times. "Constance?" she shouted. "Hello? Are you here?" When this didn't get a response, Ruth stepped into the back office.

She eyed Dorothy's old bedroom through the other door, but nothing seemed disturbed. Ruth grabbed a roll of clear tape from the office desk, then headed back to reception. She marched through the sitting area into a kitchen with a table dominating the room.

Still no sign of Constance.

Ruth rested her hand on the oven, then the stove top, and finally the kettle. *All cold.* No one here recently. She snatched a pair of rubber gloves from a hook by the sink, then opened a cupboard. On the top shelf sat a box of sandwich bags. Ruth removed a few and stuffed them into her pocket with the tape.

After checking about the kitchen for anything else useful for her immediate needs, Ruth pulled on the gloves and returned to her bedroom.

Greg and Mia, like a couple of statues, stood shoulder to shoulder as Ruth edged around the outside of the room, careful where she placed her feet.

"What is she doing?" Mia breathed to Greg.

"Detective stuff."

Ruth knelt so her eyeline matched the height of the table, and she shone her phone torch across its surface. Finding nothing, she stepped behind the sofa, examined the scattered cushions, and then the upholstery, searching for any stray hairs or fibres.

Finding no clues there either, Ruth turned her attention to the bedroom area. She shone the torch on various surfaces, then knelt by the bed. "Ah-ha."

She removed the clear tape from her pocket, tore off a length, and touched it against her bedsheet. Then Ruth pressed the tape inside one of the clear food bags and held it up to the light.

"What have you found?" Greg asked.

Along with several blue fibres—Ruth only wore black and pink—was a single strand of hair. She rushed back to the sitting room, bag held high. "We have a winner." Ruth gestured Greg and Mia over. "Red hair. Blue cardigan."

Greg pulled a face. "Constance?"

"That girl we bumped into earlier?" Mia asked.

"The new owner of this place." Greg shook his head. "She probably made the beds this morning. Doesn't mean she ransacked the place."

Ruth pocketed the bag and considered calling the police, but decided against it for two reasons: firstly, nothing seemed to be missing, nothing stolen; and secondly, Sergeant Fry would answer the call. Ruth yanked off the gloves. "I don't have a fingerprint kit, so we can tidy now."

The three of them spent the next twenty minutes righting furniture and returning items to their proper places.

Ruth thought back to several months prior when someone attempted to break into her home in Surrey while Sara was away for the weekend. The intruder had damaged the latch on the study window and gained entry, but in the end had taken nothing there either. Probably been spooked by the alarm before they had the chance.

Ruth gritted her teeth. The nerve some criminals had to take things that didn't belong to them. Their lack of empathy angered her to the core, and was one of the many reasons she'd joined the force.

When they were done, Mia and Greg sat on the sofa, while Ruth dropped into the chair opposite with a heavy sigh, a bucket of sweet, milky tea in hand.

On her phone, she located the image of the B&B ledger, and the number for the Wilkinsons. "Time we found out what's so important about this locket." Ruth dialled, and someone answered right away.

"Hello?"

"Hi, sorry to bother you." Ruth activated the speaker function and set the phone on the coffee table. "Is this Mrs Wilkinson?"

"Yes?"

"The same Mrs Wilkinson who stayed at Molly's B&B in Vanmoor?"

"Who is this?"

"My name is Ruth Morgan. I believe I have your locket."

"Oh, thank goodness. We were so worried. Where did you find it?"

"Right here," Ruth lied. "At Molly's." She left out the fact she'd won it in a lucky dip. A lucky dip game no doubt orchestrated by Constance for some bizarre reason. Now all Ruth needed to do was figure out why the girl had wanted her to have the locket, only to then ransack her room trying to retrieve it. *Why the change of heart? Was she trying to frame me? Get rid of a stolen item?* Ruth cleared her throat. "I'd be happy to send it to you."

"That's very kind," Mrs Wilkinson said. "We'd be glad to pay for your trouble."

"No trouble." Ruth pulled out the locket and flipped it over in her hand. "May I ask, when did it go missing?"

"We're not sure," Mrs Wilkinson said. "Perhaps a couple of nights ago. I couldn't find it the following morning."

"And you thought someone stole it?"

There came a few seconds' pause. "Erm, we—"

"Forgive me," Ruth said. "I overheard you and your husband outside Molly's. I didn't mean to eavesdrop, but you said, 'She *stole the locket from our room.*' Who were you referring to?" As if she couldn't guess.

"Understand I was upset," Mrs Wilkinson said. "That locket has been in my family for three generations." She took a breath. "When Terry and I got back from dinner, we saw the landlady leaving our room."

Ruth's eyebrows lifted. "Dorothy?" She glanced at Greg and Mia.

They looked equally surprised.

"We startled her," Mrs Wilkinson said. "The landlady held something in her fist. The next morning, I assumed it was—"

"Your locket," Ruth finished.

"I was wrong. I feel like such a fool."

Ruth now wondered if Dorothy had taken the locket and

placed it in the lucky dip parcel. Then Constance had somehow found out. "Were you in Vanmoor for pleasure?"

"Oh, heavens no," Mrs Wilkins said in a tone of disgust. "Terry is an artist. He met with Quentin Strange, who showed interest in Terry's work, but then declined. Complete waste of our time. The whole trip was a disaster."

Ruth stared at Greg and Mia before she shook herself. "Your address, Mrs Wilkinson?"

Ruth typed the details into her phone and made a mental note that Flamingo the art gallery owner's name was Quentin, but decided she preferred Flamingo. It suited him better.

"Are the pictures still inside?" Mrs Wilkinson asked.

"Excuse me?"

"The locket. Are the pictures still there?"

Ruth hadn't thought to open it. Lockets were like diaries: private. "You want me to look?"

"Please. It would put my mind at rest."

"Sure. Hold on." Ruth undid the clasp, and a folded piece of paper fell out. "Oh."

"Are they still there?" Mrs Wilkinson asked, her voice strained.

Ruth unfolded the paper and read what was written inside.

"Hello?" Mrs Wilkinson said. "What's wrong?"

"Nothing. All good," Ruth murmured. She gathered herself and studied the sepia photographs: a handsome man and woman in their forties, dressed in Victorian clothes. "The photos are here. They're fine."

"Thank goodness. My great-great-grandparents," Mrs Wilkinson said. "Or is it great-great-great-grandparents? I can never remember."

Ruth set the locket aside and stared at the note. On it, written in red ink, were three words:

Call the police.

Ruth frowned. *Why would Dorothy want the Wilkinsons to call the police? Call them about what?*

"Are you still there?"

Ruth blinked herself back to the moment. "Yes. I am. Sorry." She cleared her throat. "Did anything unusual happen during your stay?"

"Like what?"

"Anything out of the ordinary."

"I told you the landlady was rather odd," Mrs Wilkinson said. "But apart from that, no, nothing. Why?"

Ruth stared at the note, and then looked up at Mia. "Did you happen to see a young man staying at the B&B?"

"I think we were the only guests," Mrs Wilkinson said. "I can't know that for sure, but we didn't see anyone else."

Mia's shoulders slumped.

Greg mouthed the word, "*Car.*"

"And you didn't happen to spot a black Land Rover parked across the road?" Ruth asked.

"I'm afraid not," Mrs Wilkinson said. "The village was quite dead when we arrived, and the only people here were setting up for the winter fete."

"Of course." Ruth scratched her head.

If Dorothy took the locket, planted the note, and intended to give it back to the Wilkinsons but missed her chance, then why would Constance give it to me, only to then turn our rooms upside down? Did Dorothy steal the locket, but Constance was the one to plant the note?

If so, why does Constance now want me to have the locket

and call the police? Ruth still came full circle to the same question: *Call them about what?*

"I'll get your locket to you as soon as possible," Ruth said. "Gotta go." She hung up and let out a breath.

Greg sat forward. "What's written on that note?"

Ruth held it up for them to see.

Mia's face dropped.

An hour later, refreshed from a long soak in a bath with so many bubbles they almost touched the ceiling, Ruth headed down the front path of Molly's B&B, looking forward to asking questions at the party. Greg and Mia hurried to keep up.

First, Scott had gone missing, then either Constance or Dorothy had stolen Mrs Wilkinson's locket, only for Dorothy to then have "fallen" down the stairs and died.

Constance had made sure Ruth wound up with the locket from the lucky dip bucket, of that she was certain. *Call the police for what reason, though? Did someone threaten them?* After all, the note in the locket had come before Dorothy's death. *Or did it?*

Ruth thought back. There was no way to be certain because Constance had given her the locket after Dorothy's death. *But why ask for me to call the police?* Sergeant Fry had already spoken to Constance.

Ruth considered it now vitally important to pose these questions to the young lady as a matter of urgency. Constance was the key to unravelling part of the mystery.

As Greg and Mia followed her to the gate, Ruth worked through the remaining events. They'd found Scott's car with someone else's body inside, along with the odd sheet of symbols, only to then have that body go missing, car and all.

She stopped at the gate and blew out a puff of air. All these things had to be linked, but she couldn't yet see the connection or the proper sequence of events.

"I don't understand why you want us to go to this party," Greg muttered.

"Me neither," Mia said. "People around here aren't exactly friendly to me."

"Keep quiet and observe while I mingle," Ruth said. "I'm hoping everyone from the village will be there, and this is my best chance to ask them questions. Constance is my priority, though. I must corner her and demand answers."

"You think she knows something about my brother disappearing?" Mia asked. "It has something to do with the note?"

"Of that, I'm confident," Ruth said. "Only not sure how it all slots together. I'll question everyone I can."

Mia shrugged. "I still don't think they'll say much, even to you."

"Perhaps not," Ruth said. "But we must try." She opened the gate and gestured.

They walked down Vanmoor High Street to Elsie's Bistro. Someone had removed the sheets, and now it was ablaze with lights. Balloons, streamers, and bunting filled the windows.

Ruth opened the door and stepped inside.

Around thirty people gathered in groups of five or six. As they chatted, Ruth picked out two familiar faces: Reverend Collins in an animated discussion with a woman in a wheelchair; while Flamingo hovered by the drinks table, wearing his trademark salmon suit, and a scowl.

"Nice of him to dress up for the occasion," Ruth murmured.

A buffet table ran down one side of the bistro, crammed full of loaded serving plates; everything from hors d'oeuvres and canapés to stacks of triangular sandwiches—one shaped like the Great Pyramid—and crepes, to trifles, mini apple pies, and a bewildering assortment of cakes.

Elsie had also decked out the bistro's interior with hundreds of fairy lights strung from the ceiling, lit candles, and a silver "*Grand Opening*" banner hung across the back wall.

Ruth breathed in a giddying cacophony of scents: freshly baked bread, cakes, lemon, vanilla, spices, and roasted coffee beans.

Elsie squealed, rushed forward, and beamed. "So glad you came." She jiggled up and down and took Ruth's hands. "Well? What do you think? Isn't it perfect? Please say it's perfect." Her purple beehive hairdo now had silver stars woven into it, and instead of her flowery apron, Elsie wore a black one with gold lettering spelling out the name of the bistro.

Ruth smiled back at her. "It is perfect, and I wouldn't miss it for the world. You've outdone yourself."

"I have, haven't I? Frank would be so proud of me. People love the vol-au-vents," Elsie said with pride. "I added more cream to the chicken sauce and a pinch of black pepper, like you suggested. They're wonderful." She looked over at Greg and Mia. "You must try them before they're all gone."

"Don't need to ask me twice." Greg made a beeline for the buffet table, with Mia in tow.

Several of the gathered guests glared at Mia and turned their backs on her.

"I'll fetch you a plate." Elsie released Ruth from her grasp and rushed after them, almost barrelling over Constable Bishop in the process, who still wore her police uniform.

Ruth scanned the faces of the gathered guests, but Constance didn't appear among them. However, Sergeant Fry was here, scowling at her from the corner of the room.

Ruth gave him a jaunty wave.

11

With the bistro party in full swing, Ruth kept away from the gathered crowds and studied their faces from afar. No one leapt out as being a serial killer, but there was a suspicious lady in a rain mac shoveling an outrageous amount of garlic sauce onto a pickle sandwich.

Ruth screwed up her face and shuddered.

Unquestionably a deviant.

"Here she is . . . light of my life." Trevor pushed through the crowd. He hadn't bothered to change either, and still wore his overalls. "Everythin' okay, my lovely cherub of delight?"

Ruth's cheeks flushed. "Have you been drinking?"

"A smidge." Trevor winked. "Keep that to yourself. Anyway, yer mobile mansion is on track for a full repair. Should be finished by late tomorrow afternoon if the weather behaves itself." He noticed the flicker of a frown cross Ruth's face and added, "No way I could fit the darn thing in my garage. Been workin' on it in the driveway." His face then turned serious. "Heard about Dorothy. Terrible news. Bill's cut up about it too. He's only recently done some work for 'er at the B&B."

"You knew Dorothy well?" Ruth asked.

Trevor gave a small shrug. "As far as I'm aware, she's lived in Vanmoor all her life. I moved 'ere fifteen years ago. From Cornwall. Prefer the chillier climes. Dorothy inherited the B&B from her grandmother, by all accounts." He shook his head. "And to think she lost Arthur only a couple of months back."

"Arthur?"

"Dorothy's 'usband," Trevor said. "Never met such a hardworkin' fella in all me life. Self-made millionaire. Well, that's the rumour."

Ruth's eyebrows rose. "What did he do?"

"Artist," Trevor said. "Very talented. Have one of 'is in my garage."

"The colourful landscape?"

Trevor nodded. "Arthur was one of those prolific types."

Ruth recalled all the paintings hanging on the walls of the B&B. "Last name Pennington? A. Pennington?"

"That's 'im. Real shame to lose the old guy. Arthur could paint anything 'e liked. Incredible portraits. A master of 'is craft. No one finer." Trevor lowered his voice. "He also painted some of that modern surrealist nonsense, but we can forgive 'im for that, can't we?" He waved Bill over. "Surprised old Billy Boy showed up, to be honest with yer."

"Oh, why's that?" Ruth asked.

"He's been busy lately. Fixed a squeaky door at the church, chopped down a rotten tree at the back of the library, then mended something or other in the basement 'ere." Trevor shook his head as Bill approached. "So rushed off yer feet yer missed our usual pie and chips at the One-Legged Mare."

"I did. Sorry again." Bill held out a glass of champagne to Ruth. "Here you go, young lady." He looked drawn, bags under his eyes, and kept glancing about the place.

"Young?" Ruth accepted the drink with a smirk. "Oh, if only that were true, Bill."

"Nonsense," Trevor said. "Yer in yer prime."

"Right," Bill agreed. "Decades of mischief ahead of you." He caught Elsie's eye, and his expression turned serious again. "Speaking of which, if you'll excuse me."

"Hold on," Ruth said. "Before you go, can I ask you both something?"

Bill turned back.

Ruth plucked a piece of light-coloured twine from his dark shirt and lowered her voice. "Have either of you seen a black 4x4 with a white stripe parked in the village?"

"When?" Trevor asked.

"Last week."

Trevor pursed his lips. "Can't say I 'ave." He looked at Bill.

"Nope," Bill said. "Why do you ask?"

"You both heard about Mia's brother? Scott?"

"The blonde girl?" Trevor said. "She came to my work-shop and asked about 'im a few days back. Haven't seen the lad."

Bill shook his head and looked away.

Ruth hesitated, unsure she should divulge much more, but given the fact they'd made little progress over the last few hours, she threw caution to the wind. She kept her voice low. "We found Scott's car."

Trevor's eyebrows lifted. "Yer did?"

"In the forest outside town."

"Delph Woods," Bill said. "What was it doing there?"

"That's what we were trying to figure out," Ruth said.

"That's not all." She glanced about to make sure no one eavesdropped. "We found it parked in a tunnel." She opted to leave out the fact there had been a stranger's body inside.

"Used to be an old railway tunnel," Bill said. "Closed in the seventies. Cuts right through Delph Hill."

"So what 'appened after yer found the car?" Trevor asked.

"We lost it," Ruth said.

Trevor frowned. "Yer what?"

"I called the police, and we waited by the road. But by the time Sergeant Fry had arrived, and we'd taken him to the tunnel, the car had vanished." Ruth looked between them, studying their reactions.

"Hate to break it to yer," Trevor said. "Cars don't disappear. Someone must 'ave driven it off somewhere."

Bill stared at Ruth, eyes narrowed. "You waited by the road? At the end of the old railway track? Next to the green gate?"

"Yes," she said. "Any idea how they got past us with no one noticing?"

Bill's frown deepened. "We've been through Delph Woods plenty of times," he said to Trevor.

"On our way to the river." Trevor nodded. "Great fishin spot."

"Right you are," Bill said, his expression now intense. "There's no other way out of there. Can't cut through the forest in a car. Impossible. Gates are all too narrow."

Trevor shook his head. "Whoever moved that vehicle would 'ave 'ad to . . ." He trailed off and stared at his friend.

"No other explanation." Bill's attention moved to Elsie on the other side of the room. "Please excuse me." He slinked off.

"Is something wrong?" Ruth asked. "He doesn't look

well."

Trevor shrugged. "Overworked. What with all the odd jobs, he's also spent a lot of time 'ere at the bistro, 'elping Elsie get it ready in time."

Ruth examined the piece of twine she'd plucked from Bill's shirt, and then pocketed it. "What about the car?" she asked Trevor. "You know what Bill was getting at?"

A wry smile played on his lips. "I do."

Ruth took Trevor's arm and led him to a quiet corner of the bistro. "Spill it. Where's Scott's car?"

"I don't know for certain," Trevor said.

Ruth snorted. "Come on."

"My bet is it's still there."

Ruth frowned. She was pretty sure there was no such gadget that could make an entire car transparent. Although Ruth pictured the hijinks she could get up to if she could find a Harry Potter invisibility cloak big enough to cover her entire motorhome. "You mean farther back in the tunnel?"

"Meet me by the post office at nine tomorrow mornin'," Trevor said. "I'll show yer then."

Despite the subject matter, Ruth struggled to contain a smirk. "A date?"

Trevor cleared his throat and looked flustered. "An arranged time to meet and—"

"Here you go, Grandma." Greg returned with a plate stacked so high with food that it almost touched the ceiling. "Elsie wanted you to have at least one of everything. She was very insistent."

"I see that." One sharp sneeze and Ruth would cause a fatal avalanche. She set the plate on a table in front of the window and sampled a sausage roll. "Oh my." Ruth caught subtle hints of parsley and garlic. She helped herself to two more, plus a cheese and pickle sandwich.

"Good stuff, ain't it?" Trevor popped a shrimp vol-au-vent into his mouth. "Classy grub."

Greg nodded his agreement.

Reverend Collins glided over to them. "I've been told Elsie's always had an extraordinary gift for the culinary arts. I only moved to Vanmoor last year, so I've yet to get everyone's backstories, but I can see how that would be true." He looked round at the three of them and smiled. "Good evening."

In some ways, he reminded Ruth of a gentleman she'd recently met on the *Ocean Odyssey*—Colonel Tom. They had a similar military bearing: ramrod straight backs, and precise ways of enunciating every word, as if giving orders to a platoon about to go into battle.

The reverend extended a firm hand, and they shook. "Rose, was it?"

She swallowed the rest of her sandwich. "Ruth."

"Charmed."

Obviously sensing a round of uncomfortable chitchat, Greg backed into the crowd and disappeared.

Reverend Collins eyed Trevor's tatty and oil-stained overalls with poorly disguised aversion. They stood in stark contrast to his own immaculate suit, jacket and trousers pressed to within an inch of their lives, and his polished, mirrorlike shoes. "Good evening, Trevor."

"All right, Rev." Trevor helped himself to another vol-au-vent and a handful of salted peanuts, and then washed them down with a gulp of champagne.

Ruth smiled at him. "You're so cultured."

"Don't I know it." Trevor winked.

Reverend Collins looked as though he was about to ask Ruth a question, or suggest Trevor wear a bib, when the roar of an engine drew all eyes to the road outside.

The blue Ferrari pulled to the kerb, and a tall, slender, tanned, and well-groomed man in his late sixties stepped out.

Ruth leaned in to Trevor and whispered, "Who's that?"

"That, madam," Reverend Collins said before Trevor had time to answer, "is his lordship: Giles Vanmoor."

Sergeant Fry rushed to the front door and opened it.

Lord Vanmoor swept into the room, beaming from ear to ear, flashing a symmetrical set of porcelain teeth. He held his arms wide. "Congratulations, everyone. What a fine establishment. I'm so proud."

"I gather Lord Vanmoor paid for the bistro's refurbishment," Trevor said in Ruth's ear. "As far as I can ascertain, he funds most of the village from 'is estate."

"Yes, his lordship does seem extremely generous with his finances." Reverend Collins's eyes narrowed. "Now, if you'll excuse me . . ." He joined the excited crowd now gathered around the new arrival.

Sergeant Fry shot Ruth another nasty look as he passed her, heading to the back of the bistro.

"I see yer've made friends," Trevor said as he watched him go.

"It's not my fault Greg dunked him in a tank of cold water," Ruth muttered. Having said that, she would gladly pay to see it happen again.

Trevor chuckled. "Yeah, I 'eard. Good for Greg. Knew I liked that lad. I'll treat him to another pint of ale."

Ruth nibbled on her food while Lord Vanmoor worked the room, shaking hands, accepting drinks and warm welcomes.

Greg and Mia reappeared.

"Can't find her," Greg said to Ruth.

"Who are yer lookin'for?" Trevor asked.

"Constance," Mia said. "She's not here. We asked a few people. No one's seen her."

Ruth swore under her breath. Going back to the B&B to find her was an option, but she didn't want to upset the girl. However, she had several questions regarding Scott's visit, not to mention the stolen locket.

"Constance was 'ere earlier," Trevor said. "I spotted Constance 'elping Elsie with the decorations when I popped to the post office."

"Does Constance live at Molly's?" Ruth asked.

"Only for about the last year or so," Trevor said. "She visited a lot, but moved in with Dorothy when Arthur fell ill."

"That's Dorothy's husband, right?" Mia said. "What was wrong with him? How did he die?"

"Don't know exactly," Trevor said. "Something to do with 'is liver. Or spleen. Maybe it was a kidney." He shrugged. "Poor fella was in 'is late nineties. Something was bound to give up on 'im in the end. He 'ad a good life. Well respected in the art world. Always workin' until the very end." His eyes turned glassy. "Hope I die with me boots on too."

"I see we have a new face," a booming voice said. The crowd split, and Lord Vanmoor stepped through like Moses parting the Red Sea. He beamed at Ruth, almost blinding her with shiny porcelain. "And such a pretty face too."

"This is Ruth Morgan," Reverend Collins said with a sweep of his hand. "And her grandson." He looked over his shoulder at Mia, but didn't introduce her.

Lord Vanmoor took Ruth's hand and brushed his lips across her knuckles. "A delight."

Behind his back, Greg gestured by shoving two fingers into his mouth and retching.

Ruth suppressed a smile. "Thank you, Lord Vanmoor. It's

nice to meet you." She felt like she greeted royalty. Mind you, he was the closest thing Vanmoor Village had in the way of a king. And given his name, the two must have been inextricably linked.

Greg rolled his eyes.

Mia took his hand and led him away before he got caught.

"Ruth helped Elsie with the menu," Reverend Collins said to Lord Vanmoor. "Invaluable input."

"I wouldn't say that." Ruth took a bite of a cucumber sandwich.

Lord Vanmoor looked about the bistro. "Elsie has done wonders. Simply marvellous. A solid investment, I have no doubt. Now, if you'll excuse me." He bowed and moved to the next group of starstruck guests, who cooed and fawned over him.

Ruth downed the rest of her champagne.

"Let me get yer another one," Trevor said.

"It's okay. I'll get it." Ruth was eager to work the room and find people who knew Constance and, more importantly, her current whereabouts. Not to mention Scott. "Do you want another?"

"I'd better not," Trevor said. "Got to be up early to work on yer motorhome."

"I'll be right back." Ruth made a beeline for the bar.

Mia stood at the end of the buffet table, arms crossed, watching Lord Vanmoor.

"Where's Greg?" Ruth asked.

"Bathroom."

Ruth reached for a bottle of white wine, when a scream silenced the room. Her head snapped toward the kitchen.

A woman stood in the doorway, a hand over her mouth, eyes wide.

In three steps, Ruth joined her. "What's going on?" She followed the woman's gaze.

On the tiled floor near the range cooker lay the form of a man, pale and lifeless, with a deep red impact mark to the right side of his forehead.

"Bill," Ruth breathed. "No."

Sergeant Fry pushed past Ruth, knelt by the body, and pressed two fingers to Bill's neck. After a moment, he pulled back. "He's gone."

A crowd gathered round the open kitchen door, gasping, and turning away in shock as they each took in the ghastly sight.

"What's 'appened?" Trevor stepped beside Ruth.

She placed a hand to his chest and tried to steer him away, but it was too late.

Trevor stared over her shoulder, and when he spotted his friend, his knees buckled. Ruth grabbed Trevor under the arm, and with the help of a gentleman in a black shirt, sat him in a chair.

Mia poured a glass of water and held it out to Trevor, but he slouched forward and stared at the floor.

Greg pushed through the crowd. "What's happened?"

Mia whispered in his ear, and his face dropped.

Ruth knelt in front of Trevor and rested her hands on his knees. "Take deep breaths. Deep breaths. You'll be okay."

Sergeant Fry slammed the kitchen door closed. "Now listen up, people. No one is to leave this bistro until we have everyone's statement. Understood? You're all witnesses to a murder and must remain exactly where you are." Sergeant Fry then marched over to Elsie and held out a hand. "Keys."

She fished in the front pocket of her apron and handed over a bunch. "The one with the red fob is for the front door."

"Blue is back door?"

"Yes."

"Which one is this internal kitchen door?"

"Yellow." Elsie wobbled on her feet, clapped a hand over her mouth, and mumbled, "Sick." She then rushed off to the bathroom.

Sergeant Fry motioned for Constable Bishop to join him. She hurried over, and he handed her the keys. "Check the back door and the courtyard. Then lock that door, and come straight back here. Touch nothing."

"Understood." She slipped into the kitchen.

Sergeant Fry eyed Trevor. "Is he okay?"

Ruth straightened up and rubbed his back. "Shock."

"I'll be all right," Trevor grumbled. "Don't worry about me."

A minute later, Constable Bishop returned. "The back door was already locked, sir. No sign of a forced entry." She handed him the keys.

"Interview every person here." Sergeant Fry selected the yellow key and locked the kitchen door. "I'll be back as quickly as I can."

Constable Bishop pulled a notepad from her pocket. "Where are you going, sir?"

"To call Inspector Turner." Sergeant Fry looked around the guests again. "Everyone stays put and cooperates. The sooner you answer questions, the quicker you can leave."

"Surely, you're not including me." Lord Vanmoor tugged at his shirt cuffs. "I've only just arrived. I had no hand in this affair."

"I'm sorry, sir," Sergeant Fry said, not meeting his gaze, "but until we've taken everyone's statements . . ." He stepped from the bistro and locked the front door behind him.

12

In the bistro, Ruth's attention moved from the now locked front door to Trevor, and she struggled to comprehend what was happening. "Do you need anything?" Reality had fallen away, and everyone seemed distant.

Trevor shook his head. "Give me a minute."

Ruth motioned Greg and Mia over. "Wait here," she whispered, and then she followed Constable Bishop over to a lady in a red hat.

"You were closest," Constable Bishop said. "Did you see what happened?"

The lady swallowed. "It's awful. Poor Bill. Who'd do such a terrible thing?"

Reverend Collins joined them with a look of deep concern.

"Lovely man," another woman in a blue dress with a lace collar said. "He was so selfless."

"Did you speak to Bill tonight?" Constable Bishop asked as she made notes.

They both shook their heads.

She faced a man with slicked-back hair, who clutched a

wineglass so tight his knuckles stretched white. "What about you?"

He gave a firm shake of his head and looked as though he was about to throw up.

Speaking of which, Elsie stepped from the corridor leading to the bathroom. She wiped her mouth on a tea towel.

Ruth hurried over to her. "Are you all right?"

Elsie, now a shade of green that clashed with her colourful hair, dropped into a seat. Her hands shook, and her breaths came in laboured bursts.

"Were you the last one to see Bill?" Constable Bishop asked, making Ruth jump. "I saw you coming out of the kitchen as Lord Vanmoor arrived."

Elsie hesitated. "I think so. Not sure."

"Can I ask what you were doing?"

"We—" Elsie hesitated, glanced about, and lowered her voice. "I mean— We were— Bill and I . . ."

Constable Bishop frowned at her, pen poised over the notepad.

Elsie leaned in. "We had an understanding."

"Which was?"

"A tryst," Ruth breathed through the corner of her mouth. "A dalliance. Hookup. Liaison. You know?" She eyed Reverend Collins, who now wore a look of disapproval.

Constable Bishop made a note. "And how long did this rendezvous last?"

Elsie straightened the creases in her apron. "We were only in the kitchen a few minutes before Lord Vanmoor arrived."

"And you left with Bill?" Constable Bishop asked.

"I thought he was right behind me." Elsie wiped sweat

from her neck with the tea towel. "He was getting a glass of water."

"There wasn't anyone else in the kitchen?" Reverend Collins asked.

"Of course not." Elsie looked scandalised. "I'm not that kind of woman."

Ruth looked about the crowd. "Did you see anyone else go into the kitchen after you?"

"No." Elsie's eyebrows pulled together. "At least I don't think so. I said that's when Lord Vanmoor arrived. Everyone was greeting him. I wasn't looking." Her eyes filled with tears. "I should have stayed with Bill." Her voice cracked. "I could have—"

"It's not your fault." Ruth rested a hand on her shoulder.

"Do you mind?" Constable Bishop said to Ruth. "This is an active investigation."

"How long have you waited to say those words?" Ruth smiled and bet very little happened in the village usually, but two deaths in as many days . . .

Constable Bishop shot her a nasty look.

Ruth took a step back and made a zipping motion across her lips.

Constable Bishop faced Elsie again. "Did Bill seem in good spirits this evening?"

"Now you mention it," Elsie said, "he was a bit off."

"Off?" Reverend Collins asked. "In what way?"

"Distracted. Like he had something on his mind."

"I noticed that too," Ruth said. "Do you have any idea what was bothering him?"

"Excuse me, madam," Constable Bishop said. "I'll be the one asking the questions here, if you don't mind." She cleared her throat and addressed Elsie. "Do you have any idea what was bothering him?"

"He wanted to tell me something," Elsie said in a whisper. "But that's when—"

"Lord Vanmoor arrived," Ruth and Reverend Collins said in unison.

Constable Bishop made a note.

"Did he seem off before tonight?" Ruth asked.

Elsie shrugged. "He was fine yesterday."

Constable Bishop faced Ruth. "Madam, I'm only going to ask this once more." She pointed to the other side of the room. "Please wait over there. I'll get to you later."

Ruth held up her hands and backed away. She then turned to the room at large, and said in a loud, clear voice, "Did anyone else see someone go into the kitchen after Elsie left? Right at the moment Lord Vanmoor arrived this evening? Anyone at all?"

This resulted in blank stares. However, one person thrust a hand into the air.

Constable Bishop stepped in front of Ruth before she could hurry over to Flamingo. "Quentin Strange." She made a note of his name and looked up at him. "Who did you see go into the kitchen?"

Flamingo lifted his chin and pointed across the room.

All eyes fell on Mia.

She stared round at them all. "Huh?"

"I saw you," Flamingo said in his haughty voice. "You went in there." He pointed to the kitchen door.

Several people gasped.

"No you didn't," Mia said. "And no, I didn't."

Greg stepped beside her. "She was with me the whole time. I can vouch for her."

Although Mia was unlikely to have murdered Bill, Ruth couldn't agree with her grandson. After all, that wasn't true. When Lord Vanmoor arrived, Greg had joined Ruth soon after, but it had been several minutes before Mia had. Then, at some point, Greg had left for the bathroom.

Could Mia have had enough time to slip into the kitchen when everyone's focus was on Lord Vanmoor?

Ruth couldn't rule out the possibility but also could not figure what the motive would be. After all, Bill had shown no signs of recognising Mia, or vice versa.

The room was now deadly silent, with most staring at the girl in contempt.

She waved a finger at the corner of the room, near the end of the buffet table. "I was right there the whole time. Someone must have seen me."

"Can anyone verify that?" Constable Bishop looked about. "Anyone at all?"

After a moment's pause, Reverend Collins said, "I can."

"Me too," Ruth said. Although not true, she couldn't understand why Flamingo had lied, and felt the need to stand up for Mia. *Why falsely accuse her? What's Flamingo's reasoning?* In Ruth's mind, that made him a suspect.

Constable Bishop stared at her in disbelief, but Ruth kept her best poker face. Well, canasta face. *Bridge face?* Anyway, she was sure Mia had been in the room when Lord Vanmoor had arrived, and doubted the young lady had the inclination or the will to have murdered the village handyman.

"Where were you when Bill was murdered?" Ruth asked Flamingo.

The lady in the rain mac stepped forward. "Talking with me."

Constable Bishop made a note.

Although Ruth had no reason to doubt Flamingo's alibi, she still didn't trust him. Not after denying the fact Scott had visited his gallery. He was clearly up to something.

Ruth scanned the faces of the other gathered guests. One of them had clearly snuck into the kitchen after Elsie left and before Bill had the chance to. *Did they close the door? Is that why no one else claims to have seen the murder take place? Then opened it again when they snuck out and joined the crowds of gathered guests?*

However, without a hint of a motive, unmasking the killer would be next to impossible at this stage, no matter how many questions Constable Eager Beaver asked.

Bishop addressed the room again. "Did anyone see anything suspicious tonight? Anything at all? No matter how small or seemingly insignificant. It could be important to our investigation."

This question resulted in a few mutterings and shakes of heads.

Then, at the back of the crowd, a hand rose into the air. The people parted to reveal a portly guy with a receding hairline.

"What did you see?" Constable Bishop asked him.

"I didn't see anything," the man said. "I heard something."

Ruth glided over to him. "What did you hear?"

"A scraping sound." The man pointed to the kitchen door. "From in there."

Constable Bishop wrote this down.

"After or before Elsie left the kitchen?" Ruth asked.

The man looked between them, his eyes fearful. "A few minutes ago."

"You heard a noise after Sergeant Fry locked the door?" Ruth said, incredulous.

"He's alive." Trevor jumped to his feet.

Ruth stepped to the kitchen door and turned an ear to it. Then she tried the handle, but it remained locked.

"Must have heard mice," the woman in the red hat said. "Or rats." She shuddered.

"How dare you." Elsie looked scandalised. "I'll have you know my kitchen is one hundred percent rodent and bug free. Not so much as a bacterium in there. It's spotless." She glared.

The woman in the red hat shrank away.

Ruth had to agree; when she visited earlier, every surface was sanitised, cleaner than an operating theatre.

"He's probably imagining it," Elsie muttered with a glance in the man's direction.

He recoiled at the accusation and averted his gaze.

The bell above the front door tinkled as Sergeant Fry stepped into the bistro. He looked about. "The inspector can't get here until the morning."

"Does that mean we're free to go?" Lord Vanmoor asked.

"Constable?" Sergeant Fry waved her over. "How have you gotten on so far?"

"I've taken statements." She flipped through the notebook. "Mr Jacobs said he heard a noise coming from the kitchen just now."

Sergeant Fry's brow furrowed. He strode through the crowd, unlocked the door, nudged it open and stared in disbelief. "Who did this?" He wheeled around.

Ruth edged to one side, stood on tiptoes, and peeked over the heads of the crowd. The kitchen now stood empty: no sign of Bill's body.

She gaped and muttered, "Where's he gone?" That was two bodies vanished into thin air in a single day.

"No one went in there, sir," Constable Bishop said with conviction. "I kept an eye on the door as I interviewed suspects."

"Suspects?" Lord Vanmoor said. "You still think one of us murdered the poor fellow?"

Sergeant Fry slammed the kitchen door. "Everybody out." When no one moved, he shouted, "*Out.*" As people broke from their trances and headed for the exit, he added, "But not a single person is to leave Vanmoor." Sergeant Fry glared at Ruth, Greg, and Mia in turn. "That includes visitors." He then waved a finger at them for good measure. "Step one foot outside the village without my express permission, I'll arrest you. No arguments. Are we clear?"

"Crystal." Ruth thought he was taking a big risk letting everyone go, but with no evidence pointing to a killer, and now no body or obvious clues, Sergeant Fry would find it harder to keep so many people in one place for a prolonged period. She assumed he'd dust the kitchen for prints and look for blood splatter. Those things would then take time to process.

Besides, CCTV cameras filled Vanmoor, so it was easy to make sure everyone stayed put and to track their movements, which made Ruth's trip with Trevor in the morning extremely problematic.

The guests filed out of the bistro with expressions of sadness, confusion, and some with anger.

Elsie sobbed.

Lord Vanmoor put an arm around her. "There, there, my dear. The police will catch the fellow responsible, you'll see."

She sniffed. "But where's his body?"

"A good question," Reverend Collins said. "Maybe Bill is alive, and he's crawled off somewhere. They'll find him and make sure he receives medical attention."

Elsie's face brightened. "He's alive?"

Although Ruth couldn't go along with that hypothesis, it

wasn't impossible. Perhaps Bill had a weak pulse and Sergeant Fry simply hadn't detected it. Still didn't explain how he'd gotten out of the kitchen with no keys.

Elsie opened a door next to the bistro. Inside, a set of stairs led up to the floor above the shop.

Lord Vanmoor watched her go, closed the door, and then returned to his car. He caught Ruth's eye, opened his mouth as if he was about to say something, then climbed into his Ferrari. With an eardrum-bursting roar of the engine, he raced up the street and around the corner.

"He keeps drivin' like that," Trevor stepped from the bistro, "he'll need another service." Trevor had no colour in his cheeks, and his arms hung limp by his sides.

Ruth offered him a sympathetic smile. "How are you doing?"

"I'll be fine," Trevor said in a low voice. "Once the killer's caught. And for the record, I don't think Bill's alive. Someone found a way into that kitchen and moved 'is body, if yer ask me. No other explanation." He looked over at Sergeant Fry and Constable Bishop as they left the bistro and locked the door. "The sooner they find out who did this, the better we can all rest." Trevor nodded at Ruth. "I'll see yer at nine in the mornin', outside the post office."

"You don't have to go," Ruth said. "If you don't feel like it. Have a lay-in. I can look for myself." Although, she had no immediate plan of how she would leave the village unseen.

"I've not laid in bed since I was a teenager," Trevor said. "Up at six every morning. Tomorrow will be no different. And yer'll not go alone. Too dangerous. Not after everything that's 'appened."

"Well," Ruth said. "Only if you're sure, but I have a confession." She tensed. "The car wasn't empty."

Trevor gave her an inquisitive look. "No?"

Ruth shook her head. "There was a body inside."

Trevor gawped at her. "Another one? Who?"

"Don't know," Ruth said. "A man in his twenties. Mousy blond hair."

"No idea who that is." Trevor looked over at the bistro, eyes narrowed.

"So, if you'd rather not go," Ruth said, "I'd understand entirely."

"I'll take yer myself." Trevor's gaze moved to Mia, who stood some distance away, and he lowered his voice so she couldn't hear. "After all, there's a good chance the two murders 'ave links to one another, right? Bill and that guy in the car? And if yer think yer can get to the bottom of it, yer 'ave my full support."

Ruth thought back to the dried paint on Dorothy's fingers, and the twine she'd plucked from Bill's shirt. "Three."

Trevor's brow furrowed.

"Three possible murders," Ruth elaborated. "But I think you're right—Bill and the stranger are linked in some way."

"Grandma, we don't know Dorothy was murdered," Greg said as he joined them. "It could have been an accident."

"Yer think someone killed Dorothy too?" Trevor asked with a skeptical look.

Ruth pulled the twine from her back pocket and examined it under the nearest streetlight. "This looks like a piece of old canvas." It was discoloured with age. "Was Bill into painting?"

"No," Trevor said. "Strictly a 'ammer, saw, and screwdriver kind of guy."

"Are you sure?" Ruth pressed.

"Positive. I've known Bill for years. He doesn't 'ave any paintings 'anging at 'is place. The only thing other than DIY and 'andywork that got 'is engine revvin' was fishin'. And 'e wasn't great at that." Trevor chuckled, and then his expression turned sad again.

Greg joined Mia on a nearby bench.

"Where did Arthur do his work?" Ruth asked Trevor as she pocketed the twine. "Is his studio still about?"

He frowned. "Yer know what, I'm not sure." His eyes glazed over. "That's something Bill would've known."

Ruth didn't doubt it, and she suspected Bill had been to Arthur's studio that very evening. *Another question for Constance.* "Where does Bill live?"

Trevor pointed up the road. "Round the corner a ways."

"Can we look tomorrow?" Ruth asked.

"Sure. I know where Bill keeps a spare key."

"What about Dorothy? Was she into art at all?" Ruth pictured the paint on her fingers again.

Were *she and Bill working together to clean out Arthur's old studio?*

Trevor shrugged. "Dorothy 'ad a distinct lack of coordination, and a permanent shake, so I doubt it." He sighed. "Look, I'm off to bed. I'll see you at Nine."

Ruth bid him farewell, and as she watched Trevor go, she felt more determined than ever to figure out what had happened to Dorothy, the lad in the car, and now Bill.

But uncovering the truth was going to be an uphill climb.

13

Once everyone had left the vicinity of the bistro, and the high street now stood empty, Ruth strode over to Mia, who sat on a bench next to Greg. "You're welcome to stay with us for the night, if you'd feel safer."

"Right," Greg said. "None of us can leave. The campsite is outside the village boundary."

Ruth wasn't sure that was true, but she was not about to argue with him. After all, it certainly was beyond the scope of the CCTV cameras, and she was pretty sure that was what Sergeant Fry had been getting at.

Mia hesitated. "I— I don't have a change of clothes or my toothbrush."

"I'll find you some fresh towels so you can at least have a shower," Ruth said. "But I think one night without brushing your teeth is better than risking your life."

Mia looked at Greg, smiled, and nodded.

So, they returned to the B&B, and as usual, the place seemed deserted.

"Let's see if Constance has a new toothbrush we could have." The door behind the reception desk was closed, so

Ruth rang the bell. When Constance didn't answer, she circled the desk and tried the handle. "Locked." No light came from underneath.

The three of them headed upstairs.

Ruth found some fresh towels in a cupboard on the landing, and once they were in her bedroom, she pointed out a supply of complimentary shower gel and shampoo bottles.

"Thank you." Mia grabbed a couple, along with the towel, and padded off to the bathroom.

"She looks exhausted." Ruth dropped into an armchair with a heavy sigh. "We could all do with a good night's sleep."

"She can have my bed," Greg said.

Ruth cocked an eyebrow at him.

"I'll sleep on the sofa," he added.

Ruth pointed to the connecting door. "Keep that open tonight." She then tipped her head back, shut her eyes, and massaged her temples. "Fancy making your dear old grand-mother a nice warm beverage?"

Greg flicked on the kettle. "Tea or hot chocolate?"

"Oh, this has been a chocolate kind of day." Ruth thought of Bill's vanishing corpse. Of course there had to be a logical explanation, and despite her eagerness to uncover the truth right here and now, a swirl of confusion muddled her brain. She yawned and fought to stay awake.

Ten minutes later, Mia emerged from the bathroom, drying her hair, and she sat next to Ruth.

Greg handed her a cup of hot chocolate.

"Thank you. What's the plan tomorrow?"

"There's a million CCTV cameras around the village," Ruth said. "Some of them might have picked up the killer, and your brother too." She sipped her hot chocolate. "When

I was on board the *Ocean Odyssey*, there was a security room where we could access all the cameras. They must have something like that here too." She looked at Greg. "Do you think you could locate it tomorrow?"

"It's probably at the police station," he said. "We'll have no way to access the recordings, even if we do find it."

"I already asked Sergeant Fry about the cameras," Mia said. "He told me they're deactivated."

"I don't believe him for a second," Ruth said. "He fobbed you off with a lie." He had to be hiding something. *Why not show Mia her brother's movements?* Ruth took another sip of her chocolate as she pondered, and cursed herself for not taking a picture of Bill's body when she'd had the chance. "Nonetheless, I'd like you and Mia to see if you can track down the cameras' control room. We find that, we may be able to access the recordings. Be quiet about it, though," she warned. "Don't get caught. And do not leave the village."

"You're leaving the village with Trevor tomorrow morning," Greg said.

"Yes, but we're not going far. Only to the forest. And I'm hoping Trevor has a plan." Besides, things were getting more dangerous by the second, and Ruth wanted to keep Greg and Mia busy while she snooped about a remote crime scene with Trevor.

There came a raspy meow, and Merlin slinked from his box.

Mia's eyes lit up. "Who's this?"

"Be careful," Greg said. "He's a vicious little git. Hates everyone. Scratch your eyes out given the slightest chance."

"Is he yours?" Mia asked.

"No way." Greg pointed to Ruth. "Only person who can get near Merlin without being bitten or generally mauled to death." He muttered, "If you want to know who killed Bill, I'd start with him."

The cat hopped onto the sofa, took one look at Mia, and then climbed onto her lap.

Mia stroked him. "He's lovely."

Merlin purred.

Greg gawped. "You've got to be kidding me."

Ruth hid a smirk behind her mug.

The next morning, after only a few hours' sleep despite her best efforts, Ruth sat up in bed, reading *Mrs Beeton's Book of Household Management*, to the morning chorus of Greg's ungodly snores from the other room.

Sleeping on the sofa amplified his throat rattles to alarming decibels.

Unperturbed, Ruth absorbed herself in what distractions she could: recipes for various sauces. The 1901 edition contained two hundred and forty-one of them, to be precise. There was everything imaginable from asparagus sauce to cockle, liver, and lemon. Some had to be positively radioactive.

So far, Ruth's favourite recipe was Coffee Sauce, which comprised gathering raw coffee berries, along with arrowroot, a glass of brandy—Ruth had to admit the alcoholic beverage was the part that had caught her eye—and sugar, and a pint of boiling water.

The recipe instructed the optimistic reader to roast the berries over a fire until browned, then pound them in a mortar. As if the poor berries hadn't suffered enough, next came dousing them in boiling water and then leaving them to stand. No doubt so they could take a moment to evaluate their life choices.

After straining what remained of their essence into a saucepan, one was told to add the arrowroot, or if you somehow forgot to stock that ingredient, cornflour would suffice.

Blending that mixture with the glass of brandy—which assumed you had not yet downed it—then sweetening to taste, and simmering for a further five minutes.

Total cost? 6d. Or six old British pence. Factoring in for inflation, that made it around two pounds and fifty-eight pence in modern money. *A bargain.* If nothing else, it could degrease the cooker.

With images of Dorothy, the stranger, and Bill returning to the forefront of her mind, Ruth set Mrs Beeton's tome of culinary alchemy to one side and got out of bed. She opened a pouch for Merlin, refreshed his water, and completed the enviable task of cleaning his litter tray.

After getting dressed, she then padded into the sitting room, flipped on the kettle, grabbed her oversized mug, and filled it with three tea bags, five generous spoonfuls of sugar, and half a cow's worth of milk.

She then sat in the armchair, and Merlin joined her.

Ruth thought of Bill and his disappearing body. She knew his corpse hadn't vanished. Someone most likely had moved it, and Ruth now had a pretty good idea where to— the basement. An idea she'd explore later.

Besides, if the killer had dumped Bill's body down there, that presented a few questions she was eager to solve. First was uncovering the reason they'd done that. It must mean there were clues left behind the killer didn't want the police to find.

Second was the question of how the murderer had gained access to the kitchen when Sergeant Fry had locked the door. Even though there were no windows in the kitchen, there was a back door. *Was it open?* Was *Constable Bishop mistaken? Did the killer have a spare key?* It certainly would explain how someone not only slipped into the kitchen and murdered Bill under everyone's noses, but also returned later to hide his body.

Since Elsie lived above the bistro, Ruth considered seeing her first. However, if they hadn't already done so the previous night, no one could remove the body from the basement until the following night, under the cover of darkness. So a visit to that basement could wait until Ruth returned from her excursion with Trevor.

Mia shuffled into the sitting area and yawned. "Morning."

Ruth snapped out of her thoughts. "I take it Greg's snoring woke you up?"

Mia stretched. "He snores?"

Ruth chuckled, then straightened her face when she realised Mia wasn't joking. "You didn't hear him?" In that case, they were made for each other. "Help yourself to a hot drink."

"I'm fine." Mia dropped onto the sofa.

Merlin abandoned Ruth and leapt onto the girl's lap.

"Traitor," Ruth muttered.

"Do you still want us to hunt down the CCTV control room today?" Mia asked.

Ruth nodded and checked the time. "Better get freshened up and changed." As she headed back to her bedroom, Greg's snores ceased and left nothing but a hollow ringing in her ears.

∾

Ruth left her handbag behind since she was about to hike through the woods, and she, Greg and Mia exited the B&B and headed up Vanmoor High Street. Everything was eerily quiet compared to the day before. The bistro sat in darkness, which gave it a cold and creepy vibe.

What with the previous night's tragic events, and it now being a Sunday, Ruth didn't expect Elsie to open shop. Well, not this early in the morning, but the quicker she got back with Trevor, the better.

Speaking of which, Trevor stood outside their allotted meeting spot: Vanmoor Village Post Office.

He carried a large canvas bag. "Mornin'."

"Good morning." Ruth nodded at the bag. "What's in there?"

"Yer'll see."

"Ooh, cryptic." Ruth applied some lip balm and faced Greg. "Got your phone on you? I'll call as soon as we return."

Greg held it up. He glanced at Trevor and back to Ruth. "Are you sure you don't want us to come with you?"

"It'll increase our chances of getting caught," Ruth said, which wasn't far from the truth. "But thank you for your concern." She wanted Greg and Mia to remain in the village and under the watchful gaze of the cameras.

Anyway, Trevor was low on her list of murder suspects, not that she'd formulated a list yet, and keeping Greg and Mia together and in Vanmoor was her top priority.

Ruth and Trevor waved Greg and Mia off and strode along the high street.

Ruth eyed one of the security cameras as they passed underneath. "What's your plan to get us out of the village without getting caught?"

"Already done," Trevor said. "I said to Fry we're poppin'

to my place so I can show yer the repairs. I told 'im I'd escort yer there and back."

Ruth raised her eyebrows. "Clever."

"Thanks," Trevor said in a tired voice. He looked worn out, like he hadn't slept.

"You don't have to do this."

"No," Trevor said. "I definitely do."

Ruth smiled in sympathy, and vowed to not give up until she found Bill's killer.

Five minutes later they trekked through Delph Woods. An overcast and misty day gave the forest a sinister atmosphere.

Ruth glanced over her shoulder. "At least it seems Sergeant Fry hasn't followed us. Guess he bought your fib."

Trevor stepped over a log. "Not exactly the most observant fellow, is 'e? Explains why 'e didn't find the killer last night." Trevor pointed to a low wall. "That used to be a log cabin. Burned down forty years ago."

"How do you know that?" Ruth asked. "I thought you said you've only lived here for the last fifteen?"

"Right yer are," Trevor said. "My parents brought me many times to Vanmoor when I was a child. Came most years. My great-grandmother lived in Tilsbury Cottage, a little way outside the village. I always 'ad a soft spot for that place. Of course, Vanmoor was run-down back then."

Ruth inclined her head. "It was?"

"Hardly anyone else visited. Very few knew of its existence. Not even locals." Trevor adjusted his grip on the bag. "Then Lord Vanmoor invested in the place about twenty-five, maybe thirty years ago. Done the village right up. So, when finances permitted, I moved." He stopped outside the tunnel. "Car was 'ere, right? From what yer described."

Ruth pointed inside. "There." She showed him the photos on her phone.

Trevor cringed at the images of the dead body. "Don't recognise the fella." He unzipped the canvas bag, removed two large torches, and handed one to Ruth. "Stay close to me. Got it?"

Ruth flicked it on and shone the beam down the tunnel. "Got it."

"Come on, then," Trevor said. "And watch yer step."

They walked down the tunnel in silence, the only sound of dripping water and their footfalls on gravel.

The air grew colder with every step, and Ruth shuddered.

A few minutes later, they came to a padlocked gate that spanned the full width of the tunnel, floor to ceiling.

Ruth took a few pictures, and kept her phone ready, heart hammering in her chest.

Trevor dropped the bag to the floor and removed a set of bolt cutters. "Shine the torch on the lock."

Ruth did as he asked. Trevor broke the padlock, tossed it aside, and swung the gate open.

The beam of Ruth's torch followed the tunnel as it continued ever deeper into the hillside. In the distance sat the faint outline of the Freelander. "It was here all along."

Trevor dropped the bolt cutters into his bag. "Looks that way." His brow furrowed.

"What's wrong?" Ruth asked.

"Trouble." He grabbed his torch. "Follow me."

They hurried up the tunnel, and ten feet from the car, Ruth stopped short and wrinkled her nose at the smell of burnt plastic and rubber.

The car was nothing but a blackened shell.

She took several pictures with her phone and edged down the driver's side of the vehicle. Ruth peered into the wreckage. "No body."

"Could be ash," Trevor said.

"The fire would not have gotten hot enough."

"How yer know that?"

"I used to be a police officer."

"Really?" Trevor said. "That explains it."

"I'll take that as a compliment." Ruth edged round the remnants of the car, snapping pictures as she went, hunting for any clues, but the whole lot was a charred mess. "Bones would remain." Her eyes met Trevor's. "Which means the killer took the body."

In Vanmoor, Ruth and Trevor headed down a side street on the opposite side of the village from Molly's, and on until they reached a row of town houses.

They strode up the path of the second house from the end, and halfway along, Trevor plucked a plastic owl from among the bedding plants, flipped it over, and pulled out a key.

Ruth pointed to the front door. "Looks like Sergeant Fry beat us to it."

Police tape strung across the door barred the way, and someone had fitted an extra clasp and padlock to make sure.

Trevor swore, and stuffed the key back into the owl. "Let me check the back. Stay 'ere." He hastened down the path, along the road, and then he disappeared around the corner.

As Ruth waited, she pulled her phone out and brought up the image of the sheet of symbols. It was the only clue from that poor man's death they had left, and yet she was still none the wiser as to their meaning.

If John were alive, he would've loved to work out what they represented, and an image of her late husband appeared, as so often he did when she needed him the most.

He had a serene, inquisitive expression.

"I know." Ruth smiled. "You'd figure out what the symbols mean." She returned to her memory of their Egypt trip, and followed John from one burial pit to another, his excitement growing with every minute they spent hunched down, examining hieroglyphs and tool marks, careful not to disturb them. Now and again, Ruth would stick her head up like a meerkat and have a look about, but no one came.

And so by the time they'd realised the tour bus was gone, the sun had started its descent. They were miles from the nearest civilisation, had no idea which direction they should walk to find people, and only had half a bottle of water between them.

As night fell, things had looked decidedly bleak, but it turned out to be one of the best experiences of Ruth's life.

They'd spent the following hours huddled together, a little cold, but not afraid. They'd talked—with John first chatting about the ancient Egyptians, how they built the pyramids using farmers' labour during their offseasons, and not slaves, as most people had assumed. Then he reminisced about his childhood hunting for fossils with his father.

In that moment, Ruth had felt happy and content in John's arms. Somehow, they both knew it would be okay, that someone would find them eventually.

In the end, everything worked out: the tour bus returned the next morning—having finally figured out they were two people short of a full group—and a few bottles of water later, John and Ruth were as right as rain.

"Tape across the back door, padlock too," Trevor said, pulling Ruth from her memories. "We could smash our way in?"

She recoiled at the thought of breaking and entering. That would be a step too far. "I don't expect to find much." It could wait. Ruth stared at the house. "Did Bill have any enemies?"

Trevor scoffed. "No."

Ruth looked at him. "What about Sergeant Fry or the gallery owner? Any run-ins with them?"

"Bill got on with everyone," Trevor said. "He'd be the first to step between people's arguments and defuse the situation. I 'ave no idea why someone would want 'im dead. It doesn't make sense."

"He did seem off last night, though, didn't he?"

Trevor shrugged. "Overworked."

"What do you think of Sergeant Fry?"

"A short temper. Bit of a fool sometimes, but 'armless enough. Don't see 'im bein' a killer, though."

"Do you know anything else about him?" Ruth pressed. "Anything that may help?"

Trevor looked away for a moment as he thought, and then he shook his head. "Never bothered to get to know the guy."

"What about the gallery owner?" Ruth asked. After all, he'd pointed an accusing finger in Mia's direction.

"Quentin?" Trevor laughed. "He wouldn't say boo to a goose."

Ruth took one last look at Bill's house and turned around. "Let's go."

The two of them walked back to Vanmoor High Street,

where they parted ways, with Trevor heading back to his workshop, promising to finish up with the motorhome repairs. Ruth, for her part, verbalised her solemn vow to find Bill's killer. This seemed to ease Trevor's grief, if only ever so slightly.

Ruth then sent a text message to Greg, arranging to meet him and Mia back at the B&B in a little while. Ruth had a couple of other things to do first, and after the disaster of losing the car evidence, she didn't want to leave any stone unturned.

So, with a renewed determination to get to the bottom of what she still considered *three* murders in such a short span of time, Ruth went to the post office and shipped the locket back to its rightful owners, sans the note.

14

Back on Vanmoor High Street, Ruth pressed the intercom buzzer on Elsie's door.

"Come on, come on." Ruth bounced from foot to foot and looked about, eager for Sergeant Fry or Constable Bishop not to spot what she was up to.

After what felt like an excruciatingly long wait, Elsie answered, "Hello?"

Ruth leaned in to the intercom, her voice hushed, "Elsie, it's Ruth Morgan."

A short pause followed before she replied, "What can I do for you, Mrs Morgan?" Elsie sounded both drained and wary.

"Do you mind if I speak to you for a minute?" Ruth said in a soft tone. "It's important. I promise not to take up too much of your time."

Another pause, this one longer, and then the lock on the door buzzed.

Ruth glanced up and down the high street to make sure no one watched, then pushed the door open and headed up a flight of stairs.

Elsie greeted her at the top. She wore a pink bathrobe, and her hair was a mess. To drive home the point she hadn't slept much, if at all, Elsie wore no makeup and had bags under each eye.

"Really sorry to bother you." Ruth followed her into a sitting room.

A riot of floral patterns assaulted Ruth's senses, forcing her back a step. The wallpaper and borders, the upholstery, carpet, and curtains; even the coffee table had a flowery sheet draped over it.

Ruth blinked, waiting for her eyes to adjust to the flowery ambush.

Photo frames crammed every available surface, filled with images of Elsie through the years, each time accompanied by a strikingly handsome man—chiselled jaw, sharp features, dark eyes.

Ruth leaned in to one photo of the couple that stood out: the man wore a military uniform, with a younger Elsie in a floral dress. Both beamed at the camera, arms interlocked.

"My late husband," Elsie said. "Frank."

"He was in the army?" Ruth asked.

"Frank was a captain. He died a couple of years ago. I miss him terribly."

Ruth eyed a frame filled with service medals. "A war hero too." Her gaze then moved to another photograph; in this one Elsie and her husband were in their mid-thirties. Behind them stood a recognisable but decidedly dilapidated Vanmoor High Street, with cracked pavements, paint peeling from buildings, rotten timber, and crumbling brickwork. "Wow."

"I keep that as a reminder of how far we've come," Elsie said. "Vanmoor was on the verge of total decay until we stepped in."

Ruth faced her. "We?"

"Lord Vanmoor, Arthur, Dorothy . . . we turned it around. Took years, but we got there." Elsie lifted her chin. "If it wasn't for us, developers would have taken over and flattened what history remained." Her expression became intense. "I have lived here my entire life, my parents, their parents, generations of Jacobs. I could not see Vanmoor demolished. I refused to let that happen." She shook her head. "Not on my watch."

"Ah, that's right," Ruth said. "You're the head of the parish council." She looked back at the photo. "Well, you've done an amazing job. Congratulations."

Her single-minded determination had clearly saved the village from extinction.

"That's why you wanted a bistro here," Ruth muttered. "Makes sense."

"Frank and I always wanted to open one together," Elsie said. "It was his dream too, but then his health failed."

Ruth faced her. "I'm sorry."

Elsie sighed. "Frank made me promise I'd do everything in my power to fulfill our dream."

"And so you have." Ruth smiled. "The bistro is a triumph."

Elsie sat in one armchair, while Ruth lowered herself into one opposite.

"I know who killed him." Elsie stared at the floor. "Bill, I mean."

Ruth sat forward, shocked by this sudden proclamation. "You do?"

Elsie didn't meet Ruth's gaze. "They argued."

"Who?"

"Bill and Karen."

"Karen?" Ruth asked. "Oh, you mean Constable Bishop?" This also caught her by surprise.

"Bill helped set up the buffet tables and put out food before everyone arrived." Elsie adjusted her bathrobe. "Karen showed up to bring some extra plates. They started arguing."

"What about?" Ruth said, still taken aback by this revelation.

"I didn't catch all of it. I was in the kitchen." Elsie clenched her fists. "Bill was angry about something. He said he'd bring the whole thing crashing down if she didn't own up to her involvement."

"Involvement in what?" Ruth said in barely a whisper.

This certainly would explain Bill's odd behaviour at the party.

"I have no idea. Karen kept repeating that she didn't know what he was on about, but Bill wouldn't take her word for it. He told her to own up to it." Elsie's expression darkened. "I fear she's done something terrible."

Like murder.

Ruth cast her mind back to the previous night and couldn't recall seeing Bill and Constable Bishop interacting.

Were *they avoiding each other?*

"What happened then?" Ruth asked Elsie.

"Karen left, and said she'd speak to Bill again once he'd calmed down. That's when I came out of the kitchen. Bill looked agitated, and I asked if there was anything I could do to help, but he shrugged it off. Told me it was fine. Nothing to worry about." Tears rolled down Elsie's cheeks. "If I'd known what was about to happen . . ."

"Hey." Ruth scooted to the edge of her seat, leaned forward, and rested a hand on Elsie's knee. "It's not your fault."

Elsie sniffed and blew her nose into a handkerchief.

Ruth still couldn't picture where Constable Bishop had been at the time of Bill's murder. Also, Sergeant Fry had locked the door to the kitchen right after the killing, so it couldn't have been Constable Bishop who'd moved the body, unless she'd done it when he'd asked her to check the back door. Ruth screwed up her face. Was *there enough time?*

"What's wrong?" Elsie asked.

Ruth shook herself and sat back. "Did anyone else hear Bill and Constable Bishop's argument?"

"Constance was helping me in the kitchen," Elsie said. "I'm not sure if she heard, though. She didn't react, so I guess she didn't."

Ruth's eyebrows rose. "Why wasn't Constance at the party?" She still wanted to catch up with the girl.

"She was supposed to come and help. Maybe she's unwell."

"Where is Constance now?"

Elsie shrugged.

"Has she got a mobile phone?" Ruth asked.

"I usually just go to Molly's and find her."

Ruth pursed her lips.

Constance hadn't served breakfast during their stay either. And given the fact it was a B&B, that only provided half its advertised promise.

"It's unlike her to not show up," Elsie continued. "Constance is a good girl. But I don't think you'll get much from her. She's fragile. Best to leave her alone. She does whatever she can to avoid conflict." Elsie looked away and muttered, "Maybe she got spooked by the argument."

Ruth inclined her head. "What do you mean?"

So far, Constance was an enigma, so any details, no matter how small, were welcome.

Elsie looked back at her. "Well, and this is strictly between you and me, but only last week Dorothy shouted at her. I don't know what it was about either," she added in response to Ruth's inquisitive look. "That, coupled with her great-aunt's death not long after . . ." Elsie said in a low voice. "The guilt must be too much for the poor girl."

Ruth nodded. She would still seek out Constance, but also do her best to be gentle with the girl. However, right now, she had a more pressing matter at hand. "Are you not opening the bistro for a few days?"

"I'm opening again at twelve today," Elsie said. "Once Sergeant Fry says I can." She glanced at a clock on the mantelpiece. "I can't put it off forever. I've got a business to run."

Elsie's drive and tenacity impressed Ruth, and Ruth was also positive there was no task Elsie couldn't accomplish if she put her mind to it. "Is Sergeant Fry in there now?"

"He left thirty minutes ago. Says he's done, but to wait for the all-clear."

"Can I take a look at the kitchen?" Ruth asked.

Elsie's eyes widened. "Now? That wouldn't be proper." She then whispered, "It's a crime scene."

"If Sergeant Fry's finished," Ruth said, "it's no longer active." She softened her expression. "I promise to be careful. I'll wear gloves at all times." She had spotted a box of disposable ones next to the kitchen door the previous day.

"I don't know." Elsie squirmed in her seat. "Sergeant Fry took the keys and said not to let anyone in until he says it's okay." She swallowed. "Come by this afternoon. When I'm there, and we're open. You can look as much as you want then."

"That would be too late," Ruth said. "All remaining evidence would have been wiped clean."

"Evidence?" Elsie looked doubtful. "You don't imagine Bill crawled off somewhere? I think he's alive."

Ruth's gaze drifted around the room. "You must have a spare set of keys, though?"

Elsie hesitated. "Yes, but—"

"I used to be a police officer." Ruth straightened the creases in her skirt. "Trained as a detective." She looked up at Elsie and smiled.

Elsie stared back at her.

"You have my word not to disturb anything," Ruth continued. "I'll be as quick as I can. All I want is a little peek." She clasped her hands and tried not to show her impatience or raise her voice. "Please? I told Trevor I'd help find Bill's killer. I want to keep that promise."

"And Sergeant Fry told me he'll get to the bottom of it," Elsie said. "It wouldn't do for you to get involved. I say wait to hear what he's uncovered."

"Do you know when the inspector will arrive?" Ruth asked.

"Is he still coming?"

"Oh, I'm sure Sergeant Fry will do an excellent job regardless," Ruth lied, and gave Elsie an imploring look. "Let me have a peek in there. A little glimpse, that's all. I'll be in and out before you know it."

"You won't find anything," Elsie said.

This caught Ruth by surprise. "Why do you say that?"

"Because Sergeant Fry has already been in there twice this morning and hasn't found anything." Elsie's tone grew agitated.

She had a point, but Sergeant Fry was unlikely to have looked in the basement. Ruth didn't want to explain her theory to anyone else, so kept quiet.

Elsie stared at her for a while longer. "You're not going to give up, are you?" She huffed. "Fine. You must be quick, though. He will be furious with me if he finds out."

Ruth crossed her heart. "You have my word."

"I still say you're wasting your time."

They both stood.

Elsie opened an ornate musical box on the mantelpiece, removed a spare set of keys to the bistro, and handed them to Ruth.

"Does anyone else have a set of these?" Ruth asked.

Elsie vehemently shook her head. "I won't allow it. I'm the only one with keys, and I have to be there at all times. No one else is allowed in there on their own." Her eyes glazed over. "Apart from today. Never again, though."

"The blue one is for the back door?" Ruth wanted to check the rear of the building, as it was the most likely place the killer had gained entry. Plus, she didn't want to make it obvious she was going in. The cameras stood a greater chance of picking her up entering via the front door.

"Yes, blue is back," Elsie said. "Are you sure you want to do this?"

Ruth winked, and a rush of excitement coursed through her. She squeezed Elsie's shoulder, left the sitting room, and headed down the stairs.

"Mrs Morgan?"

She stopped and turned back. "Call me Ruth."

"Please don't touch anything. I've got it all just the way I like it. I'd hate for things to get messed up after all my hard work. Five minutes only?"

Ruth was about to point out that Bill had died in there and you couldn't get any more messed up than that, but bit her tongue. "You have my word."

Once she'd stepped foot back onto Vanmoor High

Street, Ruth kept her head low, coat collar up, and made a beeline for the nearest alleyway.

She tried to look casual, but knew her outward appearance betrayed her inner thoughts, so she did what any other sensible person would do trying to look less conspicuous: she hastened her pace.

Ruth found the nearest alleyway two shops down from the bistro and raced down it. At the end, she hung a left and stepped into a forecourt with several parking spaces, bins, and skips. Eight-foot-tall metal fences topped with razor wire surrounded it on all sides, and looked out of place with the rest of Vanmoor. It was as though she'd stepped through a portal and been transported to inner London.

As with the rest of Vanmoor, several cameras mounted high on the walls covered every conceivable angle, so there was no point in trying to avoid them.

Ruth only hoped Greg had found their control room and formulated a cunning plan for how to access them with no one knowing.

A concrete ramp led to a raised loading area at the rear of the bistro. Apart from the door, there seemed no other way to gain entry to the bistro, so without a spare key or a superior lockpicking ability, Ruth failed to see how the killer could have come this way.

After a surreptitious look about to make sure she was alone, Ruth opened the door and slipped into the kitchen.

Once safely inside, she flipped on the lights, and her gaze dropped to the tiled floor where Bill's body had once lain.

She stared with a mixture of sadness and determination. *Who did this and why?* She'd only known him for a few hours, but Bill had seemed like a nice guy, so she couldn't understand why someone had murdered him.

Ruth edged around the kitchen, grabbed a pair of disposable gloves from the box and slipped them on.

Then she knelt and examined the floor, but there were no signs a body had been here at all: no visible fibres, scrape marks, or blood. The floor looked clean and new, like the rest of the kitchen.

Sergeant Fry would have found the same lack of clues, and Ruth assumed that was the reason for his repeated visits: checking he hadn't missed something subtle. Although, if he had found a hair or a fibre of clothing, he would have bagged it and logged it as evidence.

Ruth scanned the cupboards around the area, hunting for signs of a struggle, then straightened and examined the worktops. Still finding nothing out of place, she made her way over to the hatch in the floor.

A metal ring sat in a recess.

Ruth activated the torch function on her phone, held her breath, and opened the hatch.

As before, the wooden steps dropped into darkness.

Ruth found a switch near the top and flipped it on.

Lights sprang on, illuminating the basement in a yellow glow. Ruth's gaze moved to the floor at the base of the steps, but there were no signs of a body there either.

She steeled herself and glanced about. This was a bad idea. She checked there was no way for the hatch to accidentally slam closed and trap her in there. Then with her heart hammering in her chest, Ruth descended the stairs, one step at a time, careful of her footing, each tread creaking under her weight because of course they bloody would.

At the bottom, Ruth's feet touched an old cobblestone floor, and she stepped into a cellar with wine racks down one wall, and crates stacked along the other.

Ruth frowned and looked about.

Still no corpse.

"What the—?" Stunned, she remained frozen on the spot.

Someone didn't shove Bill's body down here? She had been so certain. Ruth huffed and looked about at the crates and racks, unable to believe her own eyes. *Then where is he? Has the killer already moved the body again?*

She examined the steps.

Nothing.

Ruth climbed back into the kitchen and had just closed the hatch behind her when Sergeant Fry stepped into the room.

He scowled at her. "You're under arrest."

15

In the bistro's kitchen, Sergeant Fry motioned for Ruth to turn around. "Hands behind your back."

"Is this necessary?" Although, she did as he asked, not wanting to aggravate the situation further.

By his tone, Sergeant Fry wasn't in any mood to muck about. "You do not have to say anything. But it may harm your defence if you do not mention now something which you later rely on in court." He cuffed her. "Anything you do say may be given in evidence."

Unable to think of some immediate and clever way out of the predicament, and fighting not to let her cleithrophobia send Ruth into a blind panic, she allowed Sergeant Fry to lead her from the bistro.

As they headed down Vanmoor High Street, passersby muttered and pointed. No doubt they already had their suspicions that one of the strange visitors had murdered Bill, and now this walk of shame confirmed it in their minds.

As if to drive the point home, Ruth caught the odd word, like "*killer,*" "*guilty,*" and "*hanging.*"

What a charming bunch.

One elderly gentleman in a flatcap, his stooped form propped up with a walking cane, eyed Ruth and said in a sage tone, "I knew it. Makes perfect sense."

She'd never laid eyes on the fellow, let alone given him cause to suspect her of a heinous crime.

Sergeant Fry kept a tight grip on Ruth's arm, as though he expected her to break away in a desperate bid for freedom.

If she could escape the cuffs and disappear in a puff of smoke like David Copperfield, Ruth would have done that back in the kitchen, rather than being dragged through the street like a common criminal from the Dark Ages.

Quentin Strange, AKA Flamingo, stepped from the art gallery and glared at Ruth as they approached. "At it again? What has she done this time?"

"Never you mind." Sergeant Fry led her past and then stopped dead in his tracks. He turned back. "What do you mean, *again*?"

Ruth cringed and gave Flamingo an imploring look.

"She tried to trick me," he said. "Then stole something."

"I most certainly did not." Ruth was scandalised. "I would never—"

"Explain." Sergeant Fry's grip tightened on Ruth's arm, but he kept his focus on Flamingo.

The art gallery owner lifted his nose into the air and sniffed. "I saw right through her subterfuge. You must wake up pretty early to catch me out."

"Yes, yes," Sergeant Fry said in an exasperated tone. "And what did this little sneak thief do, exactly?"

"How dare you," Ruth said. "I never sneak."

"She feigned illness. Preyed on my kind nature."

Flamingo glowered at her. "Tried to take something from my desk. I caught her red-handed."

"I stole nothing," Ruth said. "Check for yourself. I was looking for tissues. Preferably ones infused with balsam. Four-ply. Ultrasoft. I have a sensitive nose."

Flamingo snarled, "A likely story."

"I do," Ruth said. "It goes all bright red and—"

"Come by later and fill out a report," Sergeant Fry said to Flamingo. "We'll add it to her list of charges." Then he led Ruth away before she could argue. "Quite a life of crime you've led."

Ruth pressed her lips together, fighting back a retort. No matter what she said now, he wouldn't hear it.

They crossed the road and headed into the police station —a compact building with a booking area not much bigger than an average bathroom. A narrow desk faced them, and Constable Bishop stood behind it.

Her eyes widened. "Ruth Morgan?"

"Book her," Sergeant Fry said.

"Oh, are you also a custody sergeant?" Ruth asked the officer with a thinly disguised hint of sarcasm.

"She's what we've got." Sergeant Fry released Ruth and marched down a hallway. "Make it quick."

Constable Bishop called after him, "What am I booking her for, sir?"

"Contaminating a crime scene, suspected murder, and attempted theft." He stepped through a door at the end and slammed it behind him.

"I didn't contaminate, murder, or steal anything." Ruth turned around and showed Constable Bishop she wore disposable gloves by waggling her fingers. "While we're at it, can you please remove these cuffs? I'm not dangerous, despite what he says."

Bishop hesitated, glanced down the hallway, and then pulled a set of keys from her pocket. "Promise you won't run off?"

"I can assure you," Ruth said in a low voice, "my days of running anywhere are far behind me. Nonetheless, you have my solemn word I shall stay put." Besides, a part of her was curious to see how this played out.

Constable Bishop removed her handcuffs.

Relief washed over Ruth. "Thank you." She massaged her wrists.

Constable Bishop returned to her position behind the desk. She grabbed a clipboard and pen from a nearby hook and started filling out a booking form.

Ruth gave her name, address—which she took time to explain her home and her motorhome were separate—and, with extreme reluctance, also divulged her date of birth.

Much to Ruth's chagrin, Constable Bishop didn't seem shocked, nor did she ask for Ruth's actual birth date because she simply couldn't believe how young Ruth looked.

Instead, Bishop went through the formalities of asking about Ruth's state of health, both physical and mental.

On explaining her current mood, Ruth opted for 'irritated,' but noted she was not a direct risk to herself or anyone else, so no need for the plastic cutlery and a straitjacket.

Ruth handed over her belongings, which only consisted of her phone, lip balm, and the keys to the bistro. Constable Bishop catalogued and placed them inside a clear bag, without asking what the keys were for, which was odd considering she'd seen a similar set only the night before.

"Actually, can I call my grandson?" Ruth gestured to the phone. "He'll be so worried. I'm sure I must be entitled to at least one phone call before I am led to the gallows?"

Constable Bishop handed back her phone.

Ruth faced away from the desk, took a breath, and dialled.

Greg answered on the first ring. "Where are you? We've been waiting ages. I'm hungry."

"A forced detour," Ruth muttered.

"What are you on about? To where?"

Ruth glanced back at the constable, and said through gritted teeth, "Jail."

"What?" Greg's voice turned shrill. "Why? What happened? What did you do wrong this time?"

"Why do you automatically think I did something?"

"Because you always do."

"Do what?" Ruth said, incredulous.

"Something you shouldn't."

"I. Did. Nothing. Wrong."

"Oh, no," Greg said in a sarcastic tone. "I'm sure you've been arrested for doing absolutely nothing whatsoever. People often get arrested for no reason. It's very common."

"I'll explain later," Ruth murmured, and made a mental note to bring up his inappropriate sarcastic attitude. "It's a misunderstanding. That's all. I'll have it cleared up in no time." Ruth composed herself. "Don't worry about me, and stay where you are. If I need you, I'll call back. Love you, bye."

She hung up before Greg had time to ask more awkward questions or point all ten of his fingers at her. Besides, Ruth didn't intend to be here long. She likely had more questions for Sergeant Fry than he had for her, but Ruth would hold back as much as possible.

No point jabbing a stick at a hornet's nest.

She handed her phone over to Constable Bishop with a muttered, "Thanks."

"You haven't locked it." Constable Bishop held Ruth's phone back out to her.

"Oh, I don't ever lock it." Ruth slipped off her disposable gloves and handed them over too. "Only put it into sleep mode." She shrugged. "Wouldn't remember the code anyway."

"The newer ones use your face."

"So I'm told."

Constable Bishop slipped the phone into the bag along with the keys. "Do you understand your rights?"

"Very well. Thank you."

"Do you require legal advice or representation?"

Ruth sighed. "Not right now." But if things got heated, she wouldn't hesitate to ask. She then wondered what would happen if they wanted to subject her to a physical search, how exactly they'd carry it out. After all, modern laws required two officers of the same sex to conduct it.

She guessed they'd skip over that part, and now regretted handing over her phone voluntarily.

"Can I ask you a question?"

Constable Bishop finished with the form. "Sure."

"What were you arguing with Bill about?"

Constable Bishop's brow furrowed. "What do you mean?"

"Yesterday," Ruth said. "Someone overheard you having an argument with Bill, at the bistro, in the afternoon, I believe."

Constable Bishop shook her head. "I didn't see Bill before the party."

"But you helped out at the bistro?"

"During my lunch hour. Elsie asked me to assist her in setting up."

"And you didn't argue with Bill?" Ruth asked.

"No. Who told you I did?"

Ruth opened her mouth to continue with the questioning, when the door at the end of the hallway opened and Sergeant Fry stepped out. He looked a little less grumpy than before, but he still had an expression of someone put out by her reckless shenanigans.

He beckoned Ruth to follow him.

Ruth hurried down the hall and stopped in the doorway, eyes wide.

Instead of a cold, cell-like space with battleship grey walls, the room beyond had a Persian rug, an oak table with knurled legs, flower-patterned wallpaper Elsie would've died for, along with several landscapes depicting mountains and meadows, all painted by *A. Pennington*.

Two padded chairs sat to either side of the table. Not metal, and certainly not bolted to a concrete floor.

Ruth looked about the room with incredulity. *Have I walked into the right place?* The décor was befitting a cozy parlour from the late 1800s, rather than an interview room.

The only giveaway it was an interview room at all was the modern addition of a voice recorder perched at the far end of the table.

Sergeant Fry gestured to a chair. "Sit."

Bewildered, Ruth did as he asked.

Sergeant Fry cleared his throat and started the recorder. He then went through the usual formalities: he stated where the interview was taking place, the date, who was present, and he then asked Ruth to confirm her identity. After that, Sergeant Fry cautioned her again. Finally, he asked if she understood.

"I do." Ruth gazed at him with what she hoped was still a puzzled expression, whereas she wouldn't mind admitting to herself that her stomach tightened with unease.

Whatever happened, there was no way she'd confess to going into Elsie's basement and looking for a corpse. She wasn't sure if he'd seen her close the hatch, so she'd play dumb for as long as possible.

Sergeant Fry sat back and folded his arms. "What were you doing in there?"

Ruth clenched her fists. She hadn't yet thought of an excuse, so opted to tell the truth. "I used to be a police officer."

"I know," Sergeant Fry said. "I looked up your record."

"You did?"

"I had a feeling you might have been in the force." He scanned her up and down. "You give off that vibe."

"I do?" Although, Ruth knew what he meant. It was the same with ex-military personnel—the way they conducted themselves. You could spot it a mile off. She was about to ask if Reverend Collins had served, but Sergeant Fry's expression turned serious again.

"First of all, you called in a false report of a body in a car, and wasted my time," he said. "Now I catch you at the scene of a crime."

Ruth inclined her head. "You think the two could be related?"

"I don't see how."

"Come on," Ruth said. "Three murders and a disappearance in this tiny village? Give it a few more days, and half your population will be dead."

"Three murders?" Sergeant Fry's brow furrowed. "There was only one we're aware of—Bill—and I'm starting to think that was a prank."

Ruth rolled her eyes. "You know it wasn't, Sergeant." Even the stupidest police officer, one fresh out of training, would know Bill had been murdered. After all, Sergeant Fry had felt his pulse, or lack thereof.

He leaned forward. "I'll ask you again: what were you doing at the bistro?"

Ruth considered feigning innocence and saying she'd only been a nosey parker, or that she'd gone there to borrow something, but the truth was still best. After all, one look at the CCTV cameras would punch holes in any fibs.

Even so, she went for a middle ground approach, and let out a dramatic sigh. "If you must know, I miss it something awful."

Sergeant Fry's brow furrowed. "Miss what?"

"The police force," Ruth said, and studied his reaction.

He muttered, "Why on earth would you miss this?" Sergeant Fry seemed to mean it too.

Ruth pressed on regardless. "Investigating is in my blood." And that had more than an ounce of truth to it. "I couldn't help myself. I had to check it out."

"That's not your job." He leaned further across the table. "What did you find at the bistro?"

"Apart from freshly baked scones and more diabetes than I could shake a stick at? Nothing. I found nothing at all." Ruth sat back and looked about. "Do I get a refreshment break?"

"You've only just gotten here."

"I'm thirsty."

"I will fetch you a glass of water in a minute. Just answer my question. Why were you in the bistro kitchen?"

"I've already told you," Ruth said. "I was curious. I couldn't understand how Bill's body had vanished like that. Very odd."

"And what did you discover?" Sergeant Fry asked this as though he expected her to reveal some dark secret.

Ruth considered him for a moment. "Nothing."

He threw his hands up. "You contaminated a crime scene. You know that's an offence, which will result in a custodial sentence."

Ruth cocked an eyebrow at him.

So, he wants to play it that way, does he?

"I didn't realise it was still a crime scene," she said in a casual tone. "I'd assumed you were done with your investigation. After all, Elsie is about to open the bistro again."

"You were there the night before," Sergeant Fry snapped. "You know full well it's still an active crime scene. Don't play dumb with me."

"There were no notices to show the public it was still active," Ruth persisted in a defiant tone. "There was no tape across the entrances. No barriers to keep the hoarding masses and looky-loos at bay." She shrugged. "As I said, I assumed that meant you were done gathering evidence, and it was my turn." She fixed her gaze on him. "And before you ask me the same question again, I didn't find anything in the kitchen. You showed up before I had a proper chance to look around. I'd be happy to go back and continue my search, though."

Sergeant Fry stared at her. "How did you get inside? Where did you get the keys?"

Ruth looked away. "You can't keep me here unless you're going to charge me with something."

"Don't bet on it."

"Come on, Sergeant. I hold my hands up to putting my nose somewhere it didn't belong. I confess and promise not to do it again. Now, give me a slap on the wrists, tell me how naughty I've been, and send me on my way. You have better things to do, and you and I both know I'm not the killer."

"Perhaps not, but you clearly know something, otherwise you wouldn't be snooping about the village."

Ruth glanced at the door, weighing whether she should tell him her suspicions about Constable Bishop's time spent alone in the kitchen with the body, but since that very body wasn't in the basement, she had no evidence.

Come to think of it, Sergeant Fry had a set of keys and could have snuck in the back way while the constable had everyone distracted with questions. Ruth's stomach did a backflip at the realisation. "Is— Is the inspector on his way?"

"Why would he come now?" Sergeant Fry said. "There's no body. No crime scene to investigate."

Ruth studied him. "He's not coming?"

Sergeant Fry stood and gestured to the door.

Ruth remained seated. "I'm free to go?"

He opened the door. "Get out."

Stunned, Ruth got to her feet.

"If you remember anything important"—Sergeant Fry stepped aside to let her past—"come and see me right away."

Ruth walked into the hall. "And if I don't?"

"Leave Vanmoor and never come back." Sergeant Fry slammed the door.

Ruth stood there for a few seconds, and breathed, "He did it."

He'd been checking to see if she'd found evidence proving his involvement.

Dazed, Ruth returned to the booking desk.

Constable Bishop handed over her belongings, and as Ruth marched away from the police station, she clenched her teeth, now more determined than ever to solve these murders and find Mia's brother.

16

R uth hurried up the stairs of the B&B, and her suspicions now sat fully with Sergeant Fry. He had the means, but she still had to figure out a motive and proof, which made it even more imperative they locate the CCTV control room and verify her theory.

She needed to gain access to the recordings of the previous evening, and show that Sergeant Fry had left the bistro, gone round the back, and into the kitchen. From there, he'd either moved Bill's body into the basement or out the back way.

Then, at some point later that night, or maybe in the early morning hours, he'd moved Bill's body again and taken it somewhere else. Ruth also suspected he'd then returned later that day and scrubbed away all evidence.

All wild speculation, but basis for a solid theory.

Ruth only hoped the CCTV control room was not in the police station, but in a small building or shed somewhere else. Something easy for her to access. Otherwise, she'd have to convince Constable Bishop to let her take a look, and that seemed an impossible task.

But one problem at a time; first she had to find it.

In her room, Mia sat on the sofa with Merlin on her lap.

Greg leapt from a chair. "Are you okay?"

"We were so worried," Mia said.

Merlin opened one eye, then went back to sleep.

Ruth made herself a milky mug of tea with the customary five sugars and dropped onto the other end of the sofa with a heavy sigh. "That was interesting."

"Why were you arrested?" Greg asked. "What did you do?

Ruth rubbed her temples. "I went to check out the bistro kitchen, and the basement in particular."

Greg frowned at her. "A crime scene?"

"Not you as well." Ruth sipped her tea. "Anyway." She sat forward. "You'll never guess what I found."

Mia's lip curled in disgust. "The body."

"Nope. Nothing at all."

Greg now stared at her. "Why are you so happy about that?"

"I think the killer moved the body to the basement as a temporary measure, and then returned later to remove it entirely." Ruth looked between them. "Which increases the chance the CCTV cameras captured at least one of those events."

"Who do you suspect?" Mia asked.

"At the moment"—Ruth took another sip of tea—"my misgivings lie at the feet of Sergeant Fry."

"I knew he was a bad guy," Greg said with a look of triumph.

"Did you find Scott's car?" Mia asked.

Ruth sat back and wrapped her hands around the mug. "Kind of."

Mia's face dropped. "What happened?"

"Trevor and I found it further back in the tunnel. Behind a padlocked gate. It was burnt out. The killer destroyed the evidence." Ruth rubbed her silver cat pendant. "The body wasn't in the car, though. No bones. However, the good news is—"

"The killer must be a local," Mia said. "They knew about the tunnel and the gate."

"Sergeant Fry." Greg sat and gripped his knees. "That's why he took so long to get to us—he moved the car first, and then pretended he knew nothing about it. What a scumbag."

Although Ruth couldn't be sure of that theory either, it held some water. At least, she couldn't dismiss the idea.

Mia's cheeks drained of colour, and she slumped. "Scott's dead, isn't he?"

"No, he's not," Greg said. "Don't talk like that. We'll find him. Right, Grandma?"

Although her optimism that they'd find Scott alive and well diminished with every passing hour, Ruth remained outwardly upbeat for Mia's sake. "We'll find him safe and sound, and we won't give up until we do." She forced her patented optimistic smile back into existence. "Now, I need to prove my theory about Sergeant Fry's involvement." Ruth looked between Greg and Mia again. "How did the hunt for the CCTV control room go?"

Mia stared at the floor. "We failed."

Ruth's heart sank.

"Most of the cameras are mounted too high for us to follow, or their cables go underground." Greg stood again and paced the room. "But we did find one at the edge of the village. We followed its cables to a junction box. I think all the cameras go through that."

Ruth nodded. "Progress. So, what's the problem?"

Greg stopped pacing and sighed. "We don't know where they go from there."

"Ah." Ruth finished her tea.

"I had an idea, though," Greg said. "There are two L-shaped conduits that connect to the back of the box. Both come from the ground. The one on the right is on the village side, and I assume that's where all the cameras come in. The one on the left is where I think they're going."

"Okay," Ruth said. "So where are they going?"

"Not sure," Greg said.

"Sergeant Fry caught us before we could investigate further," Mia added. "He warned us again not to leave the village and insisted we return. We had no choice but to come back."

Ruth's eyes widened.

"Must have been right before he found you at the bistro," Greg said. "Someone probably watched us on the cameras."

"As he walked us back into Vanmoor, he got a text message and left us," Mia said.

"Last we saw of Sergeant Fry, he was marching along the high street," Greg said.

"Someone warned him," Ruth muttered. "Okay, so they told him where to find me. Interesting." She thought back. Perhaps Elsie'd had a change of heart and grassed Ruth up. Either that or someone else had spotted her sneaking round the back of the bistro. Ruth stood.

"Where are you going?" Greg asked.

"To find out where that cable goes, of course."

Mia lifted Merlin off her lap and set him aside. "If someone spotted us on the cameras and alerted Sergeant Fry, what's stopping them doing it again?"

Ruth turned to Greg. "I'm going to have to find a way to avoid them."

"I've already thought of that." He grabbed a pen and pad from a table by the door. Greg then drew a rudimentary map of Vanmoor while Ruth and Mia gathered round. "There's a couple of blind spots, here and here, but no way out of the village without being seen by at least this one camera." He marked points on the map, and then drew a path around the church.

"Well done, Gregory." Ruth patted his head. "Good job. Grandma gives you a gold star."

Mia giggled.

Greg tore the map from the pad. "I'll exchange that gold star for three cheeseburger meals and a chocolate milkshake."

Ruth pursed her lips. "Better make it a bronze star."

"Can't back out now."

Mia straightened her face. "How are we going to get past that camera at the back of the church?"

"We?" Ruth shook her head. "Oh, no. You two have done enough. I'll go alone."

"We'll have to show you exactly where the junction box is." Greg pocketed the map. "We are coming with you."

Mia gave a fervent nod.

Ruth considered them for a moment. Showing her the junction box would be fine. After all, they'd already been there without incident. She could then turn them back at the first sign of trouble. However, she needed an extra way to keep them safe. After a moment's more thought, she had a fantastic idea. "Okay," Ruth said. "You can come, but you're to follow my orders precisely, right?"

Greg's eyebrow arched. "Orders?"

"I mean it," Ruth said. "You are both to do exactly as I

say. It's getting far too dangerous . . ." She looked between them. When Ruth received nods in reply, she marched from the room, across the landing, and stepped into the jumble sale room.

The two youngsters followed her.

Greg stayed by the door, arms folded. "You have got to be joking."

"Only way to avoid detection." Ruth picked out an outfit for him and handed it over.

"You're crazy." He frowned. "There's absolutely no way I'm wearing any of this stuff. Not in a million years."

Ten minutes later, Ruth, Greg and Mia strode down the front path of Molly's B&B.

Ruth wore a fetching leather bomber jacket, a pair of trendy jeans that fit her surprisingly well, and a New York Yankees baseball cap. In her mind's eye, she looked half her age.

Whereas Greg wore a ladies' oversized faux fur coat and a giant floppy hat complete with peacock feathers. "I feel ridiculous. You did this on purpose."

"Well, I think you look fantastic." Mia wore a man's black woollen coat and a matching hat. "Very handsome."

"Really?" Greg held open the gate for her.

Mia stifled a laugh. "No." She slipped past him.

Ruth beamed at Greg.

"I'm going to ask Merlin to smother you in your sleep," he grumbled as he followed her out.

"You and I both know he wouldn't listen to you. If you mutter a single word in Merlin's direction, he'll scratch your eyes out." Ruth stepped to the kerb and looked left and right.

"Anyway, these are disguises, Gregory. We're not destined for a fashion runway. Now, how do we avoid the cameras?"

He scowled at her, pulled the map from his pocket, and gestured across the road to a gate in a low stone wall. "Through there."

Ruth winked and strode across the road with beautiful Mia and the style disaster hard on her heels. She opened the gate and hurried up a path that hugged the side of the church.

When she reached the corner of the building, Ruth held back while Greg peered into the graveyard.

"There's a camera on the library." He pointed.

Ruth peeked and spotted it high on the modern facade. "No way to avoid it, right?"

Greg shook his head. "We need to make it all the way over there." He gestured at another gate at the far side of the graveyard.

Ruth pulled back. "Look casual, everyone. As if we're visiting a grave." She circled Greg and sauntered down the path, her head bowed, as if deep in mourning.

Halfway down, she glanced over at the camera. If Sergeant Fry or anyone else saw them and figured out who they were, they'd have a lot of explaining to do. Especially Greg.

Ruth stopped at a grave topped with a stone angel, a few feet from the gate. Once Greg and Mia had joined her, she breathed through the corner of her mouth, "You go first."

After a brief pause, the two of them headed on through.

"Sorry about this," Ruth whispered to the long-since-deceased person. She crossed herself, and followed her young companions into a narrow street.

They stopped at an oak tree on the other side, where

Greg pointed to the entrance of a cottage and its front garden.

"Private property," Mia said.

"Only way." Greg indicated the wall around the grave-yard. "The camera can see us if we continue down this road."

They rounded the tree, then ducked behind a bush that ran the width of the garden. Keeping low, they jogged along it, then Greg stopped at the far end.

He peered around the corner. "I think that's it. We're in the clear." Greg straightened and stepped onto the pavement.

Ruth and Mia followed.

The three of them, acting as casual as possible, strode alongside fields flanked by trees until they reached an opening between them.

A little way inside sat the control box.

Ruth walked around it. Sure enough, as Greg had described, two conduits connected to the right side, and one to the left.

He nodded at the path. "I think it follows this."

Ruth knelt and ran her fingers over the soil at the back of the box. "The ground feels raised where they buried the cable." She stood. "I think you're right." Ruth's gaze followed the path. "Where does this lead?"

Greg brought up the map application on his phone. "Hard to tell. These trees mask the path from satellites."

"Well . . ." Ruth stepped back onto it and adjusted her baseball cap. "There's nothing else for it." She glanced back in the direction of the road. "I say we make haste, though. In case someone spotted us after all."

They hurried up the path, under the cover of the tree

canopies. Occasionally there would come a break in the hedges with a view of the fields beyond.

Five minutes of walking later, the path swept past a tall brick wall, and Greg stopped at a wooden gate.

A grey connector, like the ones on the control box, popped up from the soil, and a conduit passed through a hole in the brickwork.

Ruth read a sign on the gate:

VANMOOR HOUSE

"Inspired name." She tried the handle. "Not locked."

"We shouldn't go in there," Greg said. "It's private property."

"We just ran through someone's front garden," Mia said. "Dressed like this."

"Stay here," Ruth said. "You've both done your jobs admirably and have got us to this point. As for me? I've come too far to back out now."

Besides, there were no warnings about prosecuting trespassers, so it was fair game. A weak argument that would not hold up in a court of law, but it was the only excuse she had.

Ruth opened the gate and stepped into a garden with raised bedding and plants under snow-laden sheets. She hurried to an archway. On the other side, a lawn stretched into the distance where an Edwardian mansion dominated the landscape—grey stone and plaster, three storeys high, with steps up to a giant front door under a portico held aloft by immense pillars. The building had more windows than Ruth could count.

Greg and Mia joined her.

She stared at them and growled, "What did I just say?"

They both shrugged.

Ruth bared her teeth. "Go back."

They both shook their heads.

Ruth considered marching them back, but they didn't have time to muck about. Besides, all three of them were disguised, and they'd bolt at the first hint of trouble.

Ruth glared at her young companions, put a finger to her lips, and motioned for them to follow her.

Keeping to one side of the lawn, the three trespassers jogged to the house.

Greg looked up as they approached. "I can't see any cameras here."

"We need to act fast," Ruth said. "Look for signs of those cables."

They split up, with Mia heading left, Ruth and Greg right.

"What's the penalty for trespassing?" Greg asked.

"People have died," Ruth said. "We must do what we can to find the killer."

Mia reappeared and waved them over. "I've found it."

"That quickly?"

Ruth and Greg followed her down the side of the house, where she indicated a narrow basement window near the ground.

Ruth, Greg, and Mia lay down and peered inside.

Sure enough, banks of monitors filled one wall, with a computer rack next to them, and a control desk in front.

"There's no one here watching them," Ruth said. "No one manning the consoles."

"Doesn't need it." Greg pointed to a nearby monitor. It showed a view of Vanmoor High Street, with people coming and going. Each person had a green box overlaid with numbers and letters. "AI. It's tracking them."

"Why would Lord Vanmoor have this at his house?" Mia asked. "Shouldn't the police control it?"

"Maybe it is controlled by them remotely," Ruth said. "After all, the police station isn't very big. Or perhaps Lord Vanmoor is renting this room out to Sergeant Fry."

"No way," Greg said. "Lord Vanmoor looked proper shifty. Bet he's some kind of weird pervert."

"Either that or he cares deeply about protecting people in the village," a voice from behind them said.

Ruth, Greg, and Mia stiffened.

Lord Vanmoor stood a few feet away, wearing a frown, and holding a shotgun.

17

L ord Vanmoor stepped back as Ruth, Greg and Mia got to their feet.

Ruth cursed herself for allowing Greg and Mia to accompany her. Now she wished she had put her foot down and insisted they stay behind while she checked out the house, and was determined not to make the same mistake going forward.

That is, if we get out of this mess.

Greg raised his shaking hands. "Don't shoot."

Lord Vanmoor blinked. "Oh, this?" He draped the shotgun across his arm. "I've just returned from a hunt." He looked between them. "May I ask what you're doing? And why on earth are you dressed like that?" His gaze dropped to the basement window. "Although, I could hazard a guess at both, seeing as it's not pantomime season."

Ruth motioned for Greg to lower his hands while several excuses flashed through her thoughts, each one more ridiculous than the last.

She'd gotten to number eight on her list—"*My cat escaped, and we chased it across the countryside until we got to this house. We think it went inside. Can we take a look?"*—when she gave in. The truth was their best option. *Darn it.*

Ruth took a breath. "Last night. Bill's murder."

Lord Vanmoor nodded. "You want to check the security camera recordings? See who came and went?"

"Yes," Mia said, aghast. "You'll let us look?"

"I'm afraid Sergeant Fry has beaten you to it," Lord Vanmoor said. "He found nothing out of the ordinary. You've wasted a journey."

Greg's shoulders slumped.

Lord Vanmoor studied them. "Are you private investigators?"

"We're trying to find my brother," Mia said.

Lord Vanmoor considered her. "Yes, I heard. I'm sorry. Must be awful for you." He tugged on his collar. "However, I fear there's nothing of use on the CCTV."

"Do you mind if we have a look anyway?" Ruth asked.

Lord Vanmoor's gaze wandered for a moment, no doubt as he considered any legal implications. Finally, he looked back at them. "If it will put your minds at rest." He raised a hand. "I must insist I accompany you, and I also require you to be careful with the equipment."

Ruth rested a hand on Greg's shoulder. "My grandson is a whiz with tech." She couldn't operate a toaster without causing an unintentional dip in the national electricity grid.

"Very well," Lord Vanmoor said. "You've come all this way, and I'd hate for you to leave unsatisfied."

Ruth bowed her head in respect. "That's kind of you."

"No bother at all," he replied, although he looked bothered. "This way."

They followed him round to the front of the house.

Ruth glanced back at Greg and Mia. After being close to three murders and now having a shotgun aimed at them, she'd not get them involved in anything dangerous from here on out, no matter how much they protested. This could have been a whole lot worse, and Ruth had been reckless allowing them to come along on one of her wild excursions.

"Why do you have the CCTV recording equipment here?" she asked Lord Vanmoor as they headed up the steps. "Rather than at the police station. An odd place to keep them, no?"

"I financed and set up a state-of-the-art system here at the house last year," Lord Vanmoor said. "To protect my property. I then offered to expand its reach into the village at no extra charge. Sergeant Fry, Elsie Jacobs, and the parish council took me up on my offer." He stopped at the front door. "The rest of the village gave their blessing too. The police have full, remote access. I'm merely a facilitator."

"Is it legal?" Mia asked. "To have all that CCTV around the village?"

"Perfectly legal," Lord Vanmoor said. "It's not as if we hide the cameras." A smile twitched the corners of his mouth. "You found this place quite easily, after all."

Greg frowned. "Easy?"

The front door swung open, and a butler greeted them.

He bowed as they stepped into a grand hall with marble flooring and stairs on each side, arching up to the first floor. Doors stood to the left and right, leading to a sitting area and a library, with another closed door ahead. Oil paintings hung from the walls—portraits. No doubt ancestors and acquaintances of Lord Vanmoor and his family.

However, everything seemed slightly run-down—a threadbare rug, chipped bannisters, paint peeling from a few surfaces, cracked plaster—and generally neglected.

Lord Vanmoor clearly prioritised the village over his own house, an admirable trait. Well, his house and that flashy sports car, of course, but he could be forgiven for having at least one vice.

"This way." Lord Vanmoor opened the door between the stairs, strode down a short hallway, and then turned right into another darkened one lined with doors.

"You could get lost in here," Ruth said.

To be fair, she could struggle to find her way out of a room with only one door and a glowing sign marked, "*EXIT.*" Directions had never been her strong point.

After Ruth's first eighteen months in the Guides, with only one badge to show for it, platoon leader, and older sister, Margaret, tried to disown her and convince Ruth to leave. However, with Ruth determined to stay, the adult leaders acted, and insisted Margaret help her poor sister.

So, they hatched a cunning plan where Ruth and Margaret would work together in such a way that Margaret could obtain an advanced orienteering badge, whereas Ruth would gain a basic explorer's badge.

A perfect plan, with one flaw: they underestimated Ruth's ability to screw things up.

The adults dropped Ruth and Margaret in a forest. Ruth had to use a map and a compass, and guide them from the forest. However, Margaret's task involved reading signs in the forest, like moss on trees, and figuring out which direction was which.

Her badge sounded far more exciting than using a stupid map and compass, so Ruth threw them away and decided she'd skip the basic explorer's badge and go straight to the orienteering. That would shut everyone up and prove she wasn't as dumb as they thought.

Ruth spent the next hour following Margaret, also examining tree trunks, and looking for animal tracks, until finally, they stepped from the forest, exactly where they were supposed to.

Ruth beamed at her sister. "That was easy."

Margaret rubbed her hands together and faced her. "I'm halfway there."

Ruth's face dropped. "What do you mean, half?"

Margaret lifted her chin. "My task is to not only get out of the forest, but go to the top of Green Hill, where we'll meet Brown Owl. You can wait here, if you like." She held out her hand. "Map, please."

Ruth stared at the ground and shuffled from foot to foot.

Margaret glared at her. "Where's the map and compass, Ruth?"

"I threw them away," she said in a small voice.

"What?" Margaret screamed. "Why? Why would you do that?"

"I wanted to do your badge instead," Ruth said in a defensive tone. "Yours was way more fun. You were looking at moss and whatever."

Margaret stepped to her, eyes intense. "I need to complete it by using a map." She threw her hands up. "You've lost me a badge."

"It's okay," Ruth said with more confidence than she felt. "I remember seeing the hill on the map." She pointed to a path. "It's that way."

Margaret crossed her arms. "Are you sure?"

"Positive," Ruth said.

Margaret stared down the path. "This way?" When Ruth nodded, Margaret huffed. "Fine."

They marched down the path, which soon turned into an incline, winding higher and higher.

Another two hours later, tired, hungry, and thirsty, they finally reached the summit.

Ruth and Margaret looked about. They could see for miles.

Then Margaret's expression hardened. "Ruth." She thrust a finger at a small mound in the distance. "That's Green Hill. This is Stone Bridge Mountain."

Ruth squinted into the distance. "Oops."

"You ruin everything."

They were about to make their way down when Margaret twisted her ankle and couldn't walk.

Several hours later, the adults called mountain rescue, a helicopter picked them up, and Margaret never forgave Ruth for making her lose out on that orienteering badge.

Ruth snapped out of her memory as Lord Vanmoor opened a door at the end of the dark hallway. He led them down a flight of steps into the basement. There, he typed a code into a glowing keypad, and opened a rusty steel door to reveal the CCTV control room with its bank of monitors and control desk.

He gestured to the chair. "Feel free, young man. Please treat the equipment with care."

Greg spent the next few minutes familiarising himself with the CCTV controls and software, then nodded to Ruth.

She folded her arms. "Bring up the day Scott arrived."

Mia leaned in.

"An unusual thing to happen in such a small village as ours," Lord Vanmoor said. "For someone to go missing like that."

Ruth cocked an eyebrow. "What about Bill's murder?"

"Well, yes." He tugged at his collar. "That too."

Greg did as Ruth asked, and several screens showed various angles of Vanmoor High Street, including the B&B. "What time?"

"Around eight o'clock in the evening," Mia said. "He

stayed that night and then went to the art gallery the next morning."

Greg sped the recording on.

Mia gasped. "There he is."

The timestamp had reached 20:16 when a familiar black Freelander with a white stripe down the side drove along the high street and parked outside the church, opposite the B&B.

"Good heavens," Lord Vanmoor said. "You were right."

Ruth recorded the scene with her phone as a handsome blond lad in his twenties stepped out, removed an overnight bag from the back, and then crossed the road and walked up the path to Molly's. He rang the bell, and Dorothy answered.

"I knew she was lying," Mia said through gritted teeth. "Now I have proof."

Ruth nodded. It was nice to see Mia vindicated after all the denial and disapproving looks from the locals.

Scott stepped inside the B&B and closed the door behind him.

Ruth continued to record the screen with her phone.

Mia gripped the back of Greg's chair.

Again, he sped the recording onward until night turned to day: five o'clock, six, seven . . . at eight forty-five, Scott reappeared.

He walked to his car, opened the back, and pulled out a framed canvas.

"Pause." Ruth squinted. "What is that he's painted?"

"He's an artist?" Lord Vanmoor asked.

Mia pulled her phone from her pocket, scrolled for a moment, then held it out to Ruth.

The display showed an image of the same painting: a young woman with dark hair, wearing a delicate white dress, head bowed, standing next to a window.

Ruth's eyebrows lifted. "He's very talented. Look at that detail." As a kid, she'd longed to be an artist. Well, for about a week until she'd figured out she couldn't paint anything without it resembling a deformed hippo.

Greg resumed the CCTV recording.

Scott slipped on a backpack and headed on down the high street with the painting tucked under his arm. He then stepped into the art gallery and disappeared from view.

Mia balled her fists. "He lied too. That gallery owner."

Ruth recalled Flamingo's accusation toward Mia at the bistro party—perhaps he had an inkling who the killer might be and was deflecting suspicion.

"Quentin Strange is a busy man," Lord Vanmoor said. "He gets lots of visitors. He could well have not remembered your brother."

Ruth didn't buy that for a second. She nodded as an image of the ledger and Scott's initials flashed into her thoughts. So, Flamingo had to be in on it. *Could he be the killer?* He did not seem the type, but then most murderers didn't.

Greg sped the recording on.

Ten minutes, twenty, thirty . . .

"He's not coming out," he said.

Forty, fifty . . .

Greg resumed playback a fraction before the hour, and pointed at Scott as he strolled from the art gallery, the painting still under his arm.

Mia glanced at Ruth.

She kept her phone recording, and the four of them watched in silence as Scott headed back to the B&B.

He stopped at the end of the path, adjusted his backpack, and looked between his car and the front door. After a few seconds, he seemed to have made up his mind, strode up the path and went inside.

Mia frowned. "What's he doing?"

"Settling his bill, I shouldn't wonder," Lord Vanmoor said.

Greg once again sped the recording forward, and the hours rolled by: *midday, one o'clock, two, three, four . . . Day turned back to night.*

Mia's grip tightened on the back of the chair. "He should have left ages ago."

Evening came and went, then midnight, one o'clock in the morning, two, three, four . . .

"He's not coming back out." Tears welled in Mia's eyes.

"Stop." Ruth pointed at the screen that showed a view across the street. "His car's gone." Sure enough, the space now stood empty. "When did that happen?"

"I didn't see anyone." Greg rewound the recording and leaned in. However, at twenty past three in the morning, Scott's car appeared as if by magic. Greg paused the recording and nudged it forward a few seconds at a time. The car vanished again.

"Must be a glitch in the recording," Lord Vanmoor said. "It happens."

Greg pointed at the timestamp. It jumped from 3:20:34 to 3:27:46. He sat back. "It's missing seven minutes."

Ruth's blood ran cold. She lowered her phone and turned to Lord Vanmoor. "It appears someone has tampered with this recording." And she could hazard a good guess at who.

"Preposterous," he said. "No one would do such a thing." Although, the colour had drained from his face.

Mia crossed her arms. "Who did you say was the last person here?"

Lord Vanmoor's brow furrowed. "If you're suggesting— Sergeant Fry wouldn't do that."

"Who else has access, other than the sergeant and you?" Ruth asked.

Lord Vanmoor swallowed. "Well . . . The people who set up the system, I suppose, but they've not been here for months."

"What about this room?" Ruth gestured around them. "Who has the code for the lock?"

"Any of my staff could gain access," Lord Vanmoor said. "But why would they? Are you sure it's not a glitch?"

"There's no backup." Greg navigated through several folders. "Only this one copy, and no way to recover the missing minutes without specialised equipment and software."

"Sergeant Fry," Mia snarled. "It's him. Has to be." She turned to leave.

Ruth held out a hand to stop her, and addressed her grandson. "Bring up last night."

Once again, he did as she asked and found the moment of their arrival at the bistro party, along with everyone else. Lord Vanmoor had been the final one to arrive in his extravagant sports car.

They watched both the front and rear of the building. This go-around, Ruth kept an eye on the timestamps, ready to spot any sudden jumps.

Greg kept his finger on the fast-forward button until Sergeant Fry left the bistro, and then he returned it to normal speed.

Sergeant Fry locked the front door, hurried down the high street, crossed the road, and jogged into the police station.

Lord Vanmoor sighed. "A terrible affair."

"He was calling the inspector." Greg shuffled in his seat. "Just as he said."

Ruth shrugged. Truth was, they had no idea what Sergeant Fry had done once inside the police station. He could have been calling for a pizza for all they knew. Mind you, a delivery driver on a moped would struggle to find this village in the middle of nowhere.

Six minutes later, Sergeant Fry emerged from the station and headed back across the road. He'd almost reached the bistro when he stopped dead in his tracks.

Mia leaned in. "What's he looking at?"

Ruth searched the other screens, and then she found it —she pointed.

Constance stood at the end of the road, rigid, hands straight by her sides, staring back at Sergeant Fry.

After a few seconds' pause, he made a beeline for her.

Constance turned and hurried from the high street, up the path of the B&B, and by the time Sergeant Fry had made it round the corner, she'd slammed the door.

He hesitated at the end of path, then jogged up the road, and raced round the side of the building.

Ruth tensed. "He's going the back way."

They waited in anxious silence as the time moved on.

It was another four minutes before Sergeant Fry reappeared. He hurried from the B&B, down the high street, and into the bistro.

Greg whispered, "He killed her."

"Preposterous," Lord Vanmoor said.

Ruth stepped back. No one had shown up on the cameras moving Bill's body. "It looks like we're returning to the B&B." She nodded at Lord Vanmoor, "Thank you," and marched from the room.

18

Ruth hastened her pace toward the entrance of Vanmoor Hall, eager to get back to the village as quickly as she could and put her theory about Sergeant Fry to the test.

"Hold on."

She spun back.

Lord Vanmoor approached with a serious expression. "I have been courteous enough to allow you into my home to take a look at those recordings." He motioned to a sitting room. "The least you can do is explain what this is all about."

Greg and Mia stood next to Ruth.

She glanced at the front door. Ruth really didn't have time for this, but Lord Vanmoor was right—he'd earned an explanation. A brief one. However, she stayed put, and said, "As you know, someone murdered Bill last night."

"Are we sure it was a murder?" Lord Vanmoor asked.

Ruth opened her mouth to respond, then closed it again. Truth was, without a body to examine, she couldn't be one hundred percent certain. Of course not. That was impossible. *But what is that expression about ducks? If it walks like one and quacks like one . . . Or was it dogs?* She waved a hand in the air. "Dorothy died too."

"A tragic accident," Lord Vanmoor said. "Poor woman tripped and fell down the stairs. And so soon after her husband's passing. Her funeral is next Wednesday."

Ruth weighed whether she should say anything about her theory, but her impatience got the better of her. "Scott's car." She waggled a finger in Mia's direction but kept her focus on Lord Vanmoor. "We found it in the woods." Ruth's expression hardened. "With a body inside. Someone murdered him. No question."

Lord Vanmoor's eyebrows lifted. "Is that right?" He looked dubious. "A body, you say?" His attention moved to Mia. "Your brother?"

"We don't know," Greg said.

Lord Vanmoor stared back at Ruth. "You reported your find?"

"Yes," she said. "But by the time Sergeant Fry got there, the car and body had vanished. Convenient, wouldn't you say?" She took a breath. "Someone moved the car, went back later, and set fire to it. Destroyed all the evidence. We found it the next day."

"And you don't know the victim?" Lord Vanmoor asked.

"No idea." Ruth hadn't taken a direct picture of his face, she'd concentrated on the crime scene itself, but even so she wasn't about to share images with anyone else. They could wait for the police. "Can we go now, please? We're in a bit of a hurry." She was eager to get back.

Lord Vanmoor didn't move. "Tell me why you think Sergeant Fry did this? Why are you accusing him of murdering a valuable member of our village? Bill did plenty for us, everyone loved him, and Sergeant Fry knows that. Why on earth would he want the poor fellow dead?"

"Look." Ruth took a step toward him and lowered her voice. "I know you don't want to hear this, I get that, but he's the prime suspect right now. And Constance is missing." She nodded over his shoulder. "You saw for yourself that Sergeant Fry was the last person to see her alive."

"You think she's dead?" Lord Vanmoor said, his doubtful expression still in place. "That a police officer who's served our community for many years simply murdered Constance in cold blood, along with Bill? And that happened at a party with a raft of witnesses nearby, I might add."

Truth was, Ruth wasn't sure Constance was dead, but she had a bad feeling. "I'm going to the B&B right now to find out." All this talk was wasting time. She turned to leave.

"Let me show you something."

Ruth steeled herself and turned back, biting her lip.

Lord Vanmoor strode into the library.

Ruth looked over at Greg and Mia with an exasperated expression. They both gave noncommittal shrugs. "We haven't got time for this," Ruth murmured, but she reluctantly followed Lord Vanmoor, with the other two close behind.

They strode through a library with floor-to-ceiling shelves crammed full of antique leather-bound tomes. Then they headed through a day room with several comfy armchairs next to an open fire, and then into a study with a desk and several bureaus. Like the rest of the house, everything had a slightly worn appearance—peeling paint here, a scuff there, a few exposed strands of horsehair stuffing on the upholstery, threadbare rugs . . .

"Do you use all these rooms?" Greg asked.

"Every day." Lord Vanmoor stopped at a door. "Have to.

No hallways, you see? If I want to reach one room, undoubtedly I must walk through another. Does that count as using it?"

"Not really," Greg muttered.

Mia smirked and nudged him.

Lord Vanmoor opened the door, and they walked into a vast room sixty feet long by twenty wide, with a high ceiling covered in frescoes.

Judging by its vastness, polished floors, and giant portraits on the walls, this had once been a dining room.

However, instead of a table and chairs, glass cabinets and displays lined the room on both sides.

"Looks like a museum in here," Mia said.

"That's exactly what it is," Lord Vanmoor said with pride. "Dedicated to the mighty village of Vanmoor." He tugged at his shirt cuffs. "I open the house to the public for two months of the year. Keeps the local history alive."

Ruth peered into the first display, which held a clay pipe and several flint arrowheads.

"Its history stretches back centuries." Lord Vanmoor pointed at the model of a wattle and daub structure in another cabinet. "The first house built in the village that still survives to this very day."

Ruth leaned in. She recognised parts of its timber construction as belonging to Molly's B&B. She straightened. "Why are you showing us all this?"

Lord Vanmoor beckoned her over to another cabinet.

Inside were various photographs of the village over the years, the way it had grown and changed, with horse and cart replaced by motorcars, and gas streetlamps long gone in favour of their modern LED equivalents. One series of images showed Vanmoor's restoration, from run-down and crumbling buildings to the charming village they knew today.

"Is this Dorothy?" Mia pointed to a picture of a young woman in her twenties, wearing a white dress and summer hat.

"Indeed," Lord Vanmoor said. "Her family have been part of the village for generations." He stepped to one side and pointed at a colour photograph of a man in a military uniform. "This is what I wanted to show you before you go racing off with your accusations."

Ruth recognised the man at once—two decades younger, but unmistakably Sergeant Fry.

"Afghanistan," Lord Vanmoor said. "Your supposed murderer is a decorated war hero."

"Our country pays soldiers to kill people," Greg said.

Lord Vanmoor gave a slow nod. "A sad fact, it's true, but all in the name of defence and protection of the realm." He pulled his shirt cuffs again. "Richard Fry saved the lives of twenty men. He got word of an imminent attack against their barracks, and despite huge risk to his personal safety, he rushed in to warn them. On their way out, they came under heavy fire, and he took a bullet to the leg. Despite this, he still managed to lead everyone to safety." Lord Vanmoor focussed on Ruth. "Sergeant Fry is an outstanding member of our community and most certainly *not* a killer. Whatever crimes you think he's committed, you're wrong. He is the least likely of anyone here to have murdered someone."

"Thanks for showing me." Ruth offered Lord Vanmoor a weak smile. "We should be getting along. Oh, and thank you ever so much for your hospitality."

Lord Vanmoor bowed his head. "A pleasure."

As Ruth walked from the house with Greg and Mia, she

thought about her own father and his military service during World War II.

He'd also been a war hero and had rarely spoken about it. In fact, Ruth and Margaret only found out about their dad's exploits after his death. They'd gone through his belongings and discovered several medals, awards, and letters from grateful families.

"Now that Sergeant Fry's no longer a suspect," Mia said as they followed the path next to the trees, heading back to the village, "what's our next move?"

Ruth snapped out of her thoughts. "What? Who said he isn't a suspect?" She thrust a thumb over her shoulder. "From what I saw, he's even more likely to have murdered Bill, and that guy in the car. Constance too."

Mia's eyes widened. "You didn't buy the whole 'war hero' bit?"

"Oh, no," Ruth said. "If Lord Vanmoor says he's a hero, I believe him."

Greg frowned. "Then why do you think Sergeant Fry is still the killer?"

Ruth said in a hushed voice, "Because he came here and deleted the recordings of Scott's car being moved. I mean, who does that? If that's not got serial killer written all over it, I don't know what has." She cringed. "Sorry, Mia. I'm not saying your brother is—"

"I know." She waved off the suggestion. "I suppose I agree with you."

Ruth continued her march through the gate and back toward the village, following the path from Vanmoor Hall.

Mia and Greg jogged to keep up.

Ruth thought about confronting Sergeant Fry.

Will Constable Bishop back me up? Or is she in on it?

At the end of the path, Ruth avoided the cameras by

retracing their steps through the garden, crossing the road, and into the graveyard.

"Grandma, slow down," Greg said. "It could be dangerous to go storming in there. We need to think this through. And this fur coat is *really* hot." Sweat poured down his face.

With determination coursing through her, Ruth marched onward, weaving between the headstones, ready to uncover Sergeant Fry's crimes and put an end to his killing spree.

It all made sense: how he had access to the CCTV systems and therefore could tamper with evidence. How he'd deleted part of the recording to cover the fact he'd moved Scott's car. Then when Ruth had called, Sergeant Fry had shifted it further along the tunnel, before doubling back and making them go through the charade.

Ruth ground her teeth as she shoved open the gate, crossed the road, and headed up the path of the B&B.

At the front door, she stopped. "Stay here." She expected the killer, Sergeant Fry, to be nowhere near a murder scene. Even so, if she came across Constance's body, Ruth would shield Greg and Mia as best she could. "No arguments." Ruth took a deep breath and went inside.

As usual, the place seemed deserted.

Despite herself, Ruth sniffed the air, but couldn't detect anything untoward other than the usual musty scent. *Thank goodness.* She strode over to the reception desk.

The office door beyond was closed. Ruth rang the bell.

When no one answered, she did it again and called, "Constance?" Knowing the poor girl was unlikely to answer.

Ruth circled the reception desk. At the office door, she turned an ear to it. Hearing no sound from the other side, Ruth knocked. "Constance? Are you there?" When still no reply came, she tried the door. Finding it now unlocked, Ruth opened it and stepped into the office.

The room was sparse, save for a desk and chair by a window, and a narrow filing cabinet.

Ruth stepped to the next door, knocked, and went inside.

A single bed sat pressed against the wall, along with a bedside table with a Bible, alarm clock, and an empty glass.

She opened a wardrobe and lifted out a brown dress with a black cardigan. "This must be Dorothy's room." Ruth returned it to the wardrobe and opened the next door.

Beyond was a short hallway with several more doors. The one to the left stood open, with a compact bathroom. The door straight ahead had a barred window with a view of the backyard.

She opened a door to the right. Shelves lined the walls, packed with cleaning supplies.

Ruth returned to the reception area and looked about.

Her gaze moved to the door in a darkened corner of the sitting room. She hurried over to it and marched into the compact kitchen with its tiled floor, oak cabinets, and the old-fashioned enamel cooker straight from the 1950s.

At the far end, a door with a window also opened to the backyard, while yet another door on the left led to a pantry.

Ruth walked around the kitchen, studying the tiled floor, but she couldn't spot any signs of a struggle. No blood, at least. After her second circuit, she sighed. She wasn't sure if the lack of clues was a good thing or not.

Ruth let out a long breath, and then returned to the front door. She waved Greg and Mia in.

"Find anything?" Greg asked.

"Nothing." Ruth headed upstairs, with the other two close behind. On the landing, she hesitated. "Where's Constance's bedroom?" Instead of turning left to their suites and the now empty guest room Scott had stayed in, she went right. The door to the jumble sale room stood open.

"I'm not taking another step until I get out of this ridiculous getup." Greg threw the fur coat onto the bed and got changed.

Mia opened a door opposite to reveal another store cupboard with cleaning supplies and a vacuum cleaner.

Ruth stepped to the last door. She rapped her knuckles on the woodwork and opened it. To her surprise, what greeted Ruth was not another bedroom, but a set of wooden stairs. She headed on up. At the top, Ruth found a light switch and flipped it on.

Before her stood a vast loft space. Fairy lights and colourful silk scarves hung from wooden beams, creating a snug space.

A plush sofa with fuzzy scatter cushions sat opposite a modern TV, a coffee table filled with candles in glass jars, and a faux fur rug, all increasing the tranquil feel.

A single brass bedstead sat next to a round window that overlooked the church. The sheets were fresh, the bed recently made.

When Mia reached the top of the stairs with Greg, she gasped and raised a shaking finger.

On the wall, above an ornate sideboard, next to a wardrobe, sat Scott's painting of the woman in the white dress.

The two of them hurried over to the painting.

"She stole it?" Greg asked.

"I didn't steal it. He— He gave it to me." Constance now stood at the top of the stairs, her eyes wide. "Why are you in my room?"

19

Mia's face twisted with anger, and she stepped toward Constance, fists raised. "Where's my brother?"

"Mia." Greg went to calm her, but she pushed him back a step.

Constance shrank away. She hugged herself and looked between the three of them like a frightened animal cornered by a pack of wolves.

A rush of different emotions flooded Ruth—relief the girl was alive and well, but confused as to her part in all this, and then unease and guilt over Constance's apparent fear.

Mia thrust a finger at the painting. "Why do you have this? You stole it. You must have."

"No," Constance said in a small voice. "I'd never do that. I couldn't." She shook her head and stared at the floor. "Scott gave it to me as a present."

"Liar," Mia snarled.

Constance's frightened gaze moved toward the stairs, and she no doubt contemplated making a break for freedom.

Ruth couldn't blame her. Mia's anger wasn't helping.

Greg edged in front of the stairs, arms crossed, barring her escape.

"Why would my brother give you one of his paintings?" Mia persisted. "You stole it. I know you did. Scott would never give one away to a stranger. The gallery was supposed to buy it from him." Her lip curled, and she took another step toward the terrified girl. "If you don't tell us the truth right now, I'll—"

"That's enough." Ruth stepped between them and kept a level tone. "Let's all calm down and talk about this like rational adults." She understood Mia's anger and desperation, but raised voices and accusations would get them nowhere. Constance needed breathing space to explain her side of the story, so Ruth gestured to the sofa. "Please."

Constance hesitated and then, keeping her gaze locked on Mia, circled the room and sat down.

Doing her best to remain composed and rational, Ruth lowered herself onto the other end of the sofa. After a few seconds to gather her thoughts, she faced Constance, and kept what she hoped came across as still a neutral, relaxed expression.

Canasta face on full.

Greg remained by the top of the stairs, but he looked between them, clearly unsure how to react to Mia's outburst.

Mia, however, seemed like she wanted nothing more than to throttle answers out of Constance, which would do none of them any good.

In fact, Ruth was surprised Mia had this side to her. Although determined to find her brother, and upset about his disappearance, the girl looked about ready to explode, with her reddened face.

Ruth would have to work hard to keep the situation

under control. She took a deep, calming breath, and gave everyone an extra thirty seconds to compose themselves.

On the one hand, she was happy to see Constance alive —of course she was, thrilled—but on the other it felt like Ruth would never get to the bottom of the ongoing mystery.

The sudden appearance of an assumed dead person threw an oversized spanner into the idea of Sergeant Fry having murdered her, and Scott's painting hanging on the wall only compounded the situation.

"Let's start from the beginning." Ruth straightened the creases in her skirt. "Can you please tell us when you first met Scott?"

"I made him breakfast," Constance said in a whisper, as if afraid elevated decibels would bring Mia down on her in a torrent of abuse and violence.

The former, most likely; the latter, Ruth hoped Mia wouldn't go that far, but she was ready to use her body as a human shield if it came to it.

"When did you make him breakfast?" Ruth asked. "On the morning before he left for the gallery?"

Constance shook her head. "The night he arrived."

"How does that make any sense?" Mia snapped.

"It's all we have here," Constance said. "Breakfast. The bistro wasn't open yet, and Scott didn't want to go to the pub."

"Why not?" Ruth asked.

Constance looked away.

Ruth pursed her lips. Was *there someone at The One-Legged Purple Horse Scott was avoiding? Or did he simply not like the food?*

The CCTV evidence seemed to back this up, because they'd not spotted him leaving Molly's that night, but Ruth made a mental note to recheck the recordings if she got the chance.

"What happened next?" Mia's tone had softened, but now she sounded impatient.

"I made him breakfast," Constance repeated. "Full English. We sat in the kitchen and talked while he ate."

Ruth stared at her. Constance didn't seem like the chatty type, but if Scott was anything like Mia, he would've been an open, kind, and approachable guy. Well, like Mia when she wasn't annoyed and full of fear regarding her missing brother. Most people in the village had experienced a different side of her, but Ruth saw through the angst.

"What did you talk about?" Mia asked, now with a look of disbelief.

"He told me about his art. Showed me pictures on his phone. Scott's very talented." Constance's gaze drifted up to his painting, and tears filled her eyes. "I said I really liked that one. He was kind to me." She wrung her fingers, and her gaze dropped to her lap.

"And he gave it to you?" Mia said. "Just like that? Something that took him a couple of weeks to paint?"

"Not right away." Constance sniffed and looked at Ruth, as if begging to be believed.

Mia shook her head.

Ruth motioned for Constance to keep talking. "Scott got up the next day and had breakfast again?" she asked, wanting to understand his every move.

"Cereal and a couple slices of toast," Constance said. "He told me he was still full." She half smiled, and then it faded. "Scott went to the art gallery. I thought I wouldn't see him again. I set about cleaning."

Mia stared at her. "But you did see him again."

"Scott returned later," Constance said. "I wasn't expecting him." Her pale cheeks flushed.

"Why?" Ruth pressed. "Why did Scott come back here?"

"He was upset. Didn't want to drive right away."

"That sounds like my brother," Mia said. "When he was sixteen, he split from his girlfriend and then crashed his moped on the way home. Learned his lesson."

Ruth had once known a motorcycle instructor; he too would warn students about the potential dangers of riding a motorbike while angry. Given the fact plenty of teenagers wanted mopeds and to gain their independence as soon as they could, a high proportion of accidents were down to their inexperience and proclivity for quick anger.

This part of Constance's story added up.

Ruth composed her thoughts and once again motioned for the girl to continue talking.

"Scott said his time had been a total waste. That Quentin looked at the painting, and his portfolio, and decided against stocking any of Scott's work. His paintings weren't the right fit for Vanmoor Gallery. Scott was very unhappy."

"He'd driven over two and a half hours to get here," Greg said. "I'd be miffed too."

Ruth could believe snobby Flamingo guy had a particular standard when it came to art, but judging by the painting hanging on Constance's wall, Scott was talented, and any gallery would be more than happy to stock his paintings. Besides, Flamingo had several similar styles of artwork on his own pretentious walls.

"What happened next?" Ruth asked.

"Scott gave me the painting." Constance shuffled in her seat and kept her gaze averted from Mia's. "He thanked me for being kind and told me to have it." She looked at Ruth. "I tried not to accept it, but he insisted. Said he'd paint another one."

Ruth studied Constance for a few seconds. As far as she could ascertain, the girl told the truth. There were no hints other than the general uncomfortableness of being interrogated and intimidated by three trespassers. She was either truthful or had mastered the art of lying.

"And then?" Ruth asked.

"He left," Constance said with a shrug.

"Ah." Mia's expression turned stern again. "But he didn't leave, did he?" Her eyes narrowed. "We know he didn't. You're lying."

Constance stared back at her with a puzzled expression.

"How long was Scott here before he left for a second time?" Ruth asked.

"Five, ten minutes at the most," Constance said. "Like I say; he told me about the gallery rejection, thanked me, gave me the painting, and that was it. I asked if he'd like a drink, but he wanted to get on his way as soon as possible."

Mia shook her head.

"Back up a second," Ruth said as she tried to picture the sequence of events. "Where did Scott hand over the painting? Where were you both?" She envisioned him entering the front door like in the CCTV recording, and stepping into the reception area with the canvas tucked under his arm. "Where were you, Constance?"

"He came to find me in the kitchen."

"And where did he go after that?" Ruth asked.

Something felt off. A piece of the puzzle was missing.

Constance's forehead wrinkled in a frown. "I don't understand."

Mia continued to glare at her, and then her expression softened as she obviously came to the realisation that the angry sister act wasn't working. "Where did my brother go? You watched him leave the kitchen? Then what?"

"I saw him out."

"But you didn't," Mia said. "You can't have."

"We watched the security camera recording," Ruth said. "Scott did not return to his car."

Constance looked confused.

"He parked it across the road," Greg said. "A black Freelander with a white stripe."

"I didn't see it," Constance said.

Ruth sat back. That meant Scott had vanished into thin air, which was impossible, or someone had altered the recordings in another way, and the three of them had not spotted it during their time with Lord Vanmoor. "When you saw Scott out, what time was that?"

Constance stared at the ceiling for a few seconds. "A little after ten. I remember the clock on the office wall."

"Hold on." Ruth sat up. "Office wall?"

Constance nodded. "Scott went the back way."

"Back way?" Mia's eyebrows lifted. "You didn't say he left via a back door."

Constance's face dropped. "You didn't ask."

Ruth held up a hand for calm, and then did everything she could to keep her voice level and not shout at Constance too. "Would you be a dear and show us, please?"

Constance hesitated and then stood. "Okay."

As they followed her down the stairs, Ruth gave the other two another hard look, warning them that no matter what happened next, they had to keep their cool.

The four of them reached the landing, went down the stairs, through reception, and into the back office.

Ruth glanced at the clock on the wall as they passed.

They continued through the bedroom, into the hallway

and to the back door. Constance reached up and retrieved a key from a hook. She opened the door, and they stepped into a courtyard surrounded by low stone walls.

Constance pointed to a low gate, with a path heading up the hill beyond.

"Scott went through there?" Ruth asked.

Constance nodded. "I told him it was the quickest way."

"Quickest way to what?" Mia said.

Constance looked at her feet. "The train station."

Mia stared into the distance. "He had a car. Why would he suddenly take a train?"

Ruth scratched her chin. "How far away is the station from here?"

"A little over a mile," Greg said before Constance could respond. He held his phone and scrolled across a map. "Out of the valley and on the other side of that hill."

"But Scott drove here," Mia said. "Why would he then take the train? Makes no sense."

Ruth didn't have a definitive answer to that yet, but she could hazard a good guess. "Perhaps Scott had somewhere else to go, and he chose to not drive there. Maybe he intended to return for his car. Any other art galleries in that direction?" she asked Greg.

"Give me a minute. I'll check."

Ruth's attention moved back to Mia. "Someone could have stolen Scott's car when he was away."

"The dead guy we found?"

"What guy?" Constance asked.

Ruth gave a slow nod. "Perhaps. But I think this is good news—Scott is in another village. Would explain why we haven't found him."

"Brandeen." Greg held up his phone. "Next stop on the train route. Three art galleries."

"Three?" Ruth's eyebrows lifted. "He could've already returned to Vanmoor after visiting those, seen his car was missing, and left again. Jumped on another train." She considered going back to Lord Vanmoor and searching the recordings for later that day again. Maybe they'd missed Scott's return.

"Still doesn't explain why he'd switch his phone off," Greg said. "Unless it ran out of battery."

"What about the jump in the security footage?" Mia asked. "The missing time?"

"You heard Lord Vanmoor," Greg said. "They take a lot of pride in this village. Sergeant Fry could have known the car got stolen, and then he deleted the footage to protect Vanmoor's reputation. I wouldn't put it past him."

Ruth wasn't sure that was what had happened, but it was plausible. The car thief could have intended to hide the stolen car in the tunnel but bled out. She pictured him hiding on the other side of the churchyard wall, and waiting until Scott left. The thief may have noticed Scott leave his keys inside. At the moment, it was all speculation. Besides, none of that explained the gunshot wound.

Mia traipsed back into the building, deflated, and Greg followed.

Ruth faced Constance and lowered her voice. "What about the locket?"

Constance looked away. "Locket?"

"The one you made sure I got at the fete," Ruth said. "It had a note inside. Did you put that in there? Do you want me to call the police? Why?"

Constance didn't meet her gaze. "I don't know what you're talking about."

Ruth took a step toward her. "I know you do. Are you in danger? Can I help?"

However, Constance pulled away from her.

"What did you argue about with your Aunt Dorothy?" Ruth persisted. "Elsie told me."

Constance stared at Ruth for several seconds, but then she looked at the floor and shook her head.

Ruth sighed. She wanted answers, but also didn't want to frighten the girl with a barrage of questions, which she clearly already had done, so she would have to return to the subject later. "Come and see me when you're feeling ready. It's been a stressful time for you." She resisted the urge to demand answers from the girl, and stepped back into the building.

Constance locked the door, and they gathered in the reception area.

Ruth composed herself, trying not to show her disappointment. It was another dead end, and yet they'd made good progress. Constance clearly knew more than she was letting on. As the girl shut the office door, Ruth said to her, "Can you tell us about Sergeant Fry, and what happened last night?"

Constance stiffened and looked at the floor. "W-What?"

"We saw him chase after you," Greg said.

"He was concerned about me." Constance wrung her hands. "It was my fault. All my fault."

Ruth inclined her head. "Why was he concerned?"

"I was supposed to go to the bistro with everyone else." Constance's gaze moved to the front door. "I didn't feel like it. I went to the church to pray, while it was quiet, and I came home after. I didn't want to go to the party."

"Why not?" Mia asked.

Constance's gaze dropped to the floor, and she said in a small voice, "I've had to arrange the funeral, and speak to a solicitor about Aunt Dorothy's will. It was all up to me." She sighed and shook her head. "I miss her so much. It's not fair."

Ruth rested a hand on her shoulder. "I'm sorry. This must be so hard on you." She felt terrible for piling on the pressure on an already fragile girl.

Mia gave Greg an uneasy sidelong look, as if she too regretted the way she'd spoken to Constance.

"I still don't get why Sergeant Fry was angry you weren't at the bistro," Greg said.

A valid question.

Constance sighed. "Dad can be strict sometimes."

Several seconds of stunned silence greeted this.

Ruth unstuck her tongue. "Sergeant Fry is your father?" She let out a breath as comprehension sunk in. "He wasn't trying to kill you?" She pinched the bridge of her nose. "Of course he wasn't."

Constance frowned at her. "Why would Dad kill me?"

"Hold on," Greg said. "Why isn't he helping you with this place?" He gestured about them.

Constance's expression glazed over. "Aunty Dorothy and Dad didn't see eye to eye recently, but I can run the B&B by myself. Aunty Dorothy taught me how. Dad would help if I asked him to, but I want to do it on my own. It's mine." She looked at the floor again. "And he's got enough worries."

"Like what?" Mia asked, but Constance didn't respond.

"I think that'll do for now." Ruth forced a tremulous smile at Constance. It had been a traumatic time for all of them. "Thank you for speaking to us. Sorry again for your loss." She ushered Greg and Mia outside, and disappointment washed over her.

Another dead end.

20

That afternoon, once she'd checked that his royal highness—the lord high and mighty Merlin, king of Cat Kingdom, master of the human realm, ruler of the universe—had all the food, water, treats, cleaned litter tray, and plumped pillows his little heart desired, Ruth sat at a corner table in Elsie's bistro with Greg and Mia.

"You're just giving up?" Greg said.

"There's no more evidence to follow." Ruth examined the menu. "Sandwich or soup?" She pondered. "Both? Yes, I think both." Ruth looked up at her young companions. "What do you two want? My treat."

"I want to find my brother." Mia stared at her. "I can't abandon the search for him."

Ruth offered her a sympathetic smile. "I understand, and I'd never expect you to. I'd be the same if it were my brother, but what would you have me do? We've tried everything. If there was something else, some line of enquiry, a thread of evidence . . ." Her stomach tightened in frustration. "I'd be jumping at the chance. You know I would."

"What about the missing time in the CCTV recording?"

Greg asked. "The dumped car? You said yourself someone stole it."

Mia leaned forward and whispered, "And what about Bill's body?"

"A despicable crime," Ruth said. "But someone has since destroyed any evidence we could hope to follow. We don't know where they took Bill." She felt bad for giving up right now but had no choice. "We've explored every avenue."

Whoever was doing this was one step ahead of them.

Greg pulled the copied sheet of symbols from his back pocket and flattened it out on the table. "What about these?"

Ruth had almost forgotten about them. However, they still had no context for what the symbols could represent. They may have been something the car thief had on him, no doubt stolen from somewhere too, or they could have been the beginnings of one of Scott's art projects.

"My brother is not dead." Mia's expression intensified. "He can't be."

Ruth wanted to believe her, and a wave of guilt washed from the top of her head to the tips of her toes for not being able to help more. "I think you should try that other village. The next stop on the railway line. Why don't you go with her, Greg? Speak to the owners of the galleries. I think there's a chance Scott visited them, came back here, saw his car was missing, and now he's boarded a train, heading to his home on the other side of the country."

Mia frowned. "Look, if his phone died days ago—"

"He would have charged it up and called you by now," Greg finished with a fervent nod.

Mia squeezed his hand. "Or he would have borrowed someone else's phone to let us know he's okay."

She had a point.

Ruth pondered the events of the previous days,

searching for anything she might have missed. First of all, they'd established Sergeant Fry hadn't tried to murder Constance. He was a worried father, that was all. There was no evidence he had any involvement in Bill's murder, and without a body, it would be impossible to prove anything.

Bill could have had a heart attack and indeed crawled off somewhere. It wasn't out of the question, and stranger things happened all the time.

Ruth stood. "Decide what you want to eat," she said, trying to hide her frustration. "I'll be back in a minute, and we'll order." She waved at Elsie as she passed, strode into the bathroom with the mermaid on the door, and washed her hands.

Dorothy falling down the stairs could have been exactly that—an accident. Ruth's sixth sense could be off. After all, the coroner would have found evidence of foul play by now.

A breeze brushed Ruth's ankles as she dried her hands. "Not this again." She shivered, and her gaze dropped to the gap under the door.

Elsie needed to fit that draught excluder.

Ruth headed back into the bistro and returned to her seat.

Elsie approached, notepad in hand. "Can I take your order?"

With obvious reluctance, Greg and Mia picked out sandwiches and a bowl of fries to share, while Ruth opted for a chicken salad and tomato soup.

The little bell above the door tinkled, and Trevor stepped into the bistro. He made a beeline for their table. "Afternoon, one and all."

Ruth smiled. "How are you feeling?"

"I dunno, really," Trevor said with a small shrug. "A bit numb. Can't believe he's gone. Keepin' myself busy though.

It's all I can do." He held up the keys to the motorhome. "All finished. I would say like new, but we'll settle for *roadworthy*."

Ruth let out a sigh of relief. Finally, they were free to be on their way and get to Ivywick Island before Margaret blew her top.

Trevor set the keys on the table. "Can't pretend it was easy, but she's good for another ten thousand miles." He smirked. "Avoid any more rivers and yer'll be grand."

"I'll bear that in mind." Ruth gestured to an empty chair. "Will you join us?"

"Can't," Trevor said. "Got an errand to run, but I should be back at the workshop in time to see yer off."

"Thank you for all you've done," Ruth said. "You're a lifesaver. I really appreciate it." And that was an understatement.

"Don't mention it. Happy to be of service." Trevor tipped his cap and left the bistro.

"Please don't go yet," Mia implored Ruth. "Stay one more day. My brother has to be somewhere, and I don't believe Constance. No one can simply vanish."

"I agree," Greg said. "We can stay a while longer. Right, Grandma?"

"Vanish," Ruth muttered, and thought back to her time in the force, and a particular callout she'd attended with several other officers.

It had involved a tripped alarm at a furniture warehouse. They'd entered the building and found the office door open. Ruth had gone inside. Someone had broken open the cash tin and made off with the contents.

However, the odd thing came when they checked the CCTV recording. It had showed a figure breaking open the front door grille with a crowbar, smashing the glass, and climbing through. Five minutes later, the police had arrived.

They'd then realised that the perpetrator was still inside the building.

The four officers had searched the furniture warehouse from top to bottom, inside wardrobes, under beds, even lifting the cushions from sofas, but the robber was nowhere to be seen.

Knowing someone couldn't simply vanish, they'd continued their search, and that was when Ruth had made a discovery: a hatch in the floor of the staff toilets, big enough for a slim person to slip through, which led to the sewers.

Ruth had unclipped her torch, held her nose, and shone the beam inside in time to spot a set of feet disappearing into the darkness.

Two hours later, they had a drenched and extremely stinky perp in custody. Ruth and her partner had drawn the short straw and taken the guy into their patrol car. They'd insisted the man sit on plastic bags, but it made little difference. It had taken at least six months for the smell to finally dissipate, despite three goes with a deep cleaning service and leaving the windows permanently open.

Ruth's thoughts then turned to Bill and his vanishing corpse. "You know what," she said to Mia, "you're right." As the image of the basement hatch in the bistro kitchen's floor returned to the forefront of her mind, a renewed sense of determination came with it. "People can't vanish. It's ridiculous. Even if Bill crawled off, he has to be somewhere. Your brother too." Ruth couldn't let the mystery go unsolved. *Besides, how can I abandon Mia and her search?* Ruth glanced over at the kitchen door and lowered her voice. "Last night, when Bill died, the back door to this place was locked, right?"

Greg nodded. "According to Constable Bishop."

"And despite that, Bill's body still disappeared." Ruth must have missed something in her initial search of the basement. She reached into her handbag. "Elsie told me there's only two sets of these." Ruth pulled out the bunch of keys Elsie had loaned her earlier in the day.

"Right," Mia said. "So?"

"I'm going to hold on to them for a bit longer." Ruth dropped the keys back into her bag and put a finger to her lips. So far, with all the happenings, Elsie had clearly forgotten she'd loaned them out. Sergeant Fry must have returned his set.

"What are you planning to do?" Greg asked.

Ruth opened her mouth to respond, but Elsie stepped from the kitchen, carrying a tray loaded with food.

As she laid sandwiches, salad, and soup in front of them, Ruth glimpsed Trevor walking by.

"Excuse me for one second." Ruth hurried outside, jogged along the high street, and caught up with him outside Malcolm's Groceries. She eyed the drunken gnome in the window box and smirked.

"Something wrong?" Trevor asked. "Don't tell me yer've driven another motorhome into the river?"

"Not yet, but the day is young." Ruth looked over her shoulder. "Would you mind holding on to it for another night?"

Trevor's eyes brightened. "Decided to stay with us a little while longer? Vanmoor grown on yer then"

"Something like that."

"Fantastic." He rubbed his hands together. "Dinner on me, then. This evening at The One-Legged Mare?" His face saddened for a moment. Clearly, he'd remembered their last time with Bill. "Grandson and his new girlfriend invited too, of course."

Ruth hesitated, and then smiled. "That sounds wonderful."

Trevor kissed her hand. "Tonight. Let's say eight."

As he strode away, Ruth decided he had a delightful walk, a manly stride, a masculine gait that oozed confidence and handiness.

But one thing at a time . . .

She shook herself and returned to the bistro.

That evening, after booking another night's stay at Molly's B&B, Ruth, dressed in her usual black outfit and coat, with a pink hat, scarf and gloves, headed along Vanmoor High Street with Greg and Mia.

Two doors down from the bistro, she stopped and checked the time on her phone. "We have an hour before we meet Trevor at the pub."

Greg rolled his eyes.

"Free food," Ruth reminded him. "The bistro is closed. Perfect time." She pointed to the bench across the road. "Mia, can you keep a lookout over there? Greg, I want you to come part of the way with me and keep a lookout."

"How do we stay in contact?" Mia asked.

Greg pulled out his phone. "I'll set up a conference call between the three of us." He dialled, and they all answered. "Here." Greg handed Ruth a Bluetooth earpiece. "It's got a built-in mic." He then paired it to Ruth's phone.

She adjusted the earpiece.

"Good luck." Mia pecked Greg on the cheek and jogged to the other side of the road.

Ruth and her grandson headed down the nearest alley-way, and around the back of the bistro, out of sight of the cameras.

Greg looked over his shoulder. "What if someone saw us come down here?"

"Then we'll be prosecuted for trespassing at the very least, arrested for breaking and entering at the worst." Ruth unlocked the back door. "Stay here."

Greg stared at her. "What exactly are you up to? You didn't explain."

"You'll see."

"Is it dangerous?"

"No doubt."

"Brilliant." Greg sighed. "Any point asking you to be careful?"

"Not really."

"Can I come with you?"

"Nope."

"Awesome."

"More chance of us both getting caught." Ruth pointed to a spot on the ground at the end of the alley. "Stand right there. Don't leave Mia's line of sight. Holler if someone comes." Besides, there was no sense in them both walking into a potentially dangerous situation, and Greg's mother, Sara, would never forgive Ruth if her son got a criminal record before he'd started university.

"I should definitely come with you, Grandma."

Ruth shook her head. "Not this time."

Greg muttered under his breath, took a few steps back and whispered, "Hear me?"

"Loud and clear."

Greg looked down the alley. "Mia?"

"I'm here too."

Ruth peered about to make sure they were still alone, then slipped into the bistro's kitchen and closed the door behind her. She activated the torch function on her phone and held it above her head.

The kitchen was in its usual spotless state, and the beam of the light reflected off the stainless-steel worktops, pots, and pans.

Ruth hurried to the hatch in the floor, knelt and opened it. She flipped on the basement light and took several pictures of the hatch, and its location, before she descended the steps.

"I'm going down to the basement," she whispered.

"Please be careful," Greg said.

"Always."

"Never."

"Well, sometimes I am." At the bottom, Ruth tensed and peered up at the open hatch. *I'm okay,* she told herself and her cleithrophobia. *Not trapped. Everything's fine. There's a way out of here.* Ruth peered about the darkened basement. "Now, what did I miss last time?" She edged around the room.

First, Ruth checked the crates, her chest tight, hoping someone hadn't stuffed Bill's body into one of them, but was relieved to find only a few boxed kitchen supplies and a brand new barbeque set.

Next, Ruth examined the wine racks, lifted out a few bottles, peered between them, and ran her fingers over the brick wall at the far end of the basement.

Nothing.

She huffed out a breath and made to leave when something caught her eye. Ruth knelt in front of the nearest wine rack. A deep scratch in the floor swept from one corner in a semicircle and stopped a few inches from the side wall.

"Bingo." With a rush of excitement, Ruth ran her gloved fingers over the groove, then took several more pictures.

"What have you found?" Mia said in her ear.

Ruth stood. "I'm not sure. Maybe a hidden door." Ruth shone the light from her phone down the outside edge of the wine rack. Finding no levers or latches, she gripped the woodwork and pulled.

Nothing happened.

Ruth tried again, but it wouldn't budge, so next she examined each of the wine bottles in turn, lifting them out, looking behind, searching for a latch or a trigger, but still could not figure out how to open the secret door.

She was about to fetch Greg and ask for his help when she froze. "Wait a minute."

"What's happening?" Greg said.

"I'm fine," Ruth replied. "Give me a while longer. I've just remembered something." She hurried up the steps, through the kitchen, into the main bistro, and then to the toilet corridor. Once there, Ruth knelt, pulled off her gloves, put her hand near the floor, and felt a movement of air. However, it didn't come from the bathroom, but from under another door.

Ruth stood and opened it to find a store cupboard lined with shelves and cleaning supplies, all neatly arranged. She gripped the shelves opposite, held her breath, and pulled. The entire unit swung forward to reveal a cavity in the wall and a set of steps leading down.

"Gotcha." Ruth pressed a finger to her ear. "Greg?"

"Yeah?"

"I've found something. Give me ten minutes to check it out. Don't worry if you don't hear from me for a bit."

"I'll come with you."

"No," Ruth said. "Stay put." After taking a few pictures,

she checked that the secret door wasn't about to slam shut on her. To make sure, Ruth jammed a pack of rubber gloves under it, holding the door and shelves open. Then with the light of her phone held high, she descended the stairs.

At the bottom, a brick tunnel stretched for a hundred feet on both sides, illuminated by dim lights, and lined with doors and recessed areas. In the distance, both to the left and right, the tunnel ended in heavy black doors.

Ruth jogged to the right-hand one, but it was locked, so she hurried back up the tunnel in the opposite direction.

She faced the first door on her left with a latch. Ruth flipped it up and opened the door. It swung inward with some difficulty but revealed the bistro basement, with the wine rack sliding away from the wall. She now stood in an archway with a relief carved into the stonework above, depicting the symbol of crossed keys.

"From the sheet we found?" Ruth took several more photos of the secret door and the carving.

She then stepped back into the tunnel and was about to try one of the other doors when she spotted a recess with a metal ladder mounted to the wall.

This too had a carving behind it: an eagle.

Above the ladder sat a wooden hatch.

Ruth climbed the rungs, pushed the hatch open, and crawled onto a stone floor.

For a few seconds, she struggled to comprehend where she'd come out. She remained on all fours, with a wooden ceiling mere inches above her head, and a wooden wall a few feet in front of her. Light spilled through gaps in the planks, and a raised voice carried through.

Ruth tensed—there were no other doors, and therefore no other way out. So after making sure the hatch wouldn't close and trap her, Ruth crawled like a baby and peered out.

She was under the stage at the village hall.

Reverend Collins paced with a phone pressed to his ear. "Are you threatening me? After everything I've done for you?" His face reddened. "I know we've been over this before, and I also understand you think it's none of my business, but I feel I've earned your trust."

Ruth squinted.

Who's he talking to?

"Until the dust settles?" Reverend Collins said in an incredulous tone. "I don't know how you can say that. It's everyone's business. Every single person in the village. This has gone too far, and you know it." He waved a hand in the air. "Dorothy was right."

"Right about what?" Ruth whispered.

Reverend Collins looked in her direction.

She pulled back into the shadows and held her breath.

"What's that supposed to mean?" Reverend Collins said into the phone, and resumed pacing. "That's why I'm calling, and not coming to see you directly." His eyebrows arched. "You really believe that? She was old? It was her time? Have you listened to yourself? What about Bill?"

Ruth's blood ran cold.

"How can they both be consequences out of your control?" Reverend Collins lowered his voice. "I know what really happened." He paused. "Of course I can't prove it, and I would never—" He recoiled. "I can help. Let me do that. If you explain what—" Reverend Collins pulled the phone away from his ear and looked at the darkened display. He then grumbled under his breath and stormed from the hall.

Ruth backed through the hatch and closed it above her.

With her heart in her throat, pulse pounding at her temples, she remained frozen on the ladder, trying to figure out what that conversation meant, and who he'd been talking to.

"Consequences out of their control?" she whispered. "Consequences of what exactly?"

However, after two full minutes running the conversation back over in her mind, Ruth unstuck her hands from the rungs of the ladder and forced herself to climb down.

She jogged along the tunnel and hurried back up to the bistro store cupboard. Ruth yanked the packet of gloves free, swung the shelves closed, and shut the door.

She then hurried through the bistro into the kitchen, eager to get back to Greg and Mia.

21

Ruth, Greg, and Mia sat at a table in the far back corner of The One-Legged Purple Horse, with drinks in front of them.

"Are you going to tell us what you've found or not?" Greg asked his grandmother with a look of exasperation.

Despite being confident they were out of earshot of other patrons, and masked by the surrounding chatter, Ruth kept her voice low. "I discovered a secret passageway that runs under the village." She could barely contain her excitement and grinned at them.

Mia gave her a dubious look, whereas Greg seemed confused. Although, Ruth could almost see the cogs whirring inside his head with the all-important questions: "*But, why? What's the point? What is it for? Where does it go?*"

Ruth pressed on regardless, eager to explain, and even more keen to get back down there. "There's a lot of doors in that tunnel. Plenty of places I can explore. I have to go back. It could explain everything."

"You think my brother is down there?" Mia asked, now with a hopeful expression.

"I don't know," Ruth said. "There could be anything in those rooms." She looked about the pub to make sure no one eavesdropped, then whispered, "That's not all." Ruth leaned across the table. "I overheard Reverend Collins having a heated discussion with someone on his phone. I don't know who with, and I'm not sure what he was referring to, but the reverend said it's gone too far, and Dorothy was right, whatever that means, and he also mentioned Bill."

Mia blinked. "What about him?"

"Reverend Collins said he knows what really happened."

"We have to confront him, then." Mia went to stand, but Ruth waved her down.

"What we need to do is take this one step at a time. We can't go blundering into the unknown. We must tread carefully and not spook anyone."

They were dealing with a killer, after all.

Greg leaned back and looked up for a moment before saying, "What's that supposed to mean, though? That Dorothy knew something and then conveniently fell down a flight of stairs?" His eyebrows knitted. "And if Reverend Collins knows what really happened to Bill, why is he still keeping quiet?"

"More like he has a good idea of what happened, but no evidence," Ruth said. "That's the impression I got. It's the same problem we've faced throughout our entire time here." She clenched her fists. "I have a strong feeling the answers to our questions are down in that tunnel." Ruth stared at her companions.

"Let's go and have a look." Greg went to stand, but Ruth waved him down too.

As much as she itched to return right away, now was not the time. "I must wait until later tonight. When it's quiet.

Less chance of getting caught." Ruth took a breath to steady her nerves. "I also found a symbol carved into the stonework. It matches—"

"Evening." Trevor stood over them. "Have yer ordered yet?"

Ruth composed herself and pointed at a pint of ale in front of an empty chair. "All yours."

Trevor rubbed his hands together and dropped into the seat. "Thank you. Very much appreciated." He looked between the three of them. "Well? Yer lot been up to much?" He studied them in turn. "Why the serious faces? What's 'appened now?"

Greg and Mia sat back in an obvious attempt to seem casual, and failed miserably.

"We've been exploring everything Vanmoor has to offer," Greg said in what he clearly hoped came across as a breezy tone.

"Oh, yeah?" Trevor's eyebrows lifted. "That can't 'ave taken yer long."

"You'd be surprised," Ruth murmured. She considered Trevor for a few seconds, and then turned to Greg and held out her hand. "Give me the sheet."

Greg sat bolt upright. "What sheet?"

"You know what I'm talking about." She kept her hand outstretched. "Now, please."

As far as Ruth was concerned, Trevor was about the only person in Vanmoor they could trust. She was confident he hadn't pushed Dorothy down the stairs, killed the guy they'd found in Scott's car, kidnapped Mia's brother, and Trevor certainly hadn't murdered his best friend.

Besides, Ruth wanted to let him in on their investigation because Trevor deserved to help figure out what had happened to Bill.

Greg swallowed, and then said through the corner of his mouth, "I don't think that's a good idea, Grandma."

Ruth gave him a hard look.

"Can we talk about it first?"

Ruth didn't flinch.

Greg hesitated for a while longer, then sighed, reached into his back pocket and pulled out the sheet of paper. "I still say this is a bad idea."

Ruth took it from him, cleared a space on the table, and flattened it out. "Tell me, Trevor. You've lived here a while. Do you recognise any of these symbols?"

He leaned forward for a better look. "Can't say I do. What are they?"

"I found this one"—Ruth pointed at the crossed keys symbol—"under the bistro."

Trevor's bushy eyebrows pulled together. "Under?"

"Grandma," Greg said through clenched teeth. "How do you know we can trust him?"

"Trust me with what?" Trevor's frown deepened. "Are yer bank robbers?"

Ruth kept her focus on him and watched his reaction closely. "Someone moved Bill's body, right?"

Trevor's expression darkened in a heartbeat. "And when I find out who did it, I'll rip 'em limb from limb."

"I think someone used a tunnel under the village to do that," Ruth continued. "There's a hidden entrance in the bistro. The killer could have accessed it."

Trevor stared at her for several seconds as he seemed to ponder the validity of what she was telling him, and then his gaze dropped to the sheet of symbols. "Bistro, yer say?" He tapped the symbol of the crossed keys.

Ruth nodded.

Trevor stood and walked away.

Greg snarled, "Great. Now he's going to rat us out to Sergeant Fry."

Mia grabbed his hand. "No. Look."

Trevor stopped next to the front door, glanced about to make sure no one paid him any mind, then lifted a picture frame from the wall. He returned to their table and set it in front of them.

It was an old map of Vanmoor Village, yellowed and frayed around the edges with the passage of time, but the layout of the high street and buildings had changed very little in decades.

Trevor pointed to the symbol of the crossed keys on the sheet. "Bistro." His finger moved to the corresponding building on the map. "Right 'ere." Then Trevor indicated the symbol at the top of the sheet: a cross with a circle. "Vanmoor Church." His finger glided to the top of the map. "Here. They line up."

Stunned, Ruth stared. "It's a map." She pointed to a symbol of an eagle. "That's the village hall. I was there earlier."

"Police station." Greg tapped a triangular symbol.

Mia jabbed a finger at an elongated star. "Art gallery." She took a sharp intake of breath and pointed to a four-leaf clover. "The B&B." She looked between them. "Does that mean it also has a way down into the tunnel?"

"A hidden entrance we've missed." Ruth blew out a puff of air. "All this time we had a secret map and didn't know it." She smiled at Trevor. "You're a genius."

He sat back and sipped his beer. "Not a genius, but thanks for the compliment. Just frequented this pub enough times to remember the map on the wall, and staggered through Vanmoor's streets enough to know them like the back of me 'and."

Ruth pulled a pen from her bag and marked each location next to its corresponding symbol. When she was done,
she shook her head. "Amazing."

"Why was this symbol map in Scott's car?" Mia asked.

Greg whispered, "And who was the dead guy we found?"

"That"—Ruth folded the sheet of symbols and tucked it
into her pocket—"is what I'm going to figure out." She
resisted the urge to jump from the table and go now; they
needed to stick to the plan of waiting an hour or two, when
there was less chance someone would catch them. She
picked up a stack of menus. "First, we eat." She handed
them out.

However, their appetites remained subdued, with Ruth
only managing half her ham, egg, and chips; Mia a salad
bowl; Trevor a pie; and even Greg didn't have his customary
second helping of French fries to go with his triple-stacked
chickenburger.

An hour later, when they were done eating, Trevor said,
"Yer plannin' on goin' down there tonight?"

Ruth looked at the time on her phone: a little after nine.
"Soon."

"I'm comin' with you," he said.

"No," Greg said. "That's fine. We can handle it."

"Out of the four of us, I know the village best of all,"
Trevor said. "I can be useful."

"My grandson is right," Ruth said. "We don't want you to
get too caught up in this." She glanced about. "But there is
something else you can do for us. It's not very glamourous,
though, I'm afraid."

Trevor finished the dregs of his pint. "Name it."

"You have a car, I assume?" When Ruth received a bob
of the head in confirmation, she continued, "Could you
please fetch it, and wait for me? If I don't return in an hour,

drive to the next village, and call the police. Tell them everything."

Trevor's bushy eyebrows pulled together. "Yer don't trust Sergeant Fry, I take it?"

Greg's eyes went wide and he turned to Ruth. "What do you mean *if I don't return*?" He gestured between Mia and himself. "We're coming with you."

Ruth shook her head. "Too dangerous. You're staying with Trevor."

"But if we want to search quickly," Mia said, "it will take all three of us down there."

Greg fixed Ruth with a hard look. "What happens if you get trapped?"

Ruth flinched at the idea, but remained determined. They were getting closer to the killer, she could feel it, and there was no way she'd let Greg go blundering into the unknown.

"We're in this together," Mia said.

"You don't trust us?" Greg asked.

"It's got nothing to do with trust," Ruth said.

Greg's expression soured. "We're adults."

"I'm sorry, but my mind is made up." Ruth looked about the pub. "We can connect the phones again. Stay in touch as much as possible. With it being only me down there, we're less likely to get caught."

Greg stared at her for several seconds, then let out a breath, obviously realising he couldn't change her mind.

"Hold on a minute." Trevor's voice rose. "Yer tellin' me Sergeant Fry 'as got something to do with Bill's murder?"

Ruth lifted her hands, palms raised. "I don't know anything for sure. I'm working on assumptions only at this point, and they change, frequently." Without evidence, she had no way to know if Sergeant Fry was the killer or not.

"I know for sure it was him," Mia murmured.

Trevor narrowed his eyes.

Ruth shook her head. They were getting off track. "First things first—I need to gain access to that tunnel and have a look about."

"Now?" Mia asked.

Ruth glanced around the pub. "Now."

Trevor stood. "Back in ten minutes. I'll park next to the post office and meet yer there. Yer 'ave my number, right?"

Ruth checked her phone. "Ends in seven-oh-seven?"

"That's the one." Trevor tipped his cap and turned to leave.

"Thank you for the meal," Ruth said. "That was very kind of you."

"Yes, thank you," Mia said.

Greg nodded. "Thanks." He still looked angry at Ruth for refusing their help.

"Don't mention it." Trevor nodded at Ruth. "Help catch Bill's killer, and I'll buy yer all meals for the rest of yer lives." He hesitated as if he wanted to say something further, then left.

After downing the rest of their drinks, Ruth, Greg, and Mia stood too, and exited the pub.

Outside, Ruth shivered. "It's getting colder." She pulled her coat tight around her body and adjusted her woolly hat.

As they made their way along Vanmoor High Street, heading toward the bistro, Ruth pulled the set of keys from her handbag and said, "Stick with Trevor. No splitting up. I'll search each of those rooms down there and get back out as quickly as possible, right?"

"Got it," Mia said with a look of determination.

Greg nodded, then stopped dead in his tracks.

Ruth was about to ask what was wrong with him when she spotted the problem.

Elsie marched toward them. "There you are. I've been looking all over Vanmoor for you." She held out a hand to Ruth. "Can I have my keys back, please? I thought you'd left with them."

Ruth wanted to ask Elsie if she could take another look in the bistro's basement, but that would draw suspicion and questions. Besides, Elsie had been through enough. So, with reluctance, Ruth handed them over with a painted smile.

"You're staying another night?" Elsie asked.

If Ruth didn't know better, she would have sworn Elsie almost looked disappointed.

Ruth cleared her throat. "We're heading out first thing in the morning."

"Well, if I don't see you," Elsie said. "Thank you so much for everything you've done, Ruth. I really appreciate your help." Again, she didn't seem sincere.

"You're welcome."

Elsie waved and went inside.

As the door closed, Greg blew out a breath. "Great. Now what do we do?"

Ruth composed herself. "I'll find another way down. There was no access under the stage from the village hall side." She crossed the road, sat on the bench, and pulled the sheet of symbols from her bag. As Greg and Mia joined her, Ruth angled the sheet in the light of a streetlamp. "We're here, yes?" She pointed at the symbol that represented the bistro. "This is the police station." She indicated the triangular symbol and glanced over her shoulder at Vanmoor Bank. "Diamond."

"No way to look for an entrance there," Mia said.

"And we couldn't find the way in via the B&B," Greg said. "Unless we go take another look?"

"I suspect if we didn't spot anything out of the ordinary the first time," Ruth said, "it's either extremely well hidden or blocked off entirely."

"Then how do you get down there?" Mia asked.

Ruth ran her finger over the map, scanned the symbols and the corresponding building locations. She stopped on the cross and pointed to the end of the high street. "There."

Lights glowed from inside the church, casting a multi-coloured wash across the lawn and front path.

Greg connected their phones and tested them.

"What's the point in doing that?" Mia asked. "They lost connection last time."

"At least we can hear her before she goes down there." Greg handed Ruth a Bluetooth earpiece.

She slipped it in and stood. "Go find Trevor." Ruth pocketed her phone.

Mia gave Ruth a quick hug then hurried off hand in hand with Greg.

Ruth smiled. No matter what happened next, at least one good thing came from the days' events.

She shook herself and marched in the other direction.

"How are you going to find the entrance?" Greg said in her ear.

"Not a clue," Ruth murmured. "But I have to try." She would keep an eye out for symbols or anything else out of the ordinary.

She strode through the church gate and up the front path. At the door, Ruth opened it a few inches and peered inside. "Can't see anyone in there," she whispered, and slipped on through.

She hastened down the aisle, scanning the walls, floor and between the pews on either side.

At the end, Ruth knocked on a door and opened it. Beyond sat a compact office with an antique desk, a cabinet, and a few chairs. No Reverend Collins.

She closed the door and turned around. "Now, if I was going to hide a secret entrance . . ." Ruth stepped to the altar and circled behind it. She pursed her lips, knelt, lifted the cloth, and peered at the woodwork behind. "Bingo."

"What have you found?" Mia asked.

Ruth beamed as she studied a pair of hinges on the right side. "More than a cupboard, I'm betting." She pushed it inward, released the catch, and the door swung open. "Too easy."

Inside, a metal ladder led down through a hole in the floor.

Ruth sat and swung her legs inside. "Could be about to lose connection."

"Grandma?" Greg said.

"Yes?"

"Please be careful."

"Aren't I always?"

"No."

Ruth started the descent.

22

Beneath the church, at the bottom of the metal ladder, Ruth held her phone up high, swinging the beam of the light from side to side. She took stock of her surroundings.

Beyond stood a room twenty feet square, the ceiling held aloft by stone pillars. Various items sat under dust sheets, and thick strips of steel bolted to the wall barred the way through a door at the far end.

"Can you hear me?"

"Yes," Greg replied. "Where are you?"

"Beneath the church." Ruth lifted one of the dust sheets and used the torch on her phone to reveal a crate neatly packed with cardboard boxes, each a few inches square.

Ruth looked up at the hatch, making sure it was still open, and that she had a clear escape route.

"What's down there?" Mia asked.

Ruth refocussed on the room. "Nothing out of the ordinary."

"Trevor thinks it's a good idea you keep us updated where you are," Greg said. "And I agree. He can move the car to that part of the village, and try to keep the phone signal strong."

"Good idea," Ruth said. "But if you don't hear from me, if we should lose contact for any reason, then don't panic." She looked about. "These walls are thick. Stick to the plan," Ruth insisted. "If an hour goes by without contact, drive to the next village. Don't try to find me. Got it?" When there came no answer, Ruth said in a sing-song voice, "Oh, Gregory?"

"Yes, okay," he said. "You don't need to keep on."

"Promise me?" Ruth said. "Don't do anything stupid."

Greg paused and then said, "I promise."

"Good." Ruth frowned. "This basement room is a bit on the small side for such a big church." She'd expected a massive basement or a crypt full of coffins.

Ruth's gaze moved to the bolted door in the far wall, and then the surrounding blocks. The stonework there was a lighter grey, as opposed to the original darker masonry with flecks of black.

"Looks like someone divided this space off some time ago." Ruth stepped back to the nearest crate and opened one of the boxes. "What are these for?"

"What've you found?" Mia asked.

Inside were hundreds of rusty tacks.

Ruth lifted another dust sheet. "An artist's easel." She looked back up at the ladder and hatch. "They didn't get this down that way. Too big." Her attention rested on the bolted door again, and then she took a few pictures of the items.

Toward the corner of the room, a curtain hung from brass hooks. Ruth pulled it back to reveal another oak door in a recess.

Above it, carved into the stonework, was the cross and

circle symbol. She relayed this information to the others and reached for the handle.

"Be careful," Greg warned her.

"First sign of trouble, I'll run," Ruth said.

To be fair, that was her go-to reaction in most situations, even though running wasn't her thing. More like, waddling at speed.

She opened the door an inch, peeked through the gap, then slipped into a narrow passageway with a black door at the far end.

"Hold on. This isn't the same tunnel as earlier." Disorientated, Ruth hurried along it, but before she reached the end, another door appeared on her right.

Ruth stopped and stared up at a blank wall. "No symbol."

She tried the handle, but it wouldn't open. The door didn't have a keyhole either, which meant it was bolted from the other side.

She frowned and looked about. "I think I'm somewhere near Molly's B&B."

"You're breaking up." Greg's voice crackled. "We'll move closer."

Ruth stepped back. "Or does this lead to the library?" She consulted the symbol map. The library should've been marked by an inverted triangle with a square, and Molly's by a four-leaf clover.

Ruth continued on, opened the black door at the end, and stepped through. "Ah, here we go." The familiar tunnel stretched two hundred feet ahead, lined with doors and alcoves, and ended in another black door. "Same one as earlier." She turned to her right and faced a door with a spiral above it. Ruth consulted the sheet. "Are you there?"

"We're here," Mia's faint voice replied.

"According to this, I'm now beneath the post office." Ruth imagined Trevor parking on the road above her head. She opened the door. Beyond stood a compact room with cardboard boxes crammed floor to ceiling.

She peered into one, and her shoulders slumped in disappointment. "A boring basement room."

"What's in there?" Mia asked.

Ruth reached into the box and pulled out a roll of parcel tape. "Packing supplies."

"That's all?" Greg said.

"What were you expecting beneath a post office?" Mia said. "Pirate treasure? Bottles of hooch?"

"At least one bar of gold," he murmured.

Ruth looked inside another box filled with brown paper and string. Sure enough, yet another box revealed stacks of tissue paper. She huffed. "Not quite what I'm after." She took a few pictures anyway.

"What exactly are you hoping to find?" Mia asked. "Apart from my brother."

Ruth's eyes narrowed. "Something out of the ordinary." Truth was, she did not know what to expect, but she hoped for a clue tying together all the strange goings-on in Vanmoor Village.

Ruth backed out of the room and closed the door.

She then consulted the symbols map. "Next one." Her attention moved to a door with a hammer carved into the stonework above. "Looks like this leads right under the hardware shop. Quite appropriate really." She took a picture.

"Hudson and Co," Mia said. "The Victorian-looking shop with all that stuff outside. We're there now."

Ruth held her breath, opened the door, and peered into a darkened space. She then raised her phone, torch high.

This room had shelves and another door opposite, also bolted shut.

Keeping her eye on it, Ruth perused the shelves. Packs of acrylic, oil, and watercolour paints crammed the first, with various-sized brushes, palettes, charcoal pencils, pastels, mixing cups and inks filling the rest.

"More storage." Deflated, Ruth took pictures of these items too. So far, this wasn't what she'd hoped to find.

"Trevor's made a good point," Mia said. "If the village property owners are simply using the basements for storage, then wouldn't the tunnel also be common knowledge? He's never heard mention of it before."

Ruth agreed something like a tunnel running under the village would be talked about from time to time, especially a stretch that connected all the shops. She eyed the second door that likely led to the hardware shop itself, bolted from this side.

Something felt off.

She returned to the tunnel, consulted the map, then opened another door farther down.

The next subterranean room sat beneath Vanmoor Village Bank, and held metal cases, secured with large padlocks. Unlike the others, this room had no apparent way into the bank, which made sense from a security point of view.

Back in the tunnel, and determined not to give up, Ruth consulted the map again. "I'm going another twenty feet down." She jogged to a door with an elongated star above it. "I'm at the art gallery."

"We're moving with you." Greg's voice crackled.

Ruth stepped inside. This room had a storage rack down one side, packed full of what she at first glance thought were ancient scrolls, all rolled up and stacked. However, on closer inspection, they turned out to be old canvases with nothing painted on them.

She pulled another one out, unrolled it and examined the fibres under the beam of the phone's torch. Faint remnants of paint remained, as though someone had scrubbed the original artwork away, leaving nothing but the canvas.

Ruth grabbed a second roll and found the same thing. "Hmm." She fished in her pocket and pulled out the strand she'd plucked from Bill's shirt. The fibres matched. "Bill was here?" She returned the canvas and faced the other way.

Wooden frames stacked against the nearest wall drew her attention, along with a workbench filled with tools. Ruth picked up a small hammer with a claw and examined it. Bent and rusty old metal tacks filled a box, similar to the ones beneath the church.

"Can you hear us?" Greg's voice came, faint and still breaking up.

"Just about." Ruth examined several vats of chemicals, each one labelled with hazard stickers. A breather mask and rubber gloves hung on the wall above them.

She took pictures of everything and then stepped back through the door. "I'm in the tunnel again."

"We ... hear ... Are ..."

"Say again." Ruth adjusted the earpiece.

"We can hardly hear you," Mia's faint voice said. "Are ... coming back?"

"Not yet," Ruth said. "Stay where you are. I want to look in a couple more rooms." Her attention moved to a symbol of a backward *Z* overlaid with an arrow. She reached for the door handle, but a rattling from down the tunnel made her freeze.

Ruth's heart leapt into her throat.

The rattling increased.

She ran back into the previous room. "Someone's coming." Ruth pushed the door to, extinguished the light on her phone, and peered into the tunnel.

Sure enough, the rattling grew in intensity.

Ruth stared.

A darkened figure pushed a cart in front of them. In the cart were square, flat parcels wrapped in brown paper, each one a couple of feet square.

Ruth pulled back as the figure trundled past, then she slipped into the tunnel behind them to watch.

However, instead of entering one of the other underground rooms, as she'd expected, the figure kept going, unlocked the black door at the end, then wheeled their cart through.

Ruth adjusted her earpiece and whispered, "If you can hear me, I'm going to follow them. It's someone with a cart."

She went to race after them, but Greg's faint voice replied, "We'll come down."

"Don't you dare," Ruth growled. "Stay where you are. Do not move."

There came no reply.

"Greg?"

"Yeah?"

"If either of you get murdered to death because of me, your parents will never let it go."

Even though she'd not met Mia's mother and father, Ruth didn't like the idea of explaining how their daughter had gotten hurt, or worse.

"I'm wasting time. Stay where you are. Stick to the plan." Ruth rushed to the black door. She turned an ear to it. Hearing nothing, she opened the door and paused, stunned.

Another tunnel stretched into the distance.

The figure with the cart rounded a bend and disappeared.

Ruth jogged after them, and was instantly reminded of the fact exercise was not her thing.

As she approached the corner, Ruth slowed.

To her utter astonishment, the tunnel continued for hundreds of feet, the figure growing smaller.

This stretch of tunnel didn't have any doors, but every thirty feet sat more alcoves, about big enough for her to squeeze into, which, as she followed, Ruth made sure she did now and again, in case the cart-pusher turned back.

Onward she marched, and the tunnel now barely deviated from its course, only following a slight curve or an incline from time to time.

Ruth kept her full attention on the cart and figure ahead. "We're a long way from the village now," she murmured. *Are we heading toward Vanmoor Hall?* She wasn't sure which direction they now faced.

She checked her phone.

No signal.

Ruth couldn't say she was surprised—she was deep underground, heading away from the village, surrounded by thick stone walls on all sides. However, being out of communication with the outside world, and in particular Greg, Mia, and Trevor, sent a shiver down her spine.

Then a nasty thought hit her—if the person with the cart did an about-face, she'd be in serious trouble. Sure, she could cram inside one of the alcoves, but the cart-pusher would soon spot her.

For a couple of seconds, Ruth considered going back, but then pictured Mia's face when she found Scott safe and well, and they were reunited. A tall order, granted, but Ruth chose to remain positive.

Besides, there were still no signs to point to any other outcome, discounting the three murders, and until they stumbled on a clue or Scott's corpse, Ruth would keep her promise and plough on.

She squinted, trying to gauge by the figure's size and gait whether they were male or female. It was impossible to tell at this distance, especially as they wore a heavy coat with the hood up, but given the wide shoulders and stride, it was likely a guy.

Ruth panted as she matched his brisk pace, and her lungs burned.

The most exercise she'd had over the last couple of years was when she'd heard the news that her local cake shop were having a one-day-only closing-down sale, with an extra ten percent off for seniors. Some kind soul had told Ruth this an hour before they shuttered their doors for good, and she had literally sprinted there.

Probably burned more calories than she'd later consumed.

Almost.

Ruth darted into an alcove to catch her breath.

After a few seconds, she peered down the tunnel and then hurried on.

Another thousand feet on, the tunnel finally ended, and the figure stopped at a wide door.

Ruth once again darted into an alcove.

The figure unlocked the door and pushed the cart through.

She hurried down the tunnel. At the door, Ruth let out a breath, relieved the person hadn't locked the door behind them, and peered out.

A few seconds passed as Ruth took stock of her surroundings. A path veered from the right side of the door and headed up an incline to a concrete area where a van was parked.

Ahead was a beach, and waves lapped the shore.

"The cove on the map," she murmured.

The one Greg had mentioned when they first arrived at Vanmoor.

Ruth darted behind a bush.

As the figure with the cart reached the brow of the hill, a burly gentleman wearing dark clothes stepped from the van and opened the back doors.

The two of them then unloaded the cart.

Ruth squinted at the parcels. "Are those paintings?" She couldn't be sure, but it was a safe bet, judging by their sizes and flat shapes.

Keeping low, she circled the bushes and made her way up the hill, pushing through bracken and staying in the shadows.

At the top, Ruth ducked behind a wall.

Sure enough, the brown paper parcels did indeed look like they contained paintings, and the burly guy strapped them to the sides of the van, with blankets placed between each.

Once done loading, he handed over two silver cases, similar in size and shape to the ones beneath the bank.

The hooded figure loaded them onto the cart and headed back down the hill.

As he walked beneath a streetlight, Ruth glimpsed his face, and she gasped, "Sergeant Fry. Knew it." His stupid goatee and smug face were a dead giveaway.

Burly Guy closed the van doors, and as he drove off, Ruth still had the presence of mind to take a picture of the licence plate number with her phone. She then jogged back down the hill.

No sooner had she reached the bush when Sergeant Fry disappeared back into the tunnel and closed the door behind him. There came the familiar thunk of a deadbolt securing into place.

"Erm." Ruth looked about and winced. "How exactly am I getting back?"

23

As Trevor drove Ruth toward Vanmoor Village, following the twisting country roads, she could almost feel Greg shooting daggers at her from the back seat.

"You should have come back for us," he said.

Ruth pondered the recent events and what her next move should be. "We would've all been caught."

"Caught by whom?" Mia asked. "Who was it?"

"Right," Trevor said. "And are yer gonna explain why yer appeared a mile away? Five more minutes and I was drivin' to the next village and followin' yer instructions."

"We thought you were dead somewhere," Greg grumbled.

"Wouldn't go that far," Trevor said. "But I didn't relish the idea of explainin' to the police why yer were down a tunnel somewhere." He looked at Ruth askance. "Not sure they would 'ave believed me if I did."

"That's exactly where I was—in that tunnel." Ruth rubbed her temples as she tried to clear her mind and think it through. "It ran all the way down to the cove. Looks like it's been there for hundreds of years."

"Smuggler's Cove," Trevor said with a nod.

"Turns out, it really suits its moniker," Ruth said.

Trevor stopped the car at a set of temporary traffic lights at red.

"How come you didn't go back the way you came?" Mia asked. "What happened?"

"She followed someone with a cart," Greg said with more than a hint of annoyance. "That's the last we heard of you. Anything could have happened."

"A cart?" Trevor frowned.

"He had it loaded with paintings," Ruth said. "Put them into a van at the cove." She stared out the window, and her eyes glazed over. "And he got some silver cases in exchange. The same design I found under the bank."

"What do you think was in them?" Mia asked.

"Cash," Greg said. "What else?"

Although Ruth didn't like to guess, he was probably right. The tunnel was like an underground criminal highway.

"And who was the man yer followed?" Trevor asked. "Did yer get a good look at 'is face?"

Ruth sighed. "Yes."

Mia sat forward. "Well?"

"Sergeant Fry."

This resulted in a few seconds of silence before Greg said through tight lips, "Trevor, can you please drive us to the next village? We'll call the police."

"Not until we have enough evidence," Ruth said. "And not until we find Mia's brother." They couldn't lose sight of their primary goal. "Otherwise we might put him in danger."

Greg huffed and sat back. "What is that Fry idiot up to?"

The lights turned green, and Trevor pulled away.

They drove past a coned-off section of road with zero signs anyone had carried out any repairs. Ruth assumed the workmen had only needed to store their equipment, and here was as good a place as any. "I think it's pretty clear what's going on," she murmured. "Sergeant Fry strips old paintings down to their canvases. I found them neatly stored under the art gallery. That's the first step."

"Why does he do that?" Greg asked.

"He's an art forger." Mia's eyes widened in realisation. "Using old canvas makes them appear authentic. More likely to fool people."

"The paint supplies." Ruth pictured the basement rooms. "The boxes of old tacks. It makes sense." She pursed her lips. "If we could get our hands on one of those finished paintings, I bet we'd find it's supposedly by a famous artist. Worth a lot of money on the black market."

"Yer saying the guy with the van is a link to the criminal underworld?" Trevor's eyebrows knitted. "Yer sure?" He turned onto a narrow road flanked by trees with low over-hanging canopies. "All this 'appening in Vanmoor?"

"Don't let its sleepy appearance fool you," Ruth said. "There's a lot going on beneath the surface. Literally."

"I've lived 'ere fifteen years," Trevor said, incredulous. "Everyone is 'armless. I've never seen any 'ints of something untoward goin' on." He shrugged. "Sure, there's a few quirky characters, but Sergeant Fry a criminal mastermind?" He shook his head. "I don't think so. The fella 'asn't got two brain cells to rub together."

"You've probably seen plenty of stuff," Ruth said. "Only not realised." When this received a puzzled expression, she added, "Would you think it out of the ordinary if someone delivered old paintings to an art gallery?"

"Of course not," Trevor said.

"Packing supplies to a post office? Paint, brushes, and cleaning chemicals to a shop that sells hardware?" Ruth studied him. "Would you think any of that is strange?"

"Now, yer wait a minute," Trevor said. "Yer not for one minute suggestin' several villagers are in on it?" He snorted. "Come on."

"No, I don't think they're in on it, but if the resident police sergeant asks you to store some items in your basement, to accept a delivery here or there on his behalf, you're not going to turn him down, are you? After all, if you can't trust the police, who can you trust?"

"That means the shop owners all know about the tunnel," Mia said. "I thought we'd established they don't."

"Maybe some do." Ruth shrugged. "Not every door was open. That part of the tunnel can be locked at each end with the black doors. They likely don't know the extent of it, so don't bother to mention its existence." Ruth looked over her shoulder. "Perhaps Sergeant Fry tells them he'll use the tunnel to move stuff about. They trust him. Or maybe he picks up the deliveries and takes them down to the tunnel another way. Whatever the case, the result is the same."

"Even so, why would no one be suspicious of this goin' on?" Trevor asked with a dubious expression.

Ruth wasn't sure of the answer. "He'll have an excuse. I don't know what, though."

"Online shop," Mia said. "Tells people he's buying stuff in bulk to flog online. Might even give them a cut of the imaginary proceeds."

Ruth shrugged. "Could be."

"Let's ask someone," Greg said. "We could go to that hardware place when it opens in the morning and speak to the owner."

Ruth shook her head. "We can't risk drawing attention.

And right now, it's unimportant." She stared out the window and pictured Dorothy, Bill, and then the body in Scott's car. Some pieces suddenly dropped into place, and a gasp escaped Ruth's lips.

Greg sat forward. "What now?"

Ruth turned in her seat to face Trevor. "You told us Constance's great-uncle, Dorothy's husband, the one who died a few months back, was a fantastic artist, right?"

"Sure was."

"But you didn't tell us Constance is Sergeant Fry's daughter," Ruth said. "What's the betting great-uncle Arthur served some prison time?" She looked back at Greg. "For forging artwork."

Mia gaped at her.

Greg typed *Arthur Pennington* into his phone. "Nothing comes up. Only an old social media profile."

He held the phone so Ruth could see—it showed an old man with one arm around Dorothy's waist, both of them smiling at the camera. His soft yet lined face belied the fact he could have been a criminal. Although, contrary to popular belief, most criminals looked like anyone else.

Well, the clever ones do.

"He could have used a pseudonym," Mia said. "Lots of artists don't show their real name."

Greg tried *A Pennington* too, but that didn't return any results either.

"Arthur was the art forger," Mia said. "Then when he died—" She clapped a hand over her mouth.

Ruth nodded. "That's exactly what I'm thinking."

"Scott," Mia breathed through her fingers. "Sergeant Fry is using my brother to forge artwork." She lowered her hand, and her face twisted with anger.

"The lad is alive?" Trevor asked. "Well, that's good news."

Ruth half smiled, and although she was relieved at the possibility, they still had a long way to go to find him.

She removed the symbol map from her pocket and studied it. "I went to all these." She indicated the bank, post office, hardware store, gallery, and Elsie's bistro. Although, that last one had nothing related to art forgery in the basement. "Which puts us right back here." She pointed at the symbol of the four-leaf clover. "The B&B. It's the last place we know Scott was for sure." She thought back to the separate part of the tunnel, and the door with the missing symbol. "Ignoring Constance's version of events, Scott could've been right beneath our feet this whole time."

"In the B&B's basement?" Greg asked. "We searched the building. No entrance. How do we know there's a way down?"

"I found a door with no symbol." Ruth looked back at them. "It was bolted from the other side." Not to mention the fact the bistro had a hidden way down to the tunnel, so it stood to reason there were others.

"When we were at the B&B, we looked for Constance," Mia said. "Not a basement. We could have overlooked it."

Ruth faced forward. "Trevor, could you please take us to Molly's Bed & Breakfast?"

"My pleasure." He turned into the darkened high street.

Ruth glared at the art gallery as they passed and wondered if Flamingo played a part in all this.

Does he source the antique pictures that get stripped down to their canvas? Ruth's stomach knotted. *Is Flamingo the talent-spotter? Working with Fry to find the right artist to forge the paintings?* She then remembered the Wilkinson couple and how the husband artist had been turned away by Flamingo. *What was the problem? Not skilled enough? Not capable of pulling off the correct styles?*

Trevor backed into a space outside the church. "Want me to come with yer this time?"

Ruth forced a smile she hoped didn't betray her inner anxiety about what was to come. "Thank you for all you've done, but I think it best I try this alone again." Her gaze moved to the B&B. "Do you mind waiting, same as before, and if I don't return in . . .'"

"An hour." Trevor gave a fervent nod. "Round two. Gotcha. No problem."

Ruth took a breath and climbed from the car.

Greg and Mia followed her across the road and up the front path. The B&B was in darkness, with only a weak light above the porch illuminating the way.

"Shouldn't we check Constance is in her room?" Greg whispered as they reached the front door.

"How are we going to do that?" Mia asked. "Sneak in there? And then what? Tie her up?"

Greg shrugged. "Not a bad idea seeing as her dad is a murderer and a kidnapper. We don't know what her involvement is."

Ruth looked at the time on her phone: a little gone eleven. Hopefully, Constance would be asleep. "We could do with some face socks."

Mia's eyebrows knitted. "Face socks?"

"Yeah, you know." Ruth motioned pulling it over her head. "The ones with the little holes for your mouth and eyes."

Greg pinched the bridge of his nose. "Balaclava. She means balaclavas."

"Constance lied to us," Mia said. "Are we sure she's not in on it?"

Ruth considered the question. Even though they had no

direct evidence of Constance's involvement, her being the last person to see Scott did make it appear that way.

Could Arthur have hidden the forging operation from his grandniece? Ruth doubted it. That and the fact she was Sergeant Fry's daughter meant Constance likely had some participation. *A family affair.*

Ruth motioned for Greg and Mia to stick close and tread quietly, then she opened the door, and the three of them stepped into the gloomy reception.

The door behind the desk stood open, with the office and bedroom beyond empty.

"Where do we look?" Greg murmured.

Ruth faced Mia. "Constance told us Scott came to the kitchen to see her, right?"

Mia's eyes narrowed. "If she was telling the truth."

"I don't see any reason she shouldn't have been at that point." Ruth glanced up the stairs. "We'll start in the kitchen." She motioned for Greg and Mia to follow.

The three of them tiptoed across the reception, into the lounge, and snuck through the door to the kitchen.

Once inside, Ruth flicked on the light.

The B&B's kitchen also stood empty, with pots and pans in place, surfaces clean and clutter-free.

Ruth moved around the room, examining the tiled floor, kneeling in places for a better look, but no signs of a hatch. She stopped at the table and pictured Constance and Scott seated at it, chatting. She then turned and imagined Constance working at the range cooker the second time Scott came in, after his disappointing visit at the art gallery.

"Where did you go from here, Scott?" Ruth walked around the room again, this time opening cupboards and checking the walls for hidden entrances.

Mia and Greg did the same, hunting for signs of anything out of the ordinary.

Ruth stepped into a pantry. After examining the floor in here too, she inspected the shelves, ran her fingers over the woodwork and kept an eye out for any buttons, latches, or concealed hinges, but nothing stood out. The walls behind them seemed solid too. Ruth rapped a knuckle in a few places to be sure.

Finding nothing, she backed from the pantry.

"This is useless," Greg said. "If there's a secret hatch, it must be in another room." He turned to leave.

"Wait." Ruth pointed to the door that led to reception. "Close that and lay your coat in front of it." She gestured Mia to the back door. "Do the same, please. Remove your jacket and place it on the floor in front."

With a look of puzzlement, Greg and Mia did as Ruth asked, while she opened cupboards.

Ruth removed a bag of white flour and set it on the counter. She then rummaged through drawers until she found a turkey baster. Ruth set it on the counter too, along with a saucer.

"What are you doing?" Greg asked. "Making a cake?"

"Yes, Gregory, that's exactly what I'm doing."

"Ooh," Mia smiled. "Chocolate?"

Ruth poured a pile of the flour in the middle of the saucer, then picked it up with her left hand, the turkey baster in her right. "Mia, activate the torch on your phone and come here, please. Greg, switch off the kitchen lights." Again, they both did as she asked. "Right, with me."

Mia followed Ruth around the kitchen.

"Go nice and slow. Shine the light on the cloud of powder." Ruth knelt. "Hold your breath." Using the turkey baster, she blew a puff of flour into the air.

They both watched as the particles drifted to the tiled floor.

Ruth and Mia moved to the next spot and repeated the process—again the flour drifted to the floor.

"What on earth are you doing, Grandma?" Greg asked. "Apart from making a mess."

Ruth stopped in front of the range cooker. Using the turkey baster, she blew a small puff of flour into the air, and Mia shone her torch at the resulting cloud.

This time the particles dropped as before, but then when they reached an inch or so from the floor, they drifted away the table.

"Bingo."

24

I n the B&B kitchen, with her heart pounding in her chest, Ruth looked up at the extractor above the cooker, but the draught wasn't coming from that. "Take these." She handed Mia the saucer and turkey baster, then using the torch function on her own phone, Ruth peered under the cooker.

A metal skirt ran around the bottom edge, but still visible right behind that, in several places, were heavy-duty castors.

Ruth clambered to her feet. "This is an electric cooker, right?"

Greg joined them and pointed to a nearby switch. Someone had set it to the off position.

"That means no gas pipes." Ruth ran her fingers across the front, and then down each side.

Greg looked about. "It's all electric in here. The stove top too."

Ruth placed her palms on the front of the range cooker, shoulder-width apart, and pushed.

The entire cooker glided back with ease, slid into the

wall, and uncovered a hole in the floor with a compact spiral staircase leading down.

Greg and Mia gaped at it.

"What's the betting your brother went this way?" Ruth hadn't felt this smug since she last thrashed Greg at Monopoly.

Mia went to go down first, but he put a hand out. "It might not be safe."

"I can look after myself," Mia said with an incredulous expression. "I thought you've learned that about me."

"I have," Greg said, defensive. "I don't mean to— I was just— You have—"

Ruth crossed her arms. "Neither of you are going."

They stared at her.

"I mean it," Ruth said. "You'll stay here, and I will go down and check it out. It's too risky with all three of us blundering about the place."

Greg shook his head. "I'll go."

"No." Ruth set her jaw. "You won't. You'll remain here and keep an eye out for Constance."

Greg rolled his eyes. "Can I again remind you about the river?"

"What about it?"

"How you were happy to send me in when it suited you."

"That's different," Ruth said, trying to keep her temper under control. "The river's purpose is not to kill you. You treat it with respect, and you'll be fine. The water was slow moving, and I knew someone as fit as you would be fine."

"That's ridiculous." Greg shook his head. "You're talking rubbish."

"Listen here." Ruth waved a finger at him. "A killer's single-minded obsession is to murder people. And once they commit one murder, they often find it easier to kill others. They are evil and dangerous. I will not put you directly into harm's way." She glared at him. "Understood?"

"I'm not a kid." Greg raised his voice. "I'm nineteen, and you can't tell me what to do."

"You're my grandson," Ruth snapped back. "I can always tell you what to do, if it's for your own good. You will forever be a kid to me, and if you can't live with that, then tough."

Mia took a step toward the cooker, but Ruth blocked her path too.

"You stay," Mia said. "I'm going alone."

"No." Ruth set her jaw. "You're not."

Mia waved a finger at the stairs. "It's my brother down there."

"Exactly," Ruth said. "You're too emotional to think straight. If something happens . . ." She took a deep, calming breath. "This argument is getting us nowhere and wasting time." She rested hands on both of their shoulders. "Please trust me. I'll check it out and be back in a few minutes."

Before either of them could protest further, Ruth stepped onto the spiral staircase and descended with as much haste as she dared.

"Besides," she called over her shoulder. "I bet there's loads of spiders down here, Greg. You'd hate it."

At the bottom, Ruth switched on her phone's torch and found herself in a tunnel, not a basement as she'd expected.

High on the wall opposite was the four-leaf clover, and to the left was a door without a symbol: the one she'd found earlier, only now she was on the other side.

Ruth turned to her right and squinted down the passage-way. With her phone torch held high, she headed along it, ears straining into the darkness.

Unlike the main tunnel, this one had no other doors or

alcoves. If someone walked from the opposite direction, she had nowhere to hide.

After a minute of walking, Ruth came to an archway with an oak door. Above it was an inverted triangle with a square: the library.

Ruth held her breath and opened the door.

Beyond stood a vast space with vaulted ceilings held aloft by stone pillars, and lit by lights strung on the walls.

Down one side sat rows of easels, each painting at a different stage of completion. There was a watercolour of boats in a harbour, a portrait of an old man with a bushy white beard, and even a canvas filled with lines and blocks of bright colours.

Ruth tiptoed to an open door and peered into a darkened room. Two barred cages sat at one end, ten feet on each side, jail cells with a blond-haired figure lyin on a cot in one of them, covered in a blanket.

A wave of relief washed over Ruth as his chest rose and fell in slow rhythm, and tears formed in her eyes. She'd found him, and he was alive.

Ruth's gaze moved to the lock. "Keys." She examined a table with a phone, a couple of wallets, and a stack of paperwork with more symbols.

Someone screamed, "Scott," and rushed past.

Ruth almost leapt out of her skin.

Scott sat up, blinked, and then his eyes went wide. "Mia?" He scrambled to his feet and hurried to the bars.

Ruth turned back.

Greg stood by the door.

"I told you to wait at the B&B," Ruth said.

"Sorry. No choice." Greg stepped aside to reveal Sergeant Fry behind him with an army pistol raised.

Ruth squeezed her eyes closed.

She had blundered into these tunnels and basement rooms without the slightest amount of due care, and now, because of her foolishness, Sergeant Fry had caught all three of them. Plus, Scott—alive and well, thank goodness—had gained absolutely nothing from her reckless search.

She cursed herself for being in such a hurry.

Ruth opened her eyes and looked at Sergeant Fry and, in particular, his gun. "You don't have to do this."

His hands trembled. "And you could have stayed away, but you just had to stick your beak where it doesn't belong."

Ruth motioned to Scott inside the cell. "You know we needed to find him."

"Face the wall," Sergeant Fry snarled. "All three of you."

Ruth and Greg did as he asked, but Mia remained by the bars, next to her brother, holding his hands.

"Move or I'll kill you." Sergeant Fry's voice quavered, and he aimed the gun at her. "Now. I mean it."

Mia glared at him and then edged over to Greg.

Sergeant Fry patted all three of them down, and removed their phones and personal items. He then grabbed a key from the table and unlocked the cell. Sergeant Fry waved them in.

Mia ran to her brother and threw her arms around him.

Greg hesitated, looked over at Ruth with concern, and then walked into the cell too.

Ruth remained where she was. She kept her full attention on Sergeant Fry. "I can't go in there. I have cleithrophobia."

"I don't care what you have," he retorted. "Get in."

"You have to let us go."

Surely he couldn't keep all four of them locked up indefinitely.

"What's your plan?" Ruth asked.

This seemed to catch him off guard. Sergeant Fry glanced about, as if unsure of himself.

"Well?" Ruth pressed. "I think it would be better if you—"

Sergeant Fry waved the gun in Ruth's face. "Stop talking and get in there. *Now*."

"You need to explain what—"

He grabbed her arm.

Ruth tried to resist, but Sergeant Fry shoved her into the cell.

"Hey." Greg leapt forward, but Ruth shoved him back.

"Careful," she said through a clenched jaw.

Last thing she needed was for her grandson to get shot because of her.

Sergeant Fry slammed the cell door closed.

Ruth stiffened, squeezed her eyes shut, and murmured, "You're okay. You're okay. All fine. Everyone's here with you. It's going to be all right."

Sergeant Fry locked the door, chucked the key onto the table, and left.

Ruth's whole body shook as she dropped to the cot.

Greg rushed to her and rested his hands on her shoulders. "Deep breaths, Grandma."

Ruth pulled in a big lungful of air, and another.

Mia held her brother's hands in hers. "Are you hurt?"

He gave her a weary smile. "I've been treated well, under the circumstances. Brings whatever food I ask for." He pointed to a crate in the corner of his cell, filled with bottled water and cola drinks.

"He's used you to forge artwork?" Ruth forced herself to concentrate on him.

"This is Ruth," Mia said. "And Greg." She motioned to

him as he stepped back. "I couldn't have found you without their help. They've been very kind."

Scott let out a slow breath. "It was a trap. The gallery owner wanted to see my artwork first and gauge what styles he thought I could mimic."

"Flamingo." Ruth's eyes darkened. "They're working together."

"I've not seen him since, though," Scott said. "I guess he sticks to his gallery and lets Sergeant Fry do all the dirty work."

So, Flamingo set a trap, luring in unsuspecting artists, and then once he found a suitable one, Sergeant Fry took over.

That made sense, given the type of forgery involved, and the level of skill required to fool collectors. "He invited you in to check out your portfolio."

Scott looked at the door and lowered his voice. "I've also been teaching Constance how to paint."

"What?" Mia scoffed. "You're kidding?"

"That would take years." Greg glanced around the cell, into corners, as if making sure no spiders lurked anywhere.

Scott's attention moved back to them. "She's a fast learner but has a long way to go. I think Constance is hoping she'll take over the forgeries and there'll be no need to kidnap any more artists. She doesn't seem to approve of what's going on."

Ruth nodded slowly and got control of her shaking. "Maybe that's why she had a falling-out with her father when we were at the bistro party. That was the real reason."

"What about your painting?" Mia asked. "Did you give it to Constance? She has it hanging in her bedroom."

Scott shook his head.

Mia balled her fists. "That conniving little b—"

Ruth cleared her throat. "What can you tell us about what's going on here?"

"Ethan got here a month ago." Scott pointed to the other cell. "But he managed to escape. Grabbed my car keys, and a secret map we'd made using the symbols we could remember in the tunnel when he first brought us down here." He nodded to the table, and then a flicker of concern crossed his face. "I hope Ethan's okay. It's been days since he got out."

Ruth clambered to her feet as cold washed through her veins. "This Ethan . . ." She swallowed. "He had mousy blond hair like yours? Tanned?"

Scott's face dropped. "Is he all right?"

"He's dead," Mia murmured. "Sergeant Fry killed him. Shot him in the leg."

Scott's cheeks paled. "He can't be. He got out."

"How did Ethan escape?" Ruth walked over to the bars and studied them.

"I can't believe it." Scott shook himself and pointed at the cell next to theirs again, and in particular the padlock holding the door closed. "It wasn't secured properly. Old. Rusty." He held up a hand as Ruth stepped toward their own door. "No use."

She checked the shiny new lock, then stepped back, shaking her head as a new wave of panic threatened to wash over her. Ruth took several more deep breaths, bringing her phobia back under control.

For now, at least.

They certainly weren't getting out the same way as Ethan.

Ruth eyed the key on the table, but it was too far, even if they knotted some of their clothes together as a makeshift rope and hook.

"Ethan was going to get help." Scott's voice cracked. "I—I can't believe he's dead."

"We found him in your car." Mia put an arm around him.

Scott slumped. "This is a nightmare."

"It's not your fault," Ruth said, determined to find a way out of the cell and the mess they were in. "Why has no one come looking for Ethan?"

"He moved to the UK from La Rochelle a few months back," Scott said. "His parents are dead. He has no family."

"No friends either?" Ruth asked.

Scott shrugged. "He didn't mention any. Seemed like a loner. Good guy, though." His eyes dropped to the floor. "I really liked him. Why not bring him back? Why kill him?" He placed his head in his hands.

Ruth took a few mental steps back in time to figure out the events that had led them to this basement cell. "How did Ethan know where Sergeant Fry had hidden your car?"

"The tunnel by the woods." Scott lowered his hands. "We overheard him talking to someone on the phone. He planned to move it again. That's when Ethan escaped."

Several seconds of silence greeted this as everyone seemed to ponder their predicament.

Ruth thought about Sergeant Fry and his gun.

What does he plan on doing with Scott once the artist's usefulness has come to an end? And what about us? It's not as if he can simply let us go.

"What about Constance?" Mia asked. "You went to see her after visiting the gallery. Why?"

A valid question. After all, if Scott hadn't gone back there, none of this would have happened to him.

"I went to settle the bill," Scott said. "As I left the Bed & Breakfast for the art gallery, the landlady said the card machine was down and to come back later to settle up. I didn't have enough cash." He huffed. "So, like an idiot, I went to the gallery and showed Mr Strange my portfolio." His eyes glazed over. "Should have realised something was off." Scott focussed on Ruth. "He wanted some time to call round and decide whether to stock my work. In the meantime, he told me to return to Molly's B&B and he'd find me later with a final decision. I said I had to go back anyway, and that I'd wait in the lounge."

"Dorothy was in on all this too." Ruth blew out a puff of air. "While you waited at the B&B, that's when Sergeant Fry showed up?"

"He was already waiting for me," Scott said.

"She lied again," Mia murmured. "You didn't give Constance that painting, she took it after they kidnapped you."

Greg leaned in to Ruth and whispered, "How are we going to get out of here?"

"Right now," she said. "I have no idea."

25

In the prison cell, with a sense of hopelessness, Ruth murmured to the others, "When we don't show up outside the B&B in the next twenty minutes"—she eyed her mobile phone, along with Greg and Mia's phones on the table—"Trevor will drive to the next village and call the police."

"You mean that Trevor?" Mia raised a shaking figure.

Trevor, escorted by Sergeant Fry, staggered into the room.

"Back away," Sergeant Fry snapped at the captives, then he unlocked the cage door and shoved Trevor inside.

Greg rushed forward again. Ruth went to grab his arm, but it was too late—Sergeant Fry punched the lad on the nose, sending him reeling, then pointed the gun at him.

Ruth leapt between them with her hands raised.

Sergeant Fry's finger tightened on the trigger. "Don't ever try that again." He slammed the door closed, locked it, and marched from the room.

Greg clutched his nose.

"Are you okay?" Mia asked. "Let me see." She lifted his hands away. "Not broken. It's not bleeding either."

Greg's eyes streamed. "I'm fine. Just stings a little."

Ruth shook her head. "I appreciate the attempt, Muhammad Ali, but please don't do that again." A punch to the nose bruised his pride; a bullet to the chest would have been a lot worse, and Ruth's stomach did a backflip at the horrific thought. She'd never forgive herself if something happened to her only grandson.

Greg stared at the floor.

"Well, I messed up," Trevor said with a sheepish expression. "Didn't see 'im comin'." He winced and stretched his back.

"Did he hurt you too?" Ruth asked.

"No. Sciatica is giving me gyp." He half smiled. "All the sittin' about."

Ruth winced. "Sorry. My fault."

"How did he find you?" Mia asked.

"Camaras," Ruth said. "He must have watched us go into the B&B and then saw that Trevor waited outside. Put two and two together." It was so painfully obvious.

"Which means he definitely has remote access to them," Greg said in a nasal voice.

Trevor's gaze rested on Scott. "Yer found 'im, then? That's some good news, at least." He extended a hand. "I'm Trevor. Yer sister 'as boundless tenacity." He winked at Mia.

Scott shook his hand. "Don't I know it."

Trevor faced Ruth, and his expression dropped. "I'm sorry. I 'ad one job, and I failed miserably."

Ruth squeezed his shoulder. She regretted having gotten Trevor involved, but in an odd way was glad he was here with them. It increased their chances of figuring out a way to escape.

Trevor frowned at the empty cell next to theirs. "Why 'as 'e crammed us all in 'ere?"

"Lock's broken on the other one," Mia said.

Greg sniffed. "Now what do we do?"

"How does no one else in the village see what's going on?" Mia said with frustration.

Ruth took a calming breath and sat next to Scott. Then a thought struck her. Mia was right. It *was* odd. Ruth recalled the argument between Reverend Collins and the person on the phone. That had to be Sergeant Fry. "Have you seen or heard anyone with a slight Irish accent down here?" she asked Scott. "A man. Deep voice?"

"I've only seen Sergeant Fry and Constance."

"Are you sure?" Ruth said with a rush of excitement. "Think carefully. It's important. You have to be certain."

"I haven't seen anyone other than them."

Ruth looked away and pictured the reverend, his upright stature, polished shoes, precise way of talking and his overall military vibe. "Not military, though," she murmured. And if her hunch was right, his argument took on a whole new meaning. She smacked her forehead.

"What's wrong?" Mia asked.

"On the phone, Reverend Collins said he thought he'd earned someone's trust." Ruth looked between them. "Whose?"

Greg shrugged. "Sergeant Fry."

Ruth stood and paced, trying not to think about the fact it only took a few steps before she had to turn around again. "He said it had gone too far and Dorothy was right."

"Right about what?" Trevor asked.

"Arthur clearly ran this forgery scheme with Dorothy, and their nephew, Sergeant Fry," Ruth said. "A family business."

"And the guy who runs the art gallery," Scott reminded her.

"Right," Ruth said. "He's involved too, but it appears he remains on the periphery. I gather Sergeant Fry must use him to secure old artwork to strip for their canvases."

"That's exactly what happens," Scott said. "The less valuable old paintings are stripped away, and newer artwork painted over the top." He pointed to the other room. "There's a couple of folders filled with paintings to copy. They're all famous artists with high value, but not top tier like Picasso or Monet or anyone who would draw too much attention. I make a direct copy of artwork in private British, European, Canadian, and American collections, and I think the forgeries are sold to the Middle East and Asia."

"Maybe Quentin doesn't know the full extent of this operation," Trevor said.

Mia's lip curled. "I bet he does."

Ruth clasped her hands behind her back and continued to pace the confined area. Her thoughts returned to Reverend Collins's phone call. "Dorothy said it's gone too far. What's gone too far? Murder? Kidnapping? I think Dorothy didn't approve."

"So, Sergeant Fry pushed her down the stairs?" Greg asked with a shocked expression.

Trevor's face twisted. "His own aunt?"

Mia recoiled. "That's sick. How could he?"

Ruth couldn't agree more. "Sergeant Fry told the reverend that Dorothy was old, that it was her time."

"And Bill?" Trevor asked.

Ruth stopped pacing and pulled the twine from her pocket. "I plucked this from Bill's shirt, remember? I think he stumbled on their operation and—"

"They killed 'im for it." Trevor balled his fists.

Ruth rubbed her cat pendant and continued with her original train of thought. "Reverend Collins said on the phone he wanted to help Sergeant Fry."

"Yer tellin' us 'e found out about their forgery business and wanted in?" Trevor asked.

Mia frowned. "Why would he do that?"

Ruth took a breath. "He's a police officer." Blank expressions greeted her proclamation. "Reverend Collins. I believe he's undercover. He's trying to gain access to their operation. He wants in."

Greg looked dubious. "Why do you think that?"

"Well, apart from his general demeanour, it's a hunch," Ruth conceded. "However." She held up a finger. "The heated call with Sergeant Fry would make more sense in that context." She took a breath as she thought it through. "Dorothy had planned to back out or expose what they were up to, and Sergeant Fry killed her for it. Bill too. And he shot Ethan as he tried to escape." Ruth sighed. "Reverend Collins has seen some of this, or has a good idea of what's going on, and he's been trying to get inside to gather evidence. It would fit with what's happening down here."

"I think yer could be right about Collins," Trevor said. "He is the newest member of the village. Only moved 'ere last year."

Ruth recalled Reverend Collins saying as much at the bistro party.

"Perhaps the police got wind of the art forgeries some time ago," Scott said. "And they planted an undercover officer in Vanmoor."

"Didn't stop them kidnapping you, though," Mia said through gritted teeth.

"If Reverend Collins knows," Greg said, "and Sergeant

Fry knows he knows, then why hasn't he done something about him? He's a threat."

Ruth shrugged. "Sergeant Fry is also a police officer. He'll be cautious. Maybe part of the game. Either way, he knows Collins can't act until he has evidence, and Collins clearly hasn't found the tunnels."

The undercover officer had to be careful. One slipup and he could lose months or even years of hard work.

"I think it's a bit of a stretch," Greg said. "I mean, sure, Reverend Collins may have once been a cop, but now? How can we know for sure?"

Mia put a finger to her lips and nodded at the door.

Constance peeked around the doorframe.

Ruth approached the bars. "Hello," she said in as soft a tone as she could muster. "How are you?"

The girl pulled back.

Ruth gripped the bars. "Wait." But it was too late—Constance was gone.

It's just her. She's alone. Sergeant Fry must have gone somewhere else. Ruth could turn that to their advantage, but she needed to act fast, before he returned.

Ruth faced the others and motioned for them to huddle in a group, reducing their chances of being overheard. "I think I can prove Reverend Collins is an undercover police officer." It wasn't the best idea she'd ever had, a huge risk, but would have to do. Besides, they had nothing to lose. She addressed Greg. "Fake an asthma attack."

He stared at her. "I don't have asthma."

Ruth waved this comment away. "Fall on the floor and wheeze. Turn purple if you can. Hyperventilate. Make it look realistic. Drooling will help. This is your moment to shine."

Greg sighed. "I've never seen someone have an asthma attack. I wouldn't know what to do."

Ruth looked at Mia and kept her voice barely above a whisper. "When Greg does that, scream as loud as you can. Constance will come running." A rush of adrenaline coursed through Ruth's body. "I'll then tell her Greg needs his inhaler."

"I don't have an inhaler," Greg said in an exasperated tone.

Ruth kept her focus on Mia. "We'll also tell her Greg must have dropped it somewhere. You volunteer to go, but Constance will choose me to look instead."

"Why will she do that?" Trevor asked.

"She's frightened of her." Ruth nodded at Mia. "Constance will think she'll try and escape. She's young, fit, and agile. Feisty."

"You think I'm feisty?" Mia asked with a look of pride.

"Oodles of feistiness." Ruth winked. "Constance should pick me instead, thinking she won't have so much trouble with the oldest one here."

"I'm the oldest one 'ere," Trevor said.

"Nice of you to say." Ruth glanced at the door and lowered her voice even further. "As soon as she's let me out of this cell, someone needs to create another brief distraction."

"I can do that," Scott said.

Ruth smiled. "Thank you."

"Erm, Grandma?" Greg said.

"Then, while Constance's back is turned, I'll grab my phone." Ruth pointed to the table.

"What use will that do?" Mia asked. "There's no signal down here. And even if you make it to the surface, phoning the police will only result in calling out Sergeant Fry again."

"I don't want to phone anyone," Ruth said.

"Are yer goin' to email someone?" Trevor asked.

"Grandma." Greg moved into her line of sight and waved. "About this fake asthma attack," he whispered. "I don't—"

"Once I'm out of here, I will convince Constance to take me to the church," Ruth said in a rush. "I'll explain we were there earlier, searching for a way down, when Greg must have dropped his inhaler."

Greg threw his hands up.

"Why do you want to go to the church?" Mia asked.

"To give Reverend Collins my phone." Ruth motioned for Greg to lie on the floor. "Do it."

"But—" He shook his head. "You're missing a big problem."

Ruth inclined her head. "Which is?"

Greg swallowed. "She won't care."

"Who won't?"

"Constance," Greg said. "What makes you think she cares enough to try to save me? Her father murdered three people, including their own family member. Me dying would solve one of their problems."

"They could have killed us already," Mia said. "The fact we're alive means they're trying to avoid that scenario."

"Or he doesn't want to murder us here," Greg said. "Would be a pain to move the bodies. But he will if he has to."

Ruth pondered this for a moment. Although Greg made a good point, she wanted to give her plan a try. After all, she wasn't sure how much Constance knew about the actual murders.

Has the girl realised her father killed Dorothy? Or does

Constance think it was an accident, like the rest of the village thought?

Ruth also bet Constance didn't know about Bill because she hadn't been at the party, and she'd been a recluse since. There was a good chance no one had told her.

And Ethan?

Ruth doubted Constance knew about his death either.

"Hurry," Ruth said. "Sergeant Fry could be back at any moment."

Greg hesitated, grumbled under his breath, and then sat. "This is ridiculous. I still say it won't work." With his back pressed against the bars, Greg hyperventilated, clutched his chest, and turned a convincing shade of purple.

Ruth's eyebrows shot up. "Very good, Gregory. I don't know what you were so concerned about. I see a bright pantomime career in your immediate future."

Mia screamed.

Ruth jumped and clutched her chest.

A couple of seconds later, Constance came running.

"He's having an attack," Ruth shouted.

Constance's eyes went wide.

"Asthma," Ruth said. "He needs his inhaler."

Constance wrung her hands, shuffled from one foot to another, and kept glancing at the door, as if unsure what to do.

"*Quick,*" Ruth shouted. "*Hurry* up."

Greg rolled onto his side, wheezing, and clawed at his shirt collar. "Can't. Breathe."

Constance searched the table. "Where is it?"

"He must have dropped it," Ruth said. "Quickly. He's suffocating."

Mia stepped forward. "I'll go look."

"Not you." Constance nodded at Ruth. "Only you." She grabbed the key from the table.

"Wait." Sergeant Fry appeared at the door. He folded his arms and scowled at them. "The boy doesn't have asthma."

"Yes, he does," Mia snapped. "Hurry. He's dying."

"I searched his room," Sergeant Fry said. "And I found no sign of an inhaler." His expression darkened. "You're liars."

Ruth stared at him. "You're the one who tossed our rooms? Searching for the locket?" Her attention moved to Constance. "You wanted the Wilkinsons to call the police. You left a note."

"She didn't leave that note," Sergeant Fry said. "Dorothy did."

Ruth stared at him. "Then why did Constance go to all the trouble of making sure I got it instead?"

"Dorothy didn't get the chance to return the locket, and then when Constance found it—"

"She had a moment of guilty conscience about what you're doing down here," Ruth finished. "And gave the locket to me instead, knowing I was once a police officer."

Constance took a step back and lowered her gaze. "I'm sorry, Dad."

He squeezed her arm. "You've apologised enough."

Ruth pictured Constance at the end of the high street, and Sergeant Fry racing after her. *So now we know what that was about.*

Greg wheezed, drawing all eyes back to him.

"Right," Ruth said. "Inhaler."

Sergeant Fry snarled at Greg. "Stop pretending."

"The boy 'ad the inhaler on 'im," Trevor said. "In 'is pocket. Saw 'im use it only yesterday."

Sergeant Fry shook his head. "The boy played on the

horse racing game at the fete." He waved a finger at Greg. "You pedalled fast and won. Was out of breath, but otherwise fine. Threw a beanbag like you were playing cricket."

Greg stopped panting and sat up.

Sergeant Fry's expression softened, and he took his daughter's arm. "You need to be careful. They could have hurt you."

Constance muttered an apology and scampered off.

"Get some sleep," Sergeant Fry called after her. He then glared at Ruth. "Try pulling a stunt like that again and I'll . . ." He looked at his watch, and then left the room.

"Awesome." Greg threw his hands up. "Great idea. Really flippin' spectacular."

"Language," Ruth muttered.

Sergeant Fry returned with a chair from the other room, placed it next to the cell, and sat. He rested his gun on his lap and glowered at them.

Ruth let out a long breath, and her shoulders slumped as a wave of defeat washed over her.

Greg gave her a look as if to say, "*I told you so.*"

She poked out her tongue.

26

An hour later, now seated in the corner of the makeshift prison cell, Ruth stared at the wall, trying not to think about the fact they were trapped in here and let panic get the better of her. Instead, she thought about Sergeant Fry tossing their rooms earlier.

Constance gave me the locket, only to then tell her father. Once he'd found out what his daughter had done, he tried to put it right.

At least that means Constance has a sliver of a conscience, unlike her father.

Dorothy had planted the note in the locket as a cry for help, praying the Wilkinsons would find it when they got home and call the police. Anyone but Sergeant Fry. However, she'd failed to return the locket to their room in time, and therefore Constance had found it instead.

Ruth assumed that meant Constance had also realised, or at least suspected, her father had murdered Dorothy, which had caused the moment of betrayal.

Ruth couldn't put her finger on it, but something still felt off. Something obvious she'd overlooked. A piece of the puzzle was missing.

She looked over at Sergeant Fry. He paid them no mind and seemed like he was about to doze off. Ruth edged over to Greg, Mia, Scott, and Trevor, and whispered, "When I was six years old, I had a pet chicken called Bertie. Loved every feather on his silly little head."

Greg rolled his eyes. "Not this story again."

"One day, I let Bertie out to play in our back garden," Ruth said. "But my sister, Margaret, accidentally left the gate open, and a fox snuck in. You know what happened?"

"Bertie got eaten," Mia said.

"You'd think so." Ruth shook her head. "But no." She beamed. "They became the best of friends. It was incredible. I named the fox Larry." Ruth glanced over at Sergeant Fry again to make sure he wasn't listening. "Every day Larry would come and play with Bertie," she continued, "chasing him round the garden." Ruth chuckled. "They were so happy together."

Trevor's brow furrowed. "Is there a point to yer story?"

"Even enemies can be friends," Ruth said. "If only you can find something in common. A middle ground, so to speak. A happy place." She tipped her head in the direction of Sergeant Fry. "I'm going to make that deal and get us out of here. All I'm asking is you trust me and go along with everything I say."

Trevor nodded. "I trust yer."

"I've only just met you," Scott said, "but I'll do whatever you want."

"I'm willing to try anything if it gets us out of here," Mia said.

Ruth looked to Greg.

He shrugged. "Sure. I trust you, Grandma."

She rubbed her hands. "Now, whatever you overhear, don't react, no matter how far I take it. Pretend to be asleep. Got it?"

They all nodded their agreement.

"Wait," Mia said. "What happened to the chicken?"

"Bertie?" Ruth's brow furrowed. "I'm not sure. It was ever so strange. He up and vanished. Never saw him again. Larry the fox must have been heartbroken because I never saw him again either. Anyway . . ." As Ruth edged from the group, Scott lay on the cot with Mia perched one end, head tipped back, eyes closed.

Greg and Trevor sat on the floor, backs against the cage, chins to their chests. To an outside observer, they seemed resigned to their fates, away from the door, and in no way intimidating.

So far, so good. Now it was on her.

Ruth sauntered over to Sergeant Fry, slow, nonthreatening, and forced a smile for good measure.

He did not return it.

She leaned in close to the bars and breathed, "I want to make a deal."

Sergeant Fry glared at her. "No deal. Go away."

"You haven't heard what it is yet."

"I don't care." He waved her off.

Ruth looked back at the others, and kept her voice low, pretending she didn't want them to overhear. "I'd like to make an exchange. Something you'll be very interested in. Something that affects you directly, given the fact you're Vanmoor's senior police officer, entrusted with the lives and welfare of its residents."

Sergeant Fry stared at her for a couple of seconds, and then looked away again.

Ruth eyed his gun and took in a juddering breath as

butterflies ravaged her stomach. "It involves Constance."

This got Sergeant Fry's undivided attention. "What about her?"

Ruth tried to look casual. She picked at her nails. "Someone is out to get her."

The sergeant's eyes narrowed. "Oh, yeah?" He didn't seem convinced.

Ruth ploughed on. "This person says Constance pushed Dorothy down the stairs."

"That's a lie." Sergeant Fry balled his fists.

Ruth held up her hands. "Look, you and I know she wouldn't do such a terrible thing, Constance is an angel, but he has evidence against her. Irrefutable evidence."

Sergeant Fry eyed the others and then leaned in and asked, hushed, "He? He who?"

Ruth made a zipping motion across her lips.

Sergeant Fry snarled at her. "You're a liar." He sat back and folded his arms. "Stop wasting my time." He looked at his watch again.

Ruth had to admit, although curious to know what he was waiting for, she didn't want to hang around long enough to find out. They had to get out of here.

"I'm not lying." Ruth lifted her chin. "I can prove it."

"Let me guess." Sergeant Fry sneered. "If I free you all, you'll tell me who this mystery person is, right?"

Ruth shook her head and whispered, "Only Greg. Let him go, and I'll tell you what I know."

Sergeant Fry looked away. "I'm not letting anyone out of here."

Ruth could feel her desperate plan slipping away. It was time to go for broke. "What if I told you there's an under-cover police officer in Vanmoor Village?"

"Reverend Collins."

Ruth's mouth fell agape.

A hint of a smirk twitched the corners of Sergeant Fry's mouth. "Collins has been asking questions nonstop since he got here. He can't prove anything. He'll get bored eventually." His lip curled. "Reverend Collins isn't the first to try, and he won't be the last. He might have an idea of what we're achieving down here, but he doesn't have a clue of how we're doing it." Sergeant Fry stood and went to leave.

"What about the files?" Ruth asked.

He turned back. "What files?"

"Well, you say Reverend Collins has no proof of what you're up to, but I know otherwise. How do you think I found this place?" She gestured around them. "He has evidence. A *lot* of it. Some against Constance. Pictures. I've seen them with my own two eyes." Ruth cleared her throat. "That's also how I figured out he must be an undercover cop. I found his stashed files. All the evidence against you. And your daughter."

Sergeant Fry's face turned ashen. "Y-You're lying." Although, his shaky tone belied his words.

"You can keep saying that until you're blue in the face," Ruth said. "Makes no difference to me. But I can show you. I'll prove I'm telling the truth."

His eyes narrowed again. "Why would you do that?"

Ruth glanced over at the others, pressed her face against the bars, and whispered, "I've already told you: because you'll let Greg go."

"You've lost your mind," Sergeant Fry said. "I can't set him free. He'll call the police."

"I can guarantee you he won't."

"How?"

Ruth motioned for him to approach the bars, then said

in a quieter voice still, "Because you can threaten to kill me if he does."

Sergeant Fry still looked dubious.

"Don't tell him this"—Ruth glanced back at Greg and now spoke in barely a whisper—"but my grandson is a coward. There's no way he'll run to the police if you threaten my life and his. He wouldn't risk it. He'll leave Vanmoor and hope it all sorts itself without him."

Sergeant Fry hesitated a few seconds more, and his gaze moved over the other prisoners. Then he stood, grabbed the key, and beckoned Ruth to the door.

Even though Sergeant Fry now went along with it, Ruth knew he had no intention of honouring the deal, but he didn't need to. He probably didn't believe her about the files either, but did not want to risk her being right either.

Ruth clambered to her feet, and the second she slipped out of the cage, a huge wave of relief washed over her. She let out a slow breath, glad not to be trapped anymore.

She backed toward the table as Sergeant Fry locked the door, but he then turned around and motioned out of the room.

"Five minutes, and then you're straight back here." He aimed his gun at her, as if to drive the point home. "If you don't show me those files, or if you try anything funny . . ." He gestured. "Quickly. We haven't got much time."

"Why haven't we got much time? What's happening?"

When he didn't answer, Ruth clenched her teeth and went to follow, but Trevor called out, "Hey. Where are yer goin'? Yer 'ad better not 'urt 'er." He grabbed the bars. "Take me instead, yer coward."

Sergeant Fry snarled, "Shut up." He raised the gun.

Ruth seized her chance: she grabbed her phone and slipped it into her skirt's waistband.

Trevor backed away, hands raised. "All right. Calm down, Officer."

Sergeant Fry motioned Ruth to the door. "Go."

She hurried through, along the tunnel, and back in the direction they'd come. However, Sergeant Fry steered Ruth via another route: into the room with the packing supplies, up a flight of steps, and into the post office. He unlocked the door, and they stepped onto Vanmoor's darkened High Street.

He gripped Ruth's arm and jabbed the gun into her side. "Where are we going?"

She winced and pointed to the far end of the high street. Her plan was a long shot, so she prayed it worked.

They made their way toward Vanmoor Church and she thought about her husband, John. If he'd been alive, he would have seen this as another grand adventure. However, Ruth also pictured the anger on John's face every time Sergeant Fry waved the gun in her direction.

As they passed the B&B, Ruth let out a slow breath, and hoped Merlin would be okay. Luckily, he had enough water and cat-litter real estate to last him a couple of days, but the grumpy cat would be mad if he missed breakfast.

Ruth and Sergeant Fry pushed through the front gate and marched up the path. The church lights remained on, casting a multicoloured patchwork across the lawn and path, but everything was eerily quiet.

Ruth prayed Reverend Collins would still be up as she reached for the front door handle.

Sergeant Fry stepped to her, and his upper lip curled into a sneer. "I'll remind you not to try anything funny." He nodded at the gun and covered it with his jacket.

"Don't worry," Ruth said. "I understand completely. This

is a *funny stuff* free zone." She forced a smile, opened the door, and went inside.

Sergeant Fry shadowed her every move, and his eyes darted about the place. "Where are the files?" he whispered as they headed up the aisle.

Ruth also looked about, but Reverend Collins was nowhere to be seen. "Back office." She hoped there was an office, and that he was working in there. He'd mentioned he was a night owl, and now Ruth banked her life on that statement. She guessed the time had to be around one o'clock in the morning, but it could easily be much later.

Her best bet was the office at the far end of the church, next to the altar. Ruth held her breath, nudged it open, and peered inside. The bad news: Reverend Collins wasn't about. "Files are in here." Ruth circled the desk, sat in the chair, and opened the first drawer. "Hmm."

"What?" Sergeant Fry snapped.

Ruth tried the second drawer, then opened the third, lowermost one. "Oh."

Sergeant Fry pulled the gun from under his jacket. "You lied to me." He glanced over his shoulder.

"I didn't. They were here. I promise." Ruth removed the phone from her waistband, and as she stood, she slipped it into the drawer. "Don't shoot." She raised her hands and tried to nudge the drawer closed with her knee, but Sergeant Fry raced around the desk and grabbed her arm.

"What are you playing at?" he growled in her ear.

"Nothing," Ruth said, defensive. "I'm telling you, there were files. I saw them."

"I don't believe you. This is a trick." He leaned in close. "What was your plan? What are you trying to do?"

"Nothing," Ruth insisted. "Does he have another office? A storeroom? He must have moved the files."

"Liar." Sergeant Fry dragged Ruth across the office, and as they stepped out, a door closing made them both start.

At the far end of the church, Reverend Collins strode down the aisle.

Ruth went to scream, but Sergeant Fry clapped a hand over her mouth and hauled her back into the office. He closed the door and shoved her across the room. With the gun aimed at her chest, Sergeant Fry unbolted the other door and pushed Ruth outside.

As she stumbled down the path, she said, "Does this mean you won't let Greg go? After all, I held up my end of the deal."

Sergeant Fry muttered a swear word and jabbed the gun into her back. "Keep moving."

"I'll take that as a *no*."

∾

In the library basement, Sergeant Fry slammed the cell door closed, and Ruth tensed.

"Grandma." Greg rushed forward, but she gestured for him to stay back.

With the familiar panic of cleithrophobia gnawing at her chest, Ruth kept her focus on Sergeant Fry. She pictured her phone in Reverend Collins's desk drawer. *It's in God's hands now. Quite literally.* She had to stall for as much time as possible. "Why did you kill Dorothy? How could you?"

"I didn't."

"Sure yer didn't," Trevor said. "And Bill? What 'ad 'e done wrong?" He gripped the bars and snarled, "He found out about yer little forgery operation, and yer murdered 'im."

Sergeant Fry stepped back. "I don't know what you're

talking about. If Bill uncovered this, then why didn't he call the police?"

"Yer the police," Trevor shouted. "Scumbag."

"What about Ethan?" Scott asked. "You killed him because he escaped."

"I didn't kill him either." Sergeant Fry's attention moved to Ruth. "And we only have your word he's dead."

"You burned the evidence," Ruth said, incredulous. "Where did you move the body?"

"I don't know what you're talking about," Sergeant Fry said. "I haven't murdered anyone."

Ruth's mind raced. "Then who did? If it wasn't you or your daughter?"

Who'd gain from their deaths? Who is so desperate to keep this criminal enterprise under wraps? There's no one apart from—

Ruth gasped as something clicked into place. The night of the bistro party, right after Bill's murder, one person had felt sick and rushed off to the bathroom. Only they hadn't gone to the bathroom at all, but had used the secret access in the store cupboard, gone down to the basement, then back up to the kitchen, and dragged Bill's body away. Ruth swallowed and croaked, "Elsie?"

"You called?" Elsie stepped through the door with a look of smug contempt.

27

Ruth stared back at Elsie, struggling to believe her own eyes. The change in the woman's demeanour was striking: she now oozed venom and arrogance.

"Apologies for my tardiness," Elsie said to Sergeant Fry. "I only just got your thousand text messages." She sauntered across the room like she didn't have a care in the world. "I'll be having this back." Elsie snatched the gun from him.

Sergeant Fry averted his gaze and shrank away from her.

An image of the locket note sprang into Ruth's mind. Now it made more sense. Dorothy wasn't trying to escape Sergeant Fry, but it was her weak attempt to get away from Elsie. Constance had also attempted to free her father from Elsie's grasp.

Elsie waved the gun in Ruth's direction. "What do you think? My husband's military revolver. Glad I kept it. Has come in handy lately."

Ruth stared at Sergeant Fry. "You're not in charge at all. You only work for her."

He looked away.

Trevor pressed his face to the bars and spat at Elsie. "Yer murdered Bill. Why? Why d'ya do it?"

"He stumbled onto their operation." Ruth remembered Bill saying he'd recently worked in the bistro's basement, and her blood ran cold. "The strand of canvas on his shirt." She swallowed a dry lump in her throat and focussed on Elsie. "Bill found the tunnel."

"How could yer do that to 'im?" Trevor snarled at Elsie. "He thought the world of yer."

"I had to," Elsie said in a matter-of-fact tone. "No choice. I wasn't about to let Bill ruin all my hard work." She sounded so calm about it, as though it was normal to murder someone. "Not after everything I've gone through. I'm as devastated as you are about what happened to him."

Trevor's eyes filled with hatred. "Yer a monster."

Ruth's heart grew heavier by the second, and as the pieces fell into place, she felt terrible for not figuring out the obsessed bistro owner's involvement sooner.

Elsie's determination to succeed at all costs, her expensive kitchen, her organised way of doing things with everything in its place, the fact she was the last person to see Bill alive, her disappearance at the bistro party . . .

Trevor was right; Elsie was a monster.

"You gave me the runaround." Ruth took a deep breath as the fog lifted. "You wanted me to check out the basement and not find Bill's body. To give up the search. Then you had me arrested." Ruth's stomach tensed. "What about Dorothy?" She recalled the landlady mentioning Elsie brought fresh glazed buns to the B&B every day, and the fact a plate of them had sat on the counter the morning of her death. "You pushed her down the stairs. You murdered her too."

Sergeant Fry's face dropped. "It— It wasn't an accident?"

With her free hand, Elsie snatched up Greg's phone and examined it. "I regret what happened to Dorothy, I really do." She tried to unlock the mobile with four zeros, then tossed it back onto the table.

Sergeant Fry's face twisted with anger.

"I bet Dorothy didn't take kindly to your plan to continue her husband's legacy." Ruth motioned to Scott. "Kidnapping? Was it a step too far for her? She threatened to go to the police?" Ruth looked at Sergeant Fry askance. "The *real* police."

Elsie's grip tightened on the gun as he stared at her. "What? Dorothy lost her nerve. You know she wasn't right since Arthur's death." She inclined her head at Sergeant Fry. "Dorothy wanted the whole thing to end. Didn't care about the rest of us. Said she didn't mind going to prison." Elsie rolled her eyes. "At her age, of course she didn't care. Only had a year or two at best, but us?"

"Why are you doing this?" Mia thrust a finger at the paintings in the next room. "All to make a few quid from fake artwork?"

"A few quid?" Elsie laughed. "Arthur was a fantastic forger. Made millions over the years. How do you think we got the funding to revamp the village? Profit from the annual fete?" Elsie's face turned serious again. "Without Arthur's steady work and prodigious talents, money would have dried up decades ago."

Ruth blinked. "I thought Lord Vanmoor paid for—" She groaned.

"Wait," Greg said. "Not him too? He's in on this?"

"Oh, please." Elsie said through a tight jaw. "Lord Vanmoor is clueless, but he still needs me. If it wasn't for this revenue stream, he wouldn't have his precious estate, or his flashy car."

"You're using him to launder the money." Ruth stared at her. "Making it look like he has vast wealth and that his generosity pays for everything. He's your frontman."

Elsie leaned against the cage bars and peered in at them as though they were either animals or mild curiosities. "Arthur ran a smooth operation, and when he died, I had to take over. I grabbed the bull by the horns." She pointed to herself. "I'm the one who made the hard decisions. *Me.* Choices no one else would make." Her eyes turned dark. "This village would crumble without me, taking that Lord Vanmoor buffoon with it."

"You're insane," Mia said. "A complete lunatic."

"When Arthur died, yer big idea was to kidnap artists and force them to do yer dirty work." Trevor shook his head. "Yeah, genius. Could never last."

Elsie smirked. "They weren't about to volunteer, now, were they?" She paced back and forth. "It won't be forever. The way I understand it, Constance is turning out quite talented. Speaking of which . . ." Elsie looked to the door. "Where is she?"

"Asleep," Sergeant Fry murmured.

Ruth prayed she'd had an attack of conscience and run to the nearest village to call the police.

"You also wanted the money to keep flowing so you could launch that bistro." Ruth refocussed on Elsie, hoping to keep her talking. "It's all you care about. You don't give a hoot about the village. You're determined to win at all costs, no matter what it takes." *Like the jam competition.* "What about the other things you told me? The argument between Bill and Constable Bishop? The one between Constance and Dorothy too? All lies?" Ruth took a breath as the days' events slotted into place.

Had Elsie done that to frighten Constance into silence? Had she gotten wind of Constance's unease about the whole kidnapping situation?

"Did you put Quentin up to pointing a finger at Mia too? Made out as if she had the opportunity to murder Bill in order to muddy the water?" Ruth looked over at Sergeant Fry. "Is that why you didn't pursue the line of enquiry? Didn't follow up? Because you knew full well who murdered Bill."

Mia glared at Elsie like she'd like nothing better than to rip her apart. "And what happens to my brother once you're done with him?"

"I thought you'd never ask." An evil grin swept across Elsie's face. She addressed Sergeant Fry. "I parked my van up top." She jabbed a finger into his chest. "This has gotten out of control, and you know what must be done."

Sergeant Fry took a step back.

"What does she have on you?" Ruth asked. "What's Elsie's hold? It must be bad, otherwise—" Her breath caught. "Wait." Ruth looked to Elsie. "Your husband was in the military too." Then her attention returned to Sergeant Fry. "You're not a war hero."

Elsie chuckled as though it were a grand old joke. "Far from it."

Sergeant Fry hung his head.

Elsie stepped to the table and examined the objects: picking up each in turn, then tossing them back.

Ruth stiffened and hoped she didn't twig Ruth's mobile phone was missing.

Elise set the gun down and snatched up Ruth's lip balm. "While drunk in some seedy bar, Richard gave away the location of his platoon's temporary barracks."

Sergeant Fry eyed the pistol and then looked away.

Ruth let out a breath.

Elsie checked the label on the balm and applied some to her lips. "It was only when Richard realised his mistake did he rush back to warn them." She threw the lip balm into the corner of the room and grabbed the gun again. "Some died in the attack, didn't they, Richard?" Elsie turned from the table and glared at him.

"And you have physical proof of this?" Ruth asked. Then she muttered, "Of course you do."

Elsie's top lip twisted into a snarl. "You want everyone to know?" she said to Sergeant Fry. "What my husband showed me?" She moved toward him, her eyes intense. "You're telling me you are finally ready for me to reveal, to the entire world, what. You. Did?"

"Enough." Sergeant Fry marched from the room and reappeared a few seconds later with a fistful of cable ties.

"What are those for?" Greg asked.

Ruth groaned. "Well, I don't think he has a cable management emergency he'd like us to take care of."

While Elsie trained her gun on the captives, Sergeant Fry opened the cell and beckoned Ruth forward.

Although glad the door was now open, which went some way to easing her cleithrophobia, she didn't relish the idea of having her hands bound.

However, it being the lesser of the two evils, Ruth placed her hands together. "Not too tight, if you please. I bruise like a peach."

Sergeant Fry cable-tied her wrists.

Mia stepped back, shaking her head. "No way you're doing that to me."

Elsie tapped the barrel of her gun against the bars, drawing her attention. "You'll do as you're told, little miss, or you will sorely regret it." Her cold gaze moved to Scott.

Mia relented.

Ruth gave Greg a look, silently telling him not to resist either.

"Where are you taking us?" he asked as Sergeant Fry bound his wrists.

For a second, Trevor looked like he was about to make a break for freedom.

Elsie aimed the gun at him. "No funny business, old man."

Sergeant Fry bound Trevor's wrists next, and then finished with Scott.

Once everyone was suitably restrained, Sergeant Fry led the prisoners out, with Elsie bringing up the rear, ready to shoot anyone should they make any reckless or ill-advised sudden moves.

They trooped from the basement room, along the tunnel, and headed back up to the surface. Under the cover of darkness, they came out in the bistro kitchen and filed out back to her van.

Sergeant Fry opened the rear doors.

"Can I go up front?" Ruth asked. When she got a scowl instead of an answer, she climbed into the van with the others and sat cross-legged on the floor.

Sergeant Fry slammed the doors, and Ruth's anxiety came back into full effect. She focussed on the outside world through the front windscreen and told herself she wasn't really trapped.

Elsie slipped into the passenger seat and twisted round. "Behave yourselves. This won't take long."

Mia stared at her brother. "I'm sorry. This is my fault. If we hadn't come looking for you, this wouldn't have happened."

"Shut up," Elsie snapped as Sergeant Fry climbed into the driver's side.

Ruth couldn't agree with Mia—the blame lay at Ruth's feet, and hers alone.

A few seconds later, they were off.

"Where are we goin'?" Trevor asked.

Elsie faced the front. "Not far."

Ruth assumed they were taking them to some remote spot. Probably the same place they'd dumped Ethan and Bill's bodies. She also guessed it was somewhere on Lord Vanmoor's estate, hence Elsie's "*not far*" comment.

They drove from the alleyway and along Vanmoor High Street, heading from the village.

Ruth looked at Greg opposite her, and she frowned.

He'd undone his shoelaces on both trainers, and now looped the end of one through the cable tie at his wrists.

Ruth watched in quiet amazement as he then knotted that end to the shoelace of his other trainer. "What are you doing?"

Greg glanced over at Elsie to make sure she wasn't watching, then took up the slack on his tied shoelaces by raising his wrists. Next, Greg worked his feet up and down, left foot, right foot, left foot, right foot, faster and faster, using the shoelace like a saw.

Ten seconds later, the friction burned through the cable tie, and his hands sprang apart.

Ruth, Mia, Trevor, and Scott all gaped at him.

As they followed the winding country roads, Greg quickly repeated the process with the others' bindings, until all five of them were freed.

Trevor squeezed his shoulder and whispered, "Genius."

Ruth couldn't agree more. She pointed to each of them in turn, then motioned to the back doors, signalling that when the van next came to a stop, they'd make a break for freedom.

She received four nods in reply.

The van came to a sudden and tyre-screeching halt, throwing them all forward into one another.

A mile ahead, on the brow of the hill, several police cars blocked their way.

Ruth let out a slow breath. Reverend Collins had clearly discovered her unlocked phone and browsed through the crime scene pictures.

They were saved.

However, Sergeant Fry slammed the van into reverse, spun around, and raced back toward the village. "Now what?"

"Remain calm," Elsie said. "We move to plan B."

He pressed the accelerator hard to the floor. "Which is?"

"We'll take them back to the tunnel." Else turned in her seat to look at them. "We'll deal with you at Smuggler's Cove."

The five captives remained tight-lipped, their hands clasped in their laps.

Rut sighed with relief as Elsie faced the front again. She hadn't noticed they were no longer bound.

"This is insane," Sergeant Fry said. "We were just here."

"Not an ideal solution," Elsie said. "But it will have to do."

Sergeant Fry ripped the steering wheel hard over, and they hurtled back down Vanmoor High Street. A few seconds after that, they dove down the alleyway into the bistro's rear courtyard.

Elsie and Sergeant Fry climbed from the van.

Ruth spun onto her back and lifted her feet. The second the doors started to open, she lashed out, sending them flying.

Greg leapt past her, knocking Sergeant Fry to the tarmac.

Ruth hurried after him, with Mia right behind her, but both ground to a halt as Elsie aimed the gun at them.

Ruth winced, and stepped in front of Mia.

Someone screamed and slammed into Elsie from the side.

Ruth gaped. It was Constance.

The gun flew from Elsie's hand and skidded into the shadows. "What are you doing?" she roared, and rounded on the girl.

Sergeant Fry leapt to his feet and squared up to Greg, fists raised. He then froze as sirens wailed in the distance, and a second after that he bolted.

With a look of astonishment mixed with betrayal, Elsie watched him go, and then ran in the opposite direction.

"I've got him." Greg went to run after Sergeant Fry, but Ruth grabbed his arm. "Hey."

"Too dangerous," she said.

"He's getting away."

Ruth stared back at her grandson and not only could see the determination in his eyes, but for the first time also saw the man he'd become. She relaxed, and her grip loosened.

Greg pulled free and sprinted after Sergeant Fry, with Trevor and Scott bringing up the rear.

The police sirens grew louder.

Ruth and Mia hurried after Elsie.

"Stop, Elsie," Ruth shouted. "I hate running."

But it was no use—Elsie raced around the corner and along Vanmoor High Street.

"I'll get her." Mia sped up.

Ruth halted, bent double, and groaned. "Too. Much. Exercise." Something to her right caught Ruth's eye. Her favourite drunk gnome's butt stuck out of a window box. She'd stopped outside Malcolm's Groceries. "Sorry about this, Uncle Norman." Ruth grabbed the novelty gnome and launched it.

He sailed through the air, over Mia's head, and slammed into Elsie's back, sending her crashing to the ground in a blur of floral-patterned fabric.

Mia looked back, wide-eyed.

Ruth waved and panted, "Sorry. Bored with running."

Greg would've been proud of her overarm throw.

Two police cars raced up the high street and screeched to a stop. Reverend Collins, wearing body armour, leapt out. He hurried over to Elsie. "Put your hands behind your head, and interlace your fingers."

She did as ordered, and another officer cuffed her. He then read Elsie her rights as he loaded her into the back of a police car.

Reverend Collins nodded at Mia.

She pointed to Ruth.

Ruth smiled at the undercover officer, and wheezed, "You know, you really shouldn't look through a lady's phone. It's private." She clutched a stitch in her side.

"Had to," Reverend Collins said. "I wanted to figure out whose it was so I could return it to the rightful owner." He held the phone up inside an evidence bag. "We're going to have to keep hold of this for a while."

Of course, Under the Police and Criminal Evidence Act 1984, he had every right to. The police had the power to seize and retain property that's relevant to an investigation. Especially one loaded with photos of Vanmoor crime scenes.

"As long as you don't use up all my data stuff," Ruth said, "we'll be fine."

"I suggest you buy a phone with a little more security."

He pocketed the evidence and wrote a receipt. "You can unlock the new ones with your face."

"So I hear." Ruth took it from him, and then gasped. She looked down the high street. "Greg— Sergeant Fry—"

Reverend Collins held up a hand. "We have him in custody. Your grandson had him pinned."

"Trevor and Scott?" Ruth asked.

"Both fine. They're with him."

Ruth turned to Mia. "Go."

She raced off.

Ruth let out a slow breath and sat on the nearest bench. "Constance?"

"She's in custody too," Reverend Collins said. "I have a strong feeling she'll be the first one to strike a plea bargain."

"You could be right." Ruth leaned forward to catch her breath.

Another officer retrieved the novelty gnome.

Ruth stood and took it from her. "Thanks."

"You and your grandson will need to give statements and, of course, attend court."

Ruth looked forward to Elsie getting her comeuppance.

She returned Uncle Norman the gnome to his window box and made a mental note to buy Greg one for his birthday. After all, he could use it as a paperweight when he started university.

He'd be the envy of his fellow students.

28

Two days later, Ruth, Greg, Mia, and Scott sauntered along Vanmoor High Street for the last time. Trevor had already collected their suitcases, plus Merlin, and now waited for them at his house.

They'd almost reached the end of the road when Reverend Collins marched toward them, clutching a cardboard box.

"Now what?" Greg muttered.

Ruth had answered a thousand police questions, plus a billion phone calls from Margaret, with her sister going out of her mind and demanding she leave Vanmoor immediately or face the real prospect of being disowned and disembowelled.

Not necessarily in that order.

"I thought you'd like to know we have all the evidence we need," Reverend Collins said. "Thanks to you, Lord Vanmoor's money-laundering days are far behind him."

"What about Constable Bishop?" Ruth asked.

"She claims to not know anything about what's been going on here, and she's cooperating with the investigation."

He cleared his throat. "Our digital forensic specialists also recovered the missing recordings from the CCTV cameras." Reverend Collins looked at Scott. "We now have a complete picture of your movements on those two days." He motioned to the nearest camera. "They put these up around the village so they could make sure no one stumbled across their operation, but now we can use their own stupidity against them."

"And the bodies?" Mia asked in a low voice. "Ethan and Bill?"

Reverend Collins frowned. "We've not found them yet, but we will."

"Try Lord Vanmoor's estate," Ruth said.

"Already on it. We've discovered a bonfire with a load of burnt furniture."

The man in the baseball cap removing a nightstand from Molly's B&B flashed into Ruth's thoughts. "Of course. That was Sergeant Fry." She looked at Greg. "Remember when we first arrived? I bet he removed furniture from Scott's room."

"Right," Greg said. "Destroying evidence." He frowned. "Why not just wipe it all clean? Why burn it?"

"He panicked." Reverend Collins pointed at Mia. "She was so determined to find her brother, Richard Fry wanted to make sure there was zero chance of uncovering forensic evidence."

"He hadn't finished," Ruth said. "There's a rug in the room still."

"We have it." Reverend Collins went to leave but turned back. "I almost forgot." He held the box out to Ruth.

She took it from him. "What is it?"

"A memento." Reverend Collins strode away.

Ruth opened it, peered inside, and chuckled.

"Well?" Greg asked.

Ruth lifted out the novelty drunken gnome, and she smirked. "Uncle Norman."

Greg rolled his eyes.

Scott laughed. "Tasteful."

"I know, right?" Ruth placed it back into the box. "I'll put it on the motorhome's dashboard, in pride of place."

"You'd better not," Greg muttered.

The four of them headed from Vanmoor Village and up the hill toward Trevor's house.

"Thank you for everything you've done," Scott said. "I didn't think I was ever getting out of there."

"It was our pleasure," Ruth said. "I'm glad it all worked out." She had gotten a buzz out of uncovering the truth, but Ruth wasn't about to admit that to the others.

"Grandma likes a bit of drama," Greg said.

"And now I'd like a giant mug of tea," she said, although she disagreed with that statement. Ruth preferred the quiet life. "Once we're at least a hundred miles from here."

"You're going to visit your sister?" Mia asked.

Ruth frowned. "Don't ruin my good mood."

However, she was keen to get to Ivywick Island and resolve the many and varied relationship issues between her and Margaret.

Ruth sighed in satisfaction as her shiny motorhome came into view. It looked perfect with its giant white sides and go-faster stripes, its chrome bumpers, and the crooked TV antenna perched on top, held together with duct tape and prayers.

Britain's roads really love low-hanging branches.

Trevor had even restored the jaunty sticker to its former glory: "Home is where you park it."

Ruth beamed.

And speaking of whom, Trevor stepped from the workshop, wiping his hand on an obligatory oily rag. "Yer do realise what yer've done?"

Ruth tilted her head. "Me?"

"All of yer." Trevor motioned to the four of them. "Without the forgery money, Vanmoor Village will be bankrupt within a month." Although, he said that with a mischievous glint in his eye.

The result, although the right one, was bittersweet.

"Not true," Mia said. "With everything that's happened, the murders, kidnapping, and the whole smuggling operation . . . when that gets out, this place will become a tourist trap."

"What about Mum?" Greg said to Ruth. "Can the business sponsor the next fete or something? One of the shops?"

Ruth gave a slow nod. "I'll ask her."

"Yer daughter?" Trevor said with a puzzled look.

"Sara runs the family enterprise," Ruth said. "Took it over when my husband passed away. She's a very successful breeder, runs a cattery, even has a line of high-quality cat food, toys, beds, accessories . . . if it can be branded, she did it."

"Mum has some wealthy clients," Greg said. "She could put in a good word."

"May also bring you in some more motoring trade," Ruth said to Trevor.

He waved that comment away. "After what I charged yer, I'm set for a year."

Ruth laughed. "I bet."

Trevor's expression brightened. "That's mighty good of yer though. The whole Vanmoor investment thing."

"I think Vanmoor will be fine on its own," Ruth said.

"But Sara can be very persuasive when she gets the bit between her teeth."

"And annoying," Greg muttered.

Ruth nodded. "And annoying."

"Bossy too."

"She takes after Margaret in that regard." Ruth cleared her throat and looked over at Scott and Mia. "Would you two like to come to Ivywick Island with us? You're more than welcome. My sister can be extremely irritating, but she makes a mean expresso."

"No thank you," Mia said. "We should be getting home."

"Are you sure?" Ruth pressed. "Margaret also has a secret steak and ale pie recipe she refuses to share with me." She cupped a hand around her mouth and stage-whispered, "You could spy on her. I'd pay you."

Mia chuckled. "Tempting." She faced Greg. "Could I have a quick word before we leave?"

"Me? Erm, yeah, sure. Okay." He followed her from the house.

"I'm going to call a taxi," Scott said, and he strode away too.

Ruth watched Greg and Mia as they talked and held hands.

Greg was right—he was a grown man, a good man too, and although Ruth could finally see it, he'd always be her grandson, and he'd have to put up with her treating him that way. However, she'd learned to back off a little and let him make his own bad decisions.

Goodness knows she'd made enough of those herself.

Mia kissed Greg on the cheek, and they hugged.

"Would yer like me to turn the motorhome around, so yer don't 'ave to back out? Wouldn't want yer hittin' anything else."

"Huh?" Ruth refocussed on Trevor. "Oh. Well, it depends. How fond are you of those gates? More importantly, their current location on your property?"

"I'll move it."

"Thank you."

Trevor took a step toward the motorhome, stopped, and turned back. "Can we maybe see each other again?"

Ruth smiled. "I'd love to, but I can't date until I've resolved a few things."

Trevor nodded. "I understand."

"I do think you're a great guy," Ruth added, and meant it with all her heart. "Can we have a rain check?" Although she was more than okay living the single life, Ruth could do a lot worse than Trevor, and she did get lonely from time to time. But John's death still weighed heavily on her, even after all these years.

"I'll move yer motorhome." Trevor winked and strode toward it. "I still want yer phone number," he called over his shoulder.

"As soon as I get a new mobile, you'll be the first to have it."

"Promise?"

"Cross my heart."

Even though once the police had extracted all the photos, Ruth could ask for her old phone back, she'd decided to let them keep it in evidence, and it was a good opportunity to upgrade.

Mia gave Greg another peck on the cheek, waved at Ruth, and then headed back to the road with Scott.

Greg, now fifteen shades darker pink than he was a few minutes ago, returned.

Ruth nudged his arm. "When's the wedding?"

"We're going to meet up in a couple of months," Greg muttered.

"Ooh." Ruth beamed. "That sounds promising."

"No wedding."

"Engagement party?"

"No."

"Pre-engagement party?"

"No."

"Pre-pre-engagement party?"

Greg ground his teeth. "Not even a little one."

Ruth huffed. "Spoilsport."

Once Trevor had finished moving the motorhome, he strode over to them. "All set."

Ruth hugged him. "Thank you for everything you've done." She stepped back. "Apart from emptying my bank account."

"Yer more than welcome, young lady."

"Oh, I definitely feel young on the inside." Ruth waved. "See you." She stepped inside the motorhome. Merlin's box sat on the table. Ruth opened it and peered inside. "And how are you doing, Your Highness?"

Merlin yawned.

"Right," Ruth said. "Understandable. You've had a busy few days. Deserve a nap." She strapped the box to the table and left it open, before heading to the front and slipping into the driver's seat. "I've missed you so much," Ruth whispered, and massaged the steering wheel. "I promise to never hurt you again."

Greg chirped from somewhere in the back, "You're weird."

"You think so?" Ruth looked back to make sure Greg wasn't watching her. "Just wait until you've spent a whole day with my sister." Then she placed Uncle Norman the gnome on the dashboard and smiled. "Perfect." Ruth stared through the windscreen as she recalled the past days' events.

When she'd left the force, she had put every ounce of energy into her new culinary pursuits. Ruth had pushed that previous working life far away, and concentrated on the catering business. Until recently, it had seemed like a million years ago.

"Grandma?"

"I can feel them returning," Ruth murmured.

"Feel what returning?" Greg dropped into the passenger seat next to her and fastened his belt.

"My investigative skills."

He groaned. "Really?"

"You needn't worry, Gregory." Ruth started the engine. "We're going to my sister and brother-in-law's island." She waved to Trevor. "Why on earth would I need to investigate anything there?"

Ruth then pulled away, careful not to hit the gate posts or plunge into any rivers.

Continue reading below for a sample of . . .
MURDER ON IVYWICK ISLAND
OUT NOW

Thank you for reading! We would be incredibly grateful if you could leave a star rating or review. Your invaluable support is vital to the Ruth Morgan Mystery Series' success and can make all the difference.

To be notified of FUTURE RELEASES in the Ruth Morgan series, click on the author name "Peter Jay Black" at Amazon (on

any of Peter's book pages), and then "Follow" in the top left. OR
visit peterjayblack.com and join the free VIP list.

Also grab a FREE copy of
DEATH IN BROOKLYN
A Short Story set in the Fast-Paced
Emma & Nightshade Crime Thriller Series.

IMPORTANT
Please remember to check your spam folder for any emails. You
must confirm your sign-up before being added to the email list.

MURDER ON IVYWICK ISLAND
CHAPTER ONE

Greg Shaw screamed. Not in a deep, manly shout for attention, nor a heroic call for help, but a high-pitched squeal reminiscent of a six-year-old running from an imaginary monster.

Ruth slammed both feet onto the motorhome's brake pedal, and it took one and a half football fields in length for the behemoth to come to a juddering stop.

To be fair, not the worst braking distance she'd experienced in her tin palace.

Trevor, back in Vanmoor Village, must have upgraded the discs or whatever. Bless him.

Ruth cocked an eyebrow at her grandson as the gangly teenager's bottom jaw worked, but no words came out.

"Yes. Thank you, Gregory." She'd reacted to the almighty bang, so the scream was completely unnecessary, let alone the panicked hysteria.

This was one of those times Ruth wondered if a hapless maternity ward nurse with poor eyesight had switched her grandson for another baby. There was no way she was ever this dramatic in her youth. Sara, Greg's mother, could be intense, but still not to the extent he currently exhibited.

Greg wrung his hands, and his cheeks drained of colour. "We're going to prison," he croaked.

Maybe he gets it from his father's side of the family, Ruth mused. *That certainly would explain it.*

She set the parking brake and switched off the engine. When it had come to a rattling stop, Ruth unfastened her seat belt and said in a calm voice, "Shall we go see what's happened?" She climbed from the driver's side, eager to figure out what calamity had befallen them this time, so they could get moving again.

Ruth exited the motorhome and trooped back along the road, searching for the exact location of the dreaded impact. The mere fact she'd not seen what object they'd hit, and therefore not had the time to swerve, filled her with suspicion.

Greg trotted after her, muttering something about Ruth's terrible driving.

She took offence. Her driving style wasn't bad, more like unique. Where normal people would gauge a road too narrow for their vehicle, or a bridge too low, she'd always be up for the challenge. Gave life an extra level of excitement.

A stone wall bordered the forest to their left.

Greg squeaked and motioned to a crumbled section.

On the other side, between the trunks of two oaks, lay a man in his fifties, with a weathered face, a grizzled beard, and thinning red hair jutted from the sides of his head.

He wore a tatty parker jacket, torn at the elbows; a woollen hat with more holes than a slice of Swiss cheese;

and a pair of Doc Martens boots that looked as though they'd seen at least two world wars.

He stared unblinking at the sky.

"I said your driving would kill someone one day." Greg looked at Ruth, wide eyed. "I just assumed it would be me."

She sighed. "The day's still young." Ruth leaned over the wall for a better look. "At least he's breathing. That's a good sign."

Sure enough, the man's chest rose and fell, and then he groaned.

"I'll call an ambulance," Greg said.

"No," the man croaked. "I'll be all right." He hacked and winced. "Oh dear." His eyes spun into the back of his skull.

Ruth scanned him from top to toe. He had no visible bruises or scrapes, and no part of him oozed any type of liquid. *Interesting.* She frowned and looked him over again, then the ground nearby.

Greg slipped a phone from his pocket, but Ruth grabbed his wrist.

"What are you doing?" He tried to pull free. "This man could die."

"Not in the next minute he won't." Ruth let go of her grandson. "Stay right here. Don't move." She raced back to her beloved motorhome and circled to the front. The impact had dented the bumper and grille. "Can I not go five minutes without something dinging my house?" Ruth knelt and inspected the damage.

By the look of it, a skilled tradesperson could hammer everything back into shape. Perhaps she could find one of those handy types at their destination. Ruth glanced down the road. Which was only another mile or so. "Typical."

She ran a hand over the now concave bumper and then

rubbed her fingers together. Particles of sand. Ordinary beach sand by the feel. Her eyes narrowed.

Ruth straightened and stood at one end the bumper and grille, noting the level of the impact relative to the ground, with no damage above waist height.

"As I suspected." Fists balled, she stormed back to the crumbled wall.

The man now writhed about with his eyes squeezed shut, face twisted in agony. He moaned. "It's broken. All broken. Hurts so much. The pain. What have you done to me?"

Trembling, Greg raised his phone again, but Ruth snatched it out of his hand as she passed him.

"Hey."

Ruth stepped over the remains of the wall, then over the man too, and made her way deeper into the forest.

"Where are you going?" Greg called. "Grandma?"

She glanced back as the man opened one eye and watched her.

A little way in, Ruth looked about. "Where is it, then?"

"Where's what?" Greg said.

"I'm fading." The man slumped. "Slipping away. There's a tunnel. Bright light."

Ruth held up a hand. "Don't die just yet. I'll be right with you. Give me a minute." She took several paces farther into the forest and stepped behind one of the oaks. "Ah-ha. Here we go." She snatched up a rope . . .

MURDER ON IVYWICK ISLAND
OUT NOW

To be notified of FUTURE RELEASES in the Ruth Morgan series, click on the author name "Peter Jay Black" at Amazon (on

*any of Peter's book pages), and then "Follow" in the top left. OR
visit peterjayblack.com and join the free VIP list.*

*Also grab a **FREE** copy of*
DEATH IN BROOKLYN
*A Short Story set in the Fast-Paced
Emma & Nightshade Crime Thriller Series*

IMPORTANT

*Please remember to check your spam and promotions folders for
any emails. You must confirm your sign-up before being added to
the Ruth Morgan email list.*

PETER JAY BLACK
BIBLIOGRAPHY

DEATH IN LONDON
Book One in a Fast-Paced Crime Thriller Series
https://mybook.to/DeathinLondonKindle

Emma leads a quiet life, away from her divorced parents' business interests, but when her father's fiancée turns up dead in her mother's warehouse, she can't ignore the threat of a civil war.

Unable to call the police, Emma's parents ask her to assist an eccentric private detective with the investigation. She reluctantly agrees, on the condition that when she's done they allow her to have her own life in America, away from the turmoil.

The amateur sleuths investigate the murder, and piece together a series of cryptic clues left by the killer, who seems to know the families intimately, but a mistake leads to the slaying of another close relative.

Now dragged into a world she's fought hard to avoid, Emma must do everything she can to help catch the culprit and restore peace. However, with time running out, could her parents be the next victims?

"Pick up Death in London today and start book one in a gripping Crime Thriller Mystery series."

***

DEATH IN MANHATTAN
Book One in a Fast-Paced Crime Thriller Series
https://mybook.to/DeathinManhattanKindle

When someone murders New York's leading crime boss, despite him being surrounded by advanced security, the event throws the underworld into chaos. Before anyone can figure out how the killer did it, he dies under mysterious circumstances and takes his secret to the grave.

Emma's uncle asks her to check out the crime scene, but she's reluctant to get involved, especially after the traumatic events back in London. However, with Nightshade's unique brand of encouragement, they figure out how the killer reached one of the most protected men in the world. Their lives are then complicated further when another member of the Syndicate is murdered, seemingly by the hands of the same deceased perpetrator.

Emma and Nightshade now find themselves in way over their heads, caught up in a race against time, trying to solve clues and expose a web of deception, but will they be quick enough to stop a war?

Printed in Great Britain
by Amazon

42833190R10189